A Wedding In the Keys
A Florida Keys Novel

MIKI BENNETT

First Edition

ISBN: 0998848131
ISBN 13: 9780998848136
Library of Congress Control Number: 2018901447
WannaDo Concepts Publishing, Charleston, South Carolina

This book is dedicated to all the residents of the Florida Keys. Your bravery, tenacity and love for your islands has seen you through one of the worst storms in 2017. May love and blessings continue to be with you as you come back stronger than ever.

"Are you OK? You are white as a sheet," Mandy said, setting her handbag down and coming to sit by Bailey. "Did someone cancel? Are the weddings still on? I knew that girl sounded a bit off even when she gave me the deposit. I bet she backed out of the wedding." Mandy got up and started pacing the floor.

"Mandy, everything is OK, at least with the weddings. Everything is on schedule, and as a matter of fact, Chase came by and has agreed to do the weddings."

"Thank goodness. I was beginning to get a bit worried. So, what is the matter? I can see you hyperventilating from here."

"He asked me out on a date, and I said 'yes'," Bailey said hesitantly.

"Oh. But that is a good thing, right?" Now Mandy was sitting by Bailey's desk again, looking more relax and a bit hopeful.

"I guess, but it's tonight, and I've never been on a real date."

"Are you kidding?"

"At least not one that I can remember." Bailey said the words, then wished that she could take then back quickly. But it was already out there.

"What do you mean 'can remember'?"

Bailey took a deep breath and sighed. It was now or never to tell her boss about her past. About the accident that robbed her of her memory.

1

Chase ran his hand through his hair more than once. He felt a little frustrated at the tiny flower girl, but he made sure his feelings didn't show. If only the little one would sit still. All he needed was a few seconds to capture the picture. Instead, the four-year-old repeatedly jumped off the chair while her mother kept putting her back on. Now, as Chase watched, it was becoming a battle of wills between mother and daughter. It looked as if the tiny tot was going to win.

"Don't worry," Chase said to the frazzled mom. "I'll find another time to get the picture, maybe right before she walks down the aisle."

"I'm so sorry. I guess that little bit of candy earlier wasn't the best thing before a wedding."

Chase silently agreed, but didn't want the mother to feel bad, so he said nothing and smiled. He was used to the children of the wedding parties being a little rambunctious. At least the adults were more than happy to have their pictures taken during the wedding festivities. They posed with no problem at all.

Chase never thought that one day, he would be a wedding photographer in Islamorada, one of the islands of the tropical Florida Keys. It was a hot spot for weddings – for those that lived there and for others that traveled from near and afar. It was a beautiful place for a destination wedding, and he had photographed ceremonies all the way from Key Largo to Key West.

When Chase told his parents that he was leaving the family business to work and live in the Keys, they weren't happy, but at least they didn't react like they had when his older sister, Skylar, decided to strike out on her own. Essentially, her leaving and starting her own charter boat company in Key Largo had helped pave the way for him to exit the family business, too. His parents quietly accepted his decision to leave one of the oldest real estate firms in South Florida, but let him know that they didn't think his idea of being a freelance wildlife photographer was a profession worth pursuing.

Another chink in his plan was his girlfriend, Blair. Chase had thought that she would be excited for him, but her reaction was just the opposite. She had been very upset. They had been together for over two years, and Chase had thought that one day, they would marry. But when Blair heard his idea and what he wanted to do, she was suddenly like a different person.

Blair didn't want anything to change. She liked the social notoriety that Chase's family had in the city. And she hated the fact that Chase was walking away from family money. Blair was only with him for wealth and a social presence, and this had knocked Chase's confidence for a while. He felt betrayed because he had loved her for so many different reasons. But Blair went her way, and Chase left for the Keys.

At times, Chase guessed everyone was right, to some extent. Sometimes, he felt like he was alone in the Keys. He went through half his savings trying to make it on fishing boats, taking pictures of tourists and the great fish they caught from their deep sea fishing trips. Then, his underwater photography caught the attention of a few magazines. They used his photos in several advertisements, but he still was barely keeping his head above water.

When his sister's friend needed a photographer for a wedding, all it took was that first event for his services to become in demand. The pictures he took while they exchanged vows on the beach were breathtaking, according to the bride and groom. Now Chase knew most of the wedding planners in the Keys, and his schedule stayed very full. Best of all, he was finally making it on his own in a place he loved, following in Skylar's footsteps.

He and Skylar lived nearby each other, only a street separating him from his sister. This was great for both of them because they had always been close growing up. Plus, Chase got to see his little niece frequently. Taylor was becoming a handful, and at three years old, she was beautiful, just like her mom. Skylar's husband, Garrett, and Chase were now best friends, even though Garrett was much older than him. But on those nights when they went out for a few beers and just to talk, it was like the two men were brothers.

Chase had to admit there were times when he wondered if he had made the right decision to leave his parents' business. A sense of guilt crossed his mind when he attended the family dinners every few weeks. Even though he didn't have to go, Chase usually made a point of attending the family events on Sunday, along with Skylar and Garrett.

Chase could remember when their family was almost torn apart by their parents. His mother's drinking and his father's constant working had created a rift in the family over the years. It was Maggie, the family's housekeeper and cook that usually had helped the children, including his older sister, Mara, and his eldest brother, Harris. She did her best to keep the children from noticing that their parents were having problems. And a good job she did. It was not until they were older that Chase and his siblings could look back and see that even though they had really lacked for nothing growing up on Key Biscayne, their family had been dysfunctional in so many ways.

Chase's sisters and brother had finally taken their own route to find their way in the world. Harris was now in charge of the family real estate business, though Chase's father was still there, saying he would never truly leave or retire. Mara, his other older sister, also worked part-time, but spent most of her time with her children. And Skylar and Chase had left Miami behind and escaped to the Florida Keys.

As the wedding ceremony began, Chase moved around the beach, doing his best to stay out of the way as much as possible, but still get the shots he needed that would please the bride and groom. At 6'3" tall with light brown hair, tanned skin, and a well-toned physique, it was hard not only to stay out of the way, but not to attract the attention of a bridesmaid or two.

Chase had done his share of dating since arriving in the Keys and much more so after becoming a wedding photographer. But he had yet to meet that elusive special someone, which was fine with him. There had been one person he met since moving to the Keys that he thought might have been his other half, but it had ended with Chase being hurt once more.

After what had happened between him and Blair, then another relationship once he was living here, Chase just wanted to solidify his business. That was his number one priority right now. Not that his sister hadn't continued to try playing matchmaker on many occasions, saying that he needed a woman in his life, but he was content for now. One day, Chase Cartwright would find that woman he couldn't live without.

"So, I think I have all the pictures I need," Chase said to Mandy, the wedding planner, as they watched the wedding festivities wind down. "I'll have them sent to the bride and groom on Monday. Sound good?"

"Perfect. So glad this went well. Earlier today, I thought that maybe this wedding wasn't going to happen. Another hung-over groom and a frustrated bride. I tell ya - this business keeps you on your toes, but I wouldn't be doing anything else. We're still on for Wednesday, right? The Lawson wedding? They are flying in tomorrow. Not a big one, only the bride and groom, parents, friends – about twenty-five people - so should be an easy evening shoot." Mandy quickly looked at her phone. "Just double-checking I told you right."

"I'll be there," Chase said, waving to her and heading to his car.

2

As soon as he turned the key in the ignition, he put the air conditioner on full blast. It was warm outside today, but not as hot as it could be. But when Chase was moving from one side of a venue to another, making sure he got all the usual wedding photographs, plus ones he spied spontaneously, he became hot very quickly. The cool air coming from the car vents felt good to him.

Plus, he was hungry. He quickly took his phone out of his pocket and dialed a number.

"Hello," the woman answered, sounding as though she was in a rush.

"Hi, my most wonderful sister, who is the best mom and boat captain in the Florida Keys," Chase said smoothly.

"Come on over. I just finished fixing a pot of spaghetti."

"I knew you were my favorite sister for some reason."

"It's only because Mara is in Miami, and I'm here," Skylar said, still sounding a bit frazzled, but laughing.

"I'll be there in ten minutes."

It wasn't long before Chase was sitting on the back porch of Garrett and Skylar's home, which overlooked the large canal that led to the magnificent Atlantic Ocean. The instant he had walked in the door, his little niece wrapped her tiny arms around one of his legs, begging him to play with her.

Instead, Chase convinced her that they would have a "tea party" on the back porch, making sure her dad was included in the fun. Except Chase and Garrett weren't drinking tea. Each had a beer in their hands as Taylor sat at a small table between the two of them with her tea set, pretending to pour liquid into the tiny cups.

"You guys go out today?" Chase asked, leaning his head back and relaxing in the soft chair.

"Skylar stayed here with Taylor since Annie couldn't come over. I took out a snorkeling tour this morning, then Max took a scuba group this afternoon. The other boats were gone on fishing trips all day." Garrett was also sitting back against the chair, head relaxed, but looking over at his daughter to check on her every minute or so.

"Sounds like business is doing good."

"It's all Skylar's fault," Garrett said with a laugh. "She might not have liked the family real estate business, but she used what she learned for the boat charters. They stay booked, which is a blessing."

"Don't you have a research project coming up soon?" Chase asked, taking another swig of the ice-cold drink in his hand.

"Yep. Working with sea turtles again, but I love it. They are doing some good work down here, which helps other areas of the country. What about you?"

"Doing the wedding thing. Not complaining because it's great money. Never knew so many people wanted to get married in the Keys. Still want to put that portfolio together of the wildlife down here, especially the underwater marine life, but I just haven't had any time. Too many people falling in love."

"You know that you can come on any of the snorkel and scuba trips. Just let us know. The tourists always love your personal pictures," Garret replied.

"I need to do that. But like I said, the number of weddings taking place here just boggles my mind sometimes," Chase laughed.

"Seeing anyone special right now?" Garrett asked.

Chase looked over at Garrett as though he had grown a third head. "OK, now you sound like my sister. You're supposed to be my friend, not my personal dating guru."

"Sorry, but she worries about you. Says that you are alone too much."

"That's why I come and bother you guys all the time," Chase said. "But to answer your question, no one right now. Although, my neighbor sure wished it was different."

"You mean Maria? She still stalking you?" Garrett questioned.

"I guess you can't call it stalking, but it seems like she shows up in a lot of the same places I do. But I've learned my lesson about women."

Chase was transported back in time to a year ago, when he thought he had found the woman he wanted to spend his life with. Her name was Shari, and she had moved to the Keys on a whim, working as a waitress at a local restaurant while writing her first novel. At least that was what she had told Chase.

The pair had met when she happened to take his order, and they started flirting with each other. The two hit it off immediately, and soon, any time that was available, they were together. They had explored the Florida Keys from one end to the other. It lasted for seven months, and then, one day, Shari was gone with not a word to Chase. He went to the little house she had been renting, and it was completely empty. She wouldn't return his calls. He was completely devastated and understandably confused. This was the second time he had been burned, and he wondered if he just had a knack for picking the wrong women.

Chase did receive a letter from Shari a few weeks later, and what she had written startled him. She wrote that she was sorry, but her husband finally said he would change and had begged her to come back home. Husband? Chase thought he had known her completely, but that bit of news shook him.

Ever since, he was wary of letting himself fall for someone. He kept his dating casual, choosing to concentrate on his photography and leave romance behind.

"You know there are good women out there," Garrett said, nodding his head toward Chase's sister. "You just have to be willing to let the past go."

"Now I think you and my sister have exchanged bodies!" Chase exclaimed with a smile.

"What about me?" It seemed like his sister had materialized out of thin air and was suddenly sitting on the arm of Garrett's chair.

"Just asking Chase about his love life."

"I've given up on that," Skylar said. "He's too picky and jaded right now. But there is someone that is going to come along and knock his socks off. I can feel it."

"Well, don't hold your breath, big sister."

3

Bailey Parker needed to leave Key West – and fast. The problem was she didn't know why the desire to go was so strong, but she felt it in every fiber of her being.

She loved Key West and had been here for almost four years with not so much as a peep from anyone that she didn't know. But now, some stranger had asked about her at the restaurant she managed. She just happened to be standing behind the door when the man's voice had traveled toward her office. She peeked around the corner to see his face but she could not remember ever seeing him before. But just hearing the man say her name sent chills down her spine and set off the alarm bells in her head.

It frustrated Bailey because people she didn't know asked for her all the time at the restaurant. She was the manager, for goodness sakes. But this was different, and that was the thing that confused her. Bailey had no idea why she would react this way.

If only I could remember, she thought as she tightly squeezed her eyes shut. She was so far away from California, on a tiny island. Why these feelings now, and where would she go? She loved the Keys, and for some odd reason she had yet to understand, she knew that this was where she belonged.

Bailey had found a home in Key West, though she loved all the islands of the Florida Keys. When she became manager at the little restaurant, she seemed to fit right into life in the tropical city. She felt a kinship to these islands of south Florida. It felt right to be here, even though Bailey still had no idea why.

All she knew was after the accident, the only thing she remembered – or should she say, *felt* – was the overwhelming desire to come to the Southernmost part of the United States. The only conclusion Bailey had come to was that maybe the tranquil atmosphere of the islands would help her regain her memory. And if they would, Bailey was determined to stay somewhere in the Keys no matter who might be looking for her.

"Hey, Danny, who was that?" Bailey asked as she came around the corner, seeing the strange man exiting the restaurant and walking down the street.

"Oh, hey. I didn't know you were back. He asked for you, but I told him you weren't here. Do you want me to go catch him?" Danny started heading for the door before Bailey could utter a word.

"No," Bailey said fast, almost a bit too quickly, leaving Danny with a puzzled look on his face. "I'm sure he will be back around. I'm too busy right now to talk to anyone since we are putting this party together tonight. I'll have to talk to him later." Bailey tried to act as though the incident was no big deal, but she couldn't shake the feeling that it was time to leave this beautiful city.

Bailey always wondered when she would know she should start looking again, trying to find something that would help her remember her past. But, like the doctors and her many therapists had told her, with the type of injury she had sustained, it could take time. They also reminded her gently that she might not ever recall her past. If Bailey allowed herself to focus on that last fact, depression would settle upon her fast, so she quickly shook the errant thought from her mind, instead focusing on what she needed to do to leave Key West as soon as possible.

When Bailey had left San Diego over four years ago, the only thing she knew was that she was heading to Florida. While she was in the hospital, recovering from a life-altering injury, no one had come to visit her, and even if they did, she wouldn't have known who they were. The fall and severe blow to her head had erased all her memory.

Bailey remembered waking up that day. She learned that she was finally out of her coma that had lasted for two days. The police had informed Bailey that apparently, she had been texting and almost stepped out in front of a delivery truck. A woman behind her grabbed her by her arm, yanking her backwards, and Bailey's head took the brunt of the fall.

Bailey couldn't remember anything, and they had no way to identify her. Her phone had landed in the street, which the truck had smashed into tiny pieces with its tires. The only items that were in the small handbag on her shoulder were some cash, Tylenol, and two keys. Every few days, the officers visited to see if she could remember anything, but nothing came to her. It was like her mind was a blank slate.

The only visitor she did have was Dena Singleton, the woman that had saved her life. The first day she visited, she told Bailey again what had happened and that she had come by to check on her. But soon, Dena was visiting every day, becoming the only friend Bailey had. When Bailey was asked by the doctors to pick a name for herself, Dena helped her. In fact, the day that Bailey was able to leave the hospital, it was Dena and her husband, Stan, that came and picked her up, giving her a temporary place to stay.

The police had told Bailey that the keys they had found in her purse were to a car and a house or apartment, but there was no way to identify where they were. So, she stayed with Dena and Stan for a week. They even gave Bailey a car, helped her get her driver's license, and gave her money, which Bailey insisted would only be a loan, so she could travel across the country.

They told her that it was too soon for her to leave, but Bailey insisted. She called Dena a few times to let her know that she was OK, but then lost touch. Not knowing her past made Bailey so leery of many things, and her anxiety was sometimes more than she could handle. But her therapist in Key West had helped so much.

"Tina, I'm going to have to leave for the day. The shipments are in, and the staff is putting everything up. Prep has started, and you know the rest. I'll call later to check in, but you have my cell if you need anything," Bailey said, looking at her assistant manager.

"Are you OK?" the other woman asked.

"Fine. Why?"

"Because it is weird for Miss Work-A-Holic to just take off in the middle of the day, like I try to get you to do. Plus, you seem a bit nervous."

Bailey thought that she was acting her normal self, but then, her friend could probably read her well after all this time.

"I'm fine. Just have some errands to do."

"Then, for once, have fun. You never do this, so relax a little, OK?" Tina asked.

Bailey just smiled, gathered her purse, laptop, and any other personal items she couldn't just leave behind, and stuffed them into her handbag and tote. She would have to leave, and she hated to do this to the owners, but she knew that Tina would be there, and she was the best.

Bailey also knew this meant starting over, but she wasn't going to go very far. Islamorada would be her next stop. No one was going to drive her away from these islands because she knew there was something here that would help her find her past.

Once she reached her new city, Bailey would start from scratch. She felt good about the money she had saved this entire time. She had something to help her, but as Bailey left the city of Key West behind, she decided that after this move, she wasn't going to run anymore. If someone found her, whoever it was, she would face whatever happened head-on. She was tired of looking over her shoulder, always wondering.

Hopefully, Islamorada would be the haven Bailey had always wanted in her life.

4

Chase met Mandy at Key Largo Bay Marriott Beach Resort for the mid-week wedding. Chase liked these smaller weddings because it seemed everyone was a bit more relaxed than the more formal ones that seemed to take place on the weekends. They appeared to have fun and embrace the relaxed vibe of the islands. There were times, though, when things got a bit too rowdy, but Chase knew it would give the bride and groom more memories, even though some of the things he saw, the couple might wish they didn't have.

"You're here early," Mandy Thompson said as Chase walked up to the bar.

"Thought that I would get some more shots of this place, especially the exterior. Never know when I might be able to sell some pictures for a new brochure. Always keep a stash of photos ready." Chase sat his equipment beside him and ordered a tropical smoothie.

"No alcohol, right?" Mandy asked, scrutinizing Chase with a motherly look.

He laughed. "You know I never drink on the job. Where is that coming from?"

"I had a caterer last week that I think was more drunk than the wedding party. Thank goodness, he had an excellent assistant. I think I've heard from him every day since, apologizing. Even sent me flowers!"

"That's because you are one of the best wedding planners in the Keys. Doesn't want to get on your bad side, not that you have one."

"One of the best?" Mandy teased him.

"Right now, the best. Hey, is that the bride?" Chase said, motioning to a woman walking toward them. She was very attractive, with thick, auburn hair that fell past her shoulders and complemented her cream-colored skin. But it was her eyes, the color of blue that rivaled the waters surrounding the Keys, that caught Chase's attention.

"I'm hoping it's my interview for my new assistant."

"New assistant? What happened to Gerri?" Chase asked quickly, still not taking his gaze away from the woman approaching them.

"Quit three days ago. I've been working twenty hours a day since. I'm desperate for someone now. Hope this girl has the skills I need."

■ ■ ■

Bailey walked up to the couple sitting at the bar. She knew this was the place she had agreed to meet the wedding planner,

Mandy, but she hadn't expect the gentleman beside her. His tousled blond hair and deep blue eyes were mesmerizing. Bailey could see the ripples of toned abs underneath the shirt he wore, and his exposed arms confirmed her suspicion.

He was gorgeous, and for the first time that she could remember, she was feeling something more for a man than just friendship. There was a physical attraction to him, though they had yet to say a word to each other.

"Are you Bailey Parker?" asked Mandy, getting off the bar stool to stand in front of the young lady.

"Yes, and you must be Mandy," Bailey said, reaching her hand out to the woman. She hoped the Mandy didn't feel her hand shaking, but the anxiety of starting a new job and a new life, once again, was almost overwhelming.

"Yes, I am," said Mandy, shaking Bailey's hand.

"It's nice to meet you." Bailey kept her gaze on Mandy, but it was hard to ignore the man sitting on the barstool.

"Let's go sit over here at the table and talk. Oh, and by the way, this is Chase Cartwright, my wedding photographer."

Bailey's hand slipped into Chase's outstretched one and a tingle danced up her arm. He was even more handsome up close.

"Nice to meet you, Bailey," Chase said. "And good luck."

"Thanks."

■ ■ ■

Chase watched as the two women walked over to one of the many empty tables at the hotel's restaurant. He couldn't help but watch Bailey, as discreetly as he could. There was an instant attraction to her, something that took him by surprise.

The girl was beautiful, especially with those blue eyes. He found himself staring at the two women and being caught as Bailey slightly turned and looked in his direction. Chase quickly swiveled around, reaching for his camera bag and expertly catching it before it slid off the bar. He looked up to see Bailey with a slight smile on her face before she turned back to Mandy, who was talking while trying to show her some of the papers that were scattered across the table where they sat.

Great! Chase thought. *Now I look like an idiot.* At this point, he figured that the best thing was to retreat outside while the women talked. But he hoped that Bailey would get the job. If she did, Chase knew he would look forward to every wedding Mandy had scheduled on the books.

■ ■ ■

Bailey listened as Mandy explained the details of the job she was applying for, one she felt she was perfectly capable of doing. The business of planning weddings sounded great, a change of pace from what she had been doing for the last three years. And as an assistant and not a manager, Bailey hoped that whoever that mysterious man was would not be able to find her.

She still had that feeling in the pit of her stomach that he was seeking her out for reasons she didn't know. But what if someone was trying to find her that wanted to help her? If so, why had they waited so long to find her? No one sought her out when she went missing, so why now?

"Well, what do you think?" Mandy asked.

Bailey had been so absorbed in her thoughts that she had only half-heard what Mandy had described, but she didn't care. "It sounds great, but don't you want to know more about me?"

"Well, we talked on the phone, and you answered most of my questions, or you wouldn't be here today. Your resume looks great, and though you don't have as many references as I require, today is your lucky day. I need someone now! Like, today! Plus, your work will let me know all I need. This business can be fast-paced, can change on a dime, and we have to be able to handle problems fast and quickly. Are you up for the challenge? Because if you are, you have the job. And it would begin the minute we stand up from this table. I have a wedding taking place in a little over an hour, and I need some help. Thank goodness it is a small one."

"I would love it, but what is the pay?" Bailey hated to ask, but she was still living in a little hotel and needed to find her own place soon. Though she had her nest egg set aside to live on, she needed to make sure the money would be enough.

Mandy shook her head. "So sorry that I forgot to tell you. Just a bit frazzled since my assistant left the other day."

"Why did she leave?" Bailey wondered if something was wrong with the job that someone would leave in such a hurry, but hadn't she done the exact same thing only a few weeks ago?

"She claims she fell in love. She moved rather quickly to Chicago to be with a guy she met during one of the weddings we planned. Not the groom, of course, but his brother. Have to admit, the guy was awful cute, but Gerri left so quickly. Just hope she doesn't end up with a broken heart."

"Wow, that was a big leap of faith," Bailey said.

"Well, Bailey, most things in life are."

As soon as Mandy went over the salary, Bailey found herself filling out the necessary paperwork for her new job. She was now a wedding planner assistant. And she was glad that she had dressed appropriately for the interview because Bailey was instantly at work.

But she was also happy for another reason. If Chase Cartwright was Mandy's main wedding photographer, Bailey would be seeing more of him, and that suited her just fine.

5

Bailey's first wedding with Mandy went off without a hitch. Bailey anticipated a few of the snags they ran into and instantly helped Mandy like she was an old pro. It startled her at first that she knew what to do, but she figured it was just instinct.

But then again, the doctors and therapists had told her to watch for things like this. They could be clues to who she was before that fateful accident that stripped her of her identity.

"You were perfect today," Mandy said, giving Bailey a hug. "Are you sure you have never done this before?"

"Positive," Bailey said. As far as she knew, she was speaking the truth.

"Well, I think you're going to do just fine. Let's meet tomorrow morning around ten o'clock. I'll text you the address to the office and we'll go over the schedule. I'll show you what you'll be doing there and so on. Right now, I'm so ready to head home, soak in the bathtub, and go to bed early. I can't believe there was a time when I did this all on my own."

"I know it's only my first wedding but I can't believe you used to do this all by yourself either. It was a lot of work, but fun. I'll see you tomorrow morning." Bailey turned to walk to her car and immediately bumped into Chase.

During the wedding, Bailey had watched him when she could. He seemed to be made for this job because he knew all the right angles, poses, and just what to say to elicit a laugh or two from the wedding party. She knew his photos had to be wonderful because he was a complete natural. And it didn't hurt that he was extremely easy on the eyes.

This was the first time she had ever really felt anything for a man that she could remember. Even the entire time she lived in Key West, there had been no one special. Sure, people had set her up on blind dates, and she had gone even though anxiety would be her constant companion every time, but no one had ever intrigued her.

Bailey had been more interested in her work, and that had kept her very busy. And when she wasn't working, she learned all about the city and the Keys themselves, hoping she would find clues that would help her find out why she was drawn to the islands. But now things had changed. Now there was Chase.

"I'm so sorry," Bailey said quickly. "I didn't see you standing there." Though, how she could have missed him, she wasn't sure.

"I did come up behind you a little quickly, but I thought you heard my footsteps. But then again, you were talking to Mandy."

"Just getting some more details of my new job."

"Well, it seemed like you were a big help today. I was sure the bride was about to have a meltdown about the shells, but the flowers you grabbed were a great substitute. And Mandy kept singing your praises every time she had a chance. So, I know you made a good impression."

Bailey was sure her cheeks were a bright red because she could feel the heat emanating from them. Here was this gorgeous man right in front of her, with a sexy smile, giving her a wonderful compliment about her first day as the assistant.

"I'm glad because I needed the job. Plus, I like weddings, especially here in the Keys. They seem to be just a bit more special." Bailey reached into her handbag for her car keys. "It was nice meeting you today. I guess I'll be seeing you again. Mandy is going over the wedding schedule with me tomorrow."

"Well, you came to work during the busiest season, so I'm sure we will definitely be seeing each other. Welcome to Islamorada, Bailey," Chase said before moving out of her way.

She walked toward her car, but not before she gave him an over-the-shoulder glance with a smile.

■ ■ ■

Chase watched as Bailey made her way to the parking lot. The spark between them was undeniable. Bailey was different, and he had no way to explain what it was. Though Chase had dated before, there was something about Bailey, and he had no way to explain what it was and no one to ask why he was feeling this way.

It was obvious he couldn't talk to his sister. Skylar was always trying to set him up with someone, and if she found out about this new girl, she would find Bailey and have her over for dinner before Chase could even see Bailey again.

Maybe he could talk to Garrett, only after swearing him to secrecy. Right now, though, he watched Bailey drive away, wondering where she lived, who she was, her phone number, and so much more. He couldn't wait till he could talk to her again.

When he opened the door to his house, Chase was immediately greeted by Moose. The little mix-breed dog was only ten pounds, but the name suited him just fine. Chase remembered the day he decided to get a dog, thinking that he would be bringing home a lab mix from the rescue shelter, but one look at Moose and he was hooked. The little dog was a mix of terrier and he wasn't sure what else, but he had become Chase's constant companion. When Chase wasn't working, Moose was with him just about everywhere he went.

"Hi, there. Give me a minute, and we will go for a walk," Chase said. Moose was wagging his tail so vigorously that he was about to dust the coffee table. "I could use a little time to sit on the bench. Sound good to you?" he suggested, looking at the excited dog panting at his legs.

After grabbing a drink from the refrigerator and a few treats for Moose and the fish at the dock, Chase and the dog walked down the street to the empty bench that overlooked the water.

The little bench with the dock close by was beautiful and one of Chase's favorite places to unwind after the day. With one look at the ocean and the sky, Chase knew it wouldn't be long before he would get to witness another beautiful Florida Keys sunset.

As he watched the colors above him reflect off the water and meld into different shades as the sun made its descent toward the horizon, he secretly wished that he had brought his camera. He had plenty of sunset photos, but tonight looked as though it was going to be extra colorful. But Chase didn't have the desire that bad to go back to the house and try to get back to the dock in time. Instead, he decided to sit on the bench with Moose by his side and enjoy nature's picture show.

"Well, hi, there."

Chase knew who the woman was from her voice before she came around the corner. It was Maria, his neighbor who lived a few houses down from his. *Be polite*, he told himself.

"Hi, Maria. How are you doing?"

"Good. Thought I would come down and watch the sunset. Didn't know that I would be running into you. Mind if I share that bench with you and Moose?"

Chase doubted if what Maria said was true since he did have to walk by her house to get to get to this little spot on the island. But he slid to one side, making Moose move along with him. This way, the dog was between him and Maria. This would keep Maria at a distance since she tended to sit just a little too close for Chase's comfort.

"Looks like it's going to be really nice tonight. Haven't talked to you in a while. How have you been doing?" Maria asked.

"Fine. Just working a lot." Chase didn't want to be rude, but he wished that it was only him and Moose sitting on the bench because he wasn't into a conversation tonight, especially with his neighbor. His thoughts were still on Bailey.

"Yeah, weddings are pretty popular here lately. The restaurant received another catering gig for next week for a beach wedding at a private home. Are you shooting pics for the Roberts wedding?"

"Not sure. I haven't really looked ahead at the schedule yet."

"Let me know. I will probably be there, and maybe we can go out for a drink afterwards. Always seems nice to unwind after a stress-filled couple of hours."

Chase wished he knew a way to tactfully tell Maria that she was nice, but he just wasn't interested in her. But from the moment Chase moved onto her street, she had made a point to find him, whether he was just getting home, working in the yard, or down here on the bench.

"Well, usually, I just come home to relax. Trying to get the right pictures to please the happy couple can keep me moving around so much that I just like to kick back and relax at home."

"Then we could come back to your place and order a pizza. Maybe have a few beers."

"I'll let you know. Not even sure if I'm doing that wedding. I'm also working on the charter boat with my sister next week, too. Probably going to be pretty busy." Chase stood up, ready to go. He knew that he wasn't going to be able to enjoy the evening like he had hoped.

"You know, Chase, I'm not that bad. I wish you'd give me a chance."

Chase halted, Moose coming to stand beside him, and glanced back at Maria.

"Maria, it's not you. I'm just not looking for a relationship right now. I'm concentrating on work, building my business. I know you understand that with everything you do at the restaurant with your parents."

"But I also know that it is better to have someone to share it all with," Maria said. She came to stand beside him, so close that Chase could feel her arm brush up against his.

"Goodnight, Maria."

"Bye, Chase. See you next week."

Chase felt like the woman was boring holes into his back as he walked back down the street to his house. The bad part was that he might have partially lied to her. Today, he did meet someone that intrigued him like no other, someone that he could see spending more time with. And her name was Bailey.

6

Bailey sat on the edge of the bed and took her shoes off slowly, then flopped back on the soft pillow top. Though she felt as though every muscle in her body was worn out, she smiled.

She had enjoyed her first day on the job, every minute of it. And for some reason, Bailey appeared to know what she was doing. Maybe she had been a wedding planner before she lost her memory? She laughed at the thought because it sounded crazy to her, but it was something that she would write in her journal for future reference. Every snippet of information, even something as small as this thought, could help her piece together who she was before the accident.

And then there was Chase. Just the thought of him made her shiver all over, and Bailey couldn't erase the smile from her face. There was an attraction to him, for sure. But she had promised herself no serious relationships till she could find out about her past.

But at the thought of Chase, she wondered what she would do if she never regained her memories. For the first time that she could remember, she felt like there was a small possibility that she could build a life starting from where she was now. Except for that nagging thought that she knew someone was looking for her.

The smile suddenly disappeared. In the excitement of today, Bailey had forgotten about that man. Hopefully, he was long gone since she didn't tell anyone where she was going. Yes, she was still in the Keys, but people could get lost down here and hopefully, whoever this person was, he would lose her, too. Bailey clung to that thought, willing it so, and this helped to settle the unease that had burst forth at the thought of someone finding her.

For Bailey, it was weird to experience this. After her accident, she always wondered why no one had come to look for her. And now, it seemed someone was finally trying to find her and she ran away! Right now Bailey felt like she needed to hide away from the world, except for the fact that she knew with all her heart that she belonged in the Florida Keys.

The rumble of her stomach let Bailey know that she was hungry. She thought and couldn't remember when she had last eaten. Was it breakfast this morning? It had to be. Mandy had put her straight to work and with everything that she had done, Bailey had literally forgotten to take a break for a quick snack during the wedding. Now she laughed out loud because that just wasn't her, but the work had been so enjoyable that food had been the last thing on her mind.

Bailey made her way through the room, where stacks of boxes were lined up next to the small refrigerator and microwave that had been provided by the hotel. She had a mix of a few different foods being heated in the appliance, but microwaving something yet again wasn't very appealing to her. Even though she was tired, Bailey grabbed her handbag and headed out. It would be take-out for her, and she knew just the place. Though her choice of food wouldn't be the healthiest, she didn't care at the moment. Only that it would be just what she needed after her exciting but long day.

Before long, she was sitting outside on the porch at the Hog Heaven Bar and Grill. She loved the little restaurant not only for the food, but for the great view of the water. They even had a little beach area with a few lounge chairs, but tonight, that area was already filled with people who looked like they were celebrating something or someone.

She had come here to get an order to go, but one look at the beautiful sky and the pending sunset, Bailey ordered her food so she could sit outside and watch nature's beauty unfold before her. As she waited for her order, she was tempted to pull out her phone to check any emails, but decided to just relax instead.

"Hey, there. Mind if I join you?" Bailey looked to see a man much older than her standing with two beers in his hand. "I even brought you a beer."

"Um, thanks, but I don't drink beer and…"

"So sorry I'm late. Got held up at work." Bailey now looked to see Chase standing next to the man, and she was so grateful for the intervention. And very stunned.

"Ah, yes, I figured that was the problem," Bailey said, looking at the other gentleman and shrugging her shoulders.

Then she watched him walk away toward another woman sitting by herself at the other end of the bar.

"Thank you," Bailey said as Chase made himself comfortable in the seat next to hers.

"No problem. You come here often?" Chase said then shook his head. "Wow, that sounded so cheesy."

Bailey laughed, and it felt good. She was glad to see him not only for helping her deter the man earlier, but because Chase had still been in the forefront of her thoughts since she left the wedding venue today.

"Don't worry about it. But I do love this place. I think it's the fourth time I've been here in a week."

"Then I guess you are used to fending off unwanted suitors," Chase said with an impish grin on his face.

"Yeah, fighting them off with a stick."

"Well, I know that if I'd seen you here before today, I might have been one of those guys."

Bailey was startled a bit by Chase's comment and could only smile as her food was set before her.

"I'll have what she's having," Chase said quickly before the waitress could walk away.

"How do you know what it is?"

"It looks like a juicy, very delicious cheeseburger with a wonderful order of French fries."

Bailey grinned. "I guess that was a stupid question."

"There is never a stupid question. So, I thought you would be so tired that you would have gone home and collapsed. You were certainly very busy today."

"I did get back to the hotel and contemplated a microwave dinner, but then decided to treat myself. I guess you could say a celebration of sorts. Plus, it looks as though we are in for a wonderful sunset tonight."

"Agree with you there. I came here because I was just too lazy to cook. Thought that I would go bug my sister, but just did that not too long ago, so I don't want to wear out my welcome."

Bailey looked over at him and couldn't help but smile as she ate a few French fries. Sitting this close to him, she could see more of the features that made this man so appealing. The blond hair with those bright blue eyes had entranced her earlier. His smile was so genuine, and the very masculine undercurrent he emanated sent her senses reeling.

If these feelings kept up, Bailey wasn't sure she could keep that promise to not pursue dating now. She had to admit that she had only spent less than twenty-four hours with Chase, and he was already occupying most of her thoughts.

"So, you have a sister living nearby?" Bailey asked, trying to concentrate on the conversation and her food.

"Yeah. She owns a boat charter business, and her husband is a marine biologist. They are also the parents of the sweetest girl on the island – my three-year-old niece who loves tea parties. I get coerced into participating in one every time I show up on their door step." Chase took a sip of his beer and the waitress was quickly back with his food. "So, what about you? You here with anyone else?"

"Nope, just me," Bailey said, glancing at him.

"Independent woman. I like that."

"Well, this independent woman needs to get back to her room. I have a feeling that I might have a long day tomorrow, trying to learn the ropes at my new job. I really like Mandy, but she seems like a bit of a perfectionist, which probably isn't a bad thing in this profession. I just want to make a good impression." Bailey almost wished she hadn't said anything about Mandy to Chase because she knew the pair had been working together for a while. She hadn't meant for the comment to sound bad.

"You have no idea," Chase laughed, "but don't leave just yet. I just got my food."

"I'm sorry, but I really need to go. I guess we will be seeing each other soon, though, from the way Mandy talked about the wedding schedule."

"I have a feeling we will."

"Thanks again for my earlier rescue. And enjoy your dinner. Bye, Chase."

As Bailey left the bar and grill, she had another silly smile on her face. First, she got to work with him today and then to spend a little time with him tonight. Bailey sure hoped that this was a sign of things to come.

7

Chase lay in his bed, doing his best to fall asleep. But for the first time in such a long while, he was thinking about a woman that had most definitely piqued his interest. It felt so good to him, and yet, so scary as he thought about his past relationships with Blair and Shari. But Bailey was different. It was like she had come out of nowhere and captured his attention.

He had watched her walk out of the bar and grill tonight, her red hair swaying with her walk. But her hair wasn't all he observed. For him, Bailey had curves in the all the right places, and every step she took made him think things he shouldn't so soon after meeting her. Sitting close beside her tonight, he was able to take in more of her delicate features, like the small freckles that graced her cheeks and nose. And once more, the aqua color of her eyes. She was beautiful, and he could certainly understand why the older man at the restaurant had wanted to make her acquaintance. Except Chase was pretty sure the man had more on his mind than just a beer with Bailey. But didn't he, too?

Chase tossed and turned, but it was with a grin on his face, not a feeling of frustration. The only thing that allowed him to fall asleep was the realization that he would be seeing the girl again in the next few days. Of that, he was sure. Chase had another wedding schedule with Mandy in a few days, and now he couldn't wait for the weekend.

Even though his night had been restless, Chase was up early, his clock waking him up. He felt good this morning and instantly knew the reason why. A picture of a red-haired woman floated in his mind.

Today, he was working on the boat charter with Skylar, taking pictures of the tourists on their snorkeling trip. Hopefully, there was a scuba group, too. Chase hadn't dived in a while, and just the thought of it sounded peaceful and relaxing. He grabbed his gear by the front door and was out like a flash.

"Wow, you are here early," Skylar said as her baby brother approached the boat. "Usually, I'm wondering if you will make it on time. Plus, you are smiling. What is going on?"

"What are you talking about? I'm always on time, even if I only have minutes to spare. I still show up. I love going out in the boat with you. Plus, you always give me a time to be at the dock way before your passengers are even supposed to be here," Chase said as he looked around.

"Because I like for my *employees* to be here before them," Skylar said, coming to stand beside him, staring at him with a quizzical look. "So, are you going to tell me what's happened?"

"What?"

"Don't give me that crap. I've not seen you look this happy in a while."

"Man, you make it sound like I'm depressed all the time."

"Didn't mean it like that, and you know it. You are just different today. You can't hide it from you sister."

"It's a girl," Garrett said, seeming to appear out of nowhere.

"You met someone and didn't tell me?" Skylar said, her eyes lighting up like headlights on a very dark night. She gently punched Chase in the arm.

Chase just looked at Garrett, dumbstruck.

"I told you," Garrett said with a mischievous smile. "Sorry, but I know that look."

"She is just a work acquaintance," Chase said, knowing that he had lost this battle. There was no way Skylar was going to give this up, especially since Garrett could apparently read minds.

"I knew you would eventually hook up with a bridesmaid. It was a bridesmaid, right? Not the bride?" Skylar asked seriously.

"Really, Skylar? You think I would do that? And no, she is Mandy's new assistant. And we just met yesterday. We worked a wedding, and we will probably just see each other at weddings. Nothing more."

"The way you walked up to the boat with that goofy grin, I know so well, I can tell that it is a little more than just work for you."

Chase sighed because he had to admit that Skylar was right. Chase was thinking of Bailey and even wondered what she was doing right now. *Man, this is ridiculous! You just met her yesterday,* Chase chided himself.

"Can you please give it a rest? I've got a job to do and need to get ready without all the harassing comments."

"Well, I can't wait to meet her," Skylar said. She walked past her brother this time, giving him an excited squeeze of his arm.

■ ■ ■

Bailey was at Mandy's office at nine o'clock sharp. As she thought about the previous night, she was glad that she had gone out to eat, but Bailey never thought that she would run into Chase. She had been enjoying the evening as she sat by herself, watching the ocean water from her bar stool. But having Chase save her from the very persistent older man, then just the two of them talking for a while felt so good.

"Good morning, and thanks for being on time," Mandy said as Bailey took a seat in front of her new employer's desk. "That was a trait my last assistant didn't value very much, though she was good at her job. But I have to say, Bailey, you did wonderfully yesterday. I don't think I've ever had someone work for me that was so intuitive as to what needed to be done. Are you sure you have never done this before?"

"I'm pretty sure," Bailey said politely, knowing her response was more accurate than Mandy knew. She still could only wonder what she did for a career before that fateful day.

"Well, I typed up this list. Everyone that works for me will tell you I'm a list-maker. So, this is what I need done here at the office and when we are on the job site, I mean the weddings. I also printed up a list of our suppliers, venues, and transportation businesses. This is the important one," Mandy said, holding up a single sheet of paper. "The list of our upcoming weddings."

Mandy handed the stack of papers to Bailey. It only took a glance at the wedding list for Bailey to know that they were going to be busy, which for her right now, was perfect.

"I need you to make sure that you have this information with you at all times. I don't care if it is on a computer, tablet, phone, or paper in a notebook. I want you to have it with you always. You never know when you are going to need it. Plus, like I told you yesterday, there will be times I might have to bug you at home. It just comes with the territory."

"It's no problem. Kinda how it was with my last job as the restaurant manager, so I'm familiar with that," Bailey said as she continued to stare down at the list. "I do have a question. What is the 'D' for beside so many of the wedding party names?"

"Out-of-towners. A destination wedding. Very popular here."

"Are you the only wedding planner in town?"

"No, but I like to think that I'm the best," Mandy said with a smile. "My mom was an event planner throughout the Keys till she retired, and I worked with her till she decided to move to Arizona. She left me the business, but I decided to specialize in just weddings. At first, Mom thought I was crazy, but it's been ten years now, and she says she wishes she had thought of the idea first." Mandy got up and motioned for Bailey to follow her.

"So, here is your workspace," Mandy said as she walked to an empty desk on the other side of the partition. "I guess I should have said that you are the receptionist right now, too. I keep promising myself to hire someone, and things just get too busy. But we do need a part-time person. As a matter of fact, if you will put that on that list of to-do's I gave you, that would be great. However you want to get the word out – newspaper, social media – whichever is fine with me.

"If you have any questions, which I know you probably will, just let me know. We don't have a wedding till Saturday, which gives you a couple of days to settle in. Not much time, but after how you performed yesterday, I'm not worried. Welcome to the business, Bailey." Mandy's cell phone was ringing, and she hurried back to her desk.

Bailey sat her things at the desk and was glad that she had a beautiful glass window to look out of. Though her view was mainly of Highway 1, it didn't matter. Just being able to look at the blue sky and sunshine was wonderful.

At the restaurant in Key West, her office had been a back room. There were times when she would just go outside to stand on the sidewalk or slip through the back door to get some fresh air. That feeling of wanting to be outside was another clue that she had put on her ever-growing list of things she liked, desired, didn't care for, and so on. Hopefully, one day, all these bits of information would trigger her memory to come back to her.

Bailey tackled the list that Mandy gave her, trying to do as much as she could without disturbing her new boss. If felt weird to not be the manager, but she was so glad. She didn't want that responsibility, and right now, that felt good. She needed time to herself and not to have to worry if a business was going to survive or not based on her decisions.

From what she could tell, Mandy's business was very popular. The website needed to be updated, but only a small amount. Her social media accounts were lagging a bit behind, but it wasn't anything that Bailey couldn't handle. In fact, she enjoyed the task.

Bailey decided to put all the information that Mandy had given her earlier on her laptop, iPad, and iPhone as well. This way, she would be sure to have it with her, as the apps she used would keep everything synced. Then the paper copies, Bailey would keep here at the office, where they could always be found.

At lunchtime, Mandy had a business meeting, and Bailey stayed behind to man the office. She was glad that she had brought her lunch. She wanted to eat more healthy foods, rather than running to the local fast food stop, but it was hard keeping just the right amount of food in her little refrigerator. As soon as she could, Bailey decided that she had to get her own place.

The office was quiet as Bailey ate her sandwich, and she decided to use the computer for a little investigating. Looking over the vendor list that Mandy had given her earlier, she found out that Chase was the owner of Cartwright Outdoor Photography. She quickly searched the Internet and found his website. The picture of him that popped up on the screen made her heart race, though she had to admit the photo didn't do him justice.

When Bailey read his biography, it was more vague than she expected, but she could see where it would make someone seek out his services. His photography was beautiful, showing pictures from the islands, both on land and on or under the sea. She was surprised to see that he did underwater photography, showing sea life and even some of tourists on vacation.

But Bailey also noticed Chase's name showed up in some of Miami's high society articles. Following one website to the next, it wasn't long before Bailey figured out that Chase's family was a very prominent part of the social circles of Miami. They also had one of the oldest and most successful real estate businesses in south Florida. She read about Chase's sister, Skylar, who lived in the Keys also and had her own business doing boat charters. The more Bailey read about him, the more she was intrigued.

Before she left for the day, Bailey realized that she had accomplished about half the tasks on the to-do list. *Not bad*, she thought for her first – well, second – day on the job.

She bid Mandy goodbye and made her way to the grocery store. She needed to stock up on a few things, something she seemed to do every other day to keep some fresh food around. But now that she had a full-time job, finding an apartment or small home to rent was a very high priority. She would love to have her own place, like she did in Key West. And, from what she could tell, the monthly rent here was much better. She still had a fair amount of money to live on, so she wanted to make sure she found something she really liked. Living in the hotel was getting old very fast.

Bailey reached the store, put her handbag in the cart, and started toward the produce aisle. She grabbed her phone and found her small list. But just as she rounded the corner, her cart almost hit someone looking at the fruit juices.

"I'm so sorry," Bailey said and looked up into familiar blue eyes. It was Chase.

"Wow, it seems that we keep running into each other. Some of us, literally." He laughed, seeing how close she had come to almost hitting him in the legs.

Bailey smiled. "At least I stopped in time. I have to ask. Are you following me?"

"Um, I think I was in the store first. Remember, you almost hit me, right?"

"Uh, right," Bailey said sheepishly.

"So, no, I'm not stalking you, but I can't help but say that I'm glad that I ran into you. I was wondering how your first day on the job was. Let's say your first official day."

"Mandy is great. I have my own desk, and even though I haven't worked for a wedding planner before, I seem to be catching on quickly. I do have a bit of homework tonight, though."

"Homework?" Chase asked.

"Just have a bunch of information she wants me to keep with me at all times, and I have to put it all on my iPad and phone. So, it's dinner and computer time for me tonight."

"So, no eating out?"

"No, that's why I'm at the store. I have to come here pretty often since the fridge I have is small. But not that I'm complaining. At least I have a temporary place to stay."

"How do you cook?"

"Good ol' microwave. It will be nice when I have a stove again."

"Thinking of getting a place soon?"

"Now that I have a job, yes. But looks like it will have to wait till next week sometime. These next few days are going to be quite busy. And I saw that you are going to be at both weddings this weekend," Bailey said. The day had been good so far, but running into Chase was like the icing on top.

"I'll be there."

"You look a little sunburnt right now. You OK?"

"Oh, this is nothing," Chase said as he held out muscular arms that Bailey noticed glistened with lotion. He looked so good, his tanned skin rippling over some very taut muscles. Bailey could feel her heart beat just a little faster. This man was certainly having an effect on her that she couldn't stop. Not that she wanted it to.

"I went out on my sister's charter boat and took pictures for the tourist group she had today. Then I went back out with my brother-in-law and went for a dive. Took some underwater pics since the water was amazing. So, I guess my sunscreen didn't stay on all day."

"Aren't you supposed to reapply after being in the water?" Bailey said, not wanting the conversation to stop.

"Yeah, but I didn't have anyone to help me put it on all over." Chase sent Bailey a grin, and it was certainly flirtatious.

"Well, I'd better go. I really want to get this work done so I can either do a little reading or zone out in front of the TV. Feel like I need some down time since it looks like the next few days could be a bit hectic."

"Well whatever you decide, enjoy your evening, Bailey. I'll see you soon."

This time, it was Bailey watching Chase walk away, and she couldn't keep from staring. This man was fit from head to toe, and even though his clothing might have been loose, Bailey could see the very tone body hiding beneath. And it sent little flutters through her in a very good way.

8

Bailey looked at the checklist once more for the Anderson wedding. The wedding on the beach was set up, and the tent for the reception was ready. The hotel had been so easy to work with, having been the site of plenty of past nuptials. Bailey had checked everything at least once, if not twice, with Mandy checking behind her. The only thing missing at this point was the groom.

Bailey kept looking for the Island Time Trolley that was supposed to deliver the groom about thirty minutes ago, but they hadn't shown yet. There were still thirty minutes till the wedding, but the bride was already here, and she had asked at least a dozen times if her soon-to-be husband was already here.

When she found out that he hadn't arrived, naturally, the bride panicked and blamed it on his bachelor party last night. She went through each scenario as to why he wouldn't show up, her anxiety level rising with each dramatic scene she created.

But Bailey managed to calm her down each time, though now Bailey was getting nervous.

But then the trolley bus pulled into the parking lot, and Bailey breathed a sigh of relief. Mandy walked up behind her, sighed and said, "Thank you," while looking at the sky above. They both watched as the groom and his groomsmen filed out of the trolley, laughing and joking around. Bailey thought Mandy was going to give them all a piece of her mind. Instead, she calmed down and shooed them to the groom's room where, now, they would only be for a few short minutes.

One thing that had calmed the bride was Chase. He was there already, taking pictures of the bride and her bridesmaids, the flower girl, and more. He kept her busy once Chase saw Bailey trying to calm the poor girl down. Bailey said a silent "Thank you" to him, and Chase just gave her a wink that sent that now-familiar shiver through her body. This man really knew how to push those happy buttons for her.

As the wedding progressed, Bailey and Mandy watched in the background. But Bailey wasn't watching the ceremony. She was focused on Chase instead. She watched him as he stealthily made his way around the venue, through the guests, taking pictures of everything a newly-married couple would want on their wedding day. It was like he had a certain routine, and Bailey guessed by now, he probably did.

As the wedding began to wind down and the new husband and wife left, guests began to leave one by one. The caterer cleaned up, and the rental people picked up the tent, table, and chairs while Mandy and Bailey made sure everything was taken care of and back in place. It was only around eight o'clock in the evening, which was good. The timing had been perfect for the sunset wedding the couple had dreamed of.

"So, how did everything go?"

Chase was standing by her side now as she went over her list once more to make sure everything was done.

"Looks like we have a very happy bride and groom. And some more that happy guests," Bailey said as both she and Chase watched a few people being escorted by friends and family to their cars. The very sweet alcoholic drink the couple had picked for their special day had given more than one person reason to have someone drive them home or back to their hotel.

"I want to thank you for earlier today," Bailey said as she closed the case on her tablet and looked at Chase.

"For what?"

"Helping me to keep the bride from completely losing it. I think she was close to going over the edge. Not that I didn't blame her. I have heard that grooms – and brides, for that matter – sometimes don't show up at the altar. But after I talked to her and you started taking all those pictures, she seemed to quickly come back to the present moment."

"Taking the pictures helped to take her mind off the 'late to the party' groom. Did you ever find out what took them so long?" Chase asked, wanting to keep the conversation going with her.

"The driver of the Trolley said that they hadn't even started getting dressed when he arrived. Seems like they were scrambling around fast to get dressed. I guess the bachelor party must have lasted late into the night. I was just glad that there were no bad hangovers. That would have made for an angry bride and a not-so-great way to start the honeymoon," Bailey commented.

"It wouldn't be the first time I've seen it happen. And I have been to some weddings where one or the other – bride or groom – doesn't show. Let's just say it's not a happy time, and things get mighty awkward really fast."

"Yes, I can certainly see that it would," Bailey said as she thought about what it would be like to be left at the altar. "But now it's off to home to go to bed. We have to do this again tomorrow, but much smaller, thank goodness. And I need to go catch up with Mandy real quick. See ya then?" Bailey asked, smiling at Chase.

"Looking forward to it."

■ ■ ■

Chase arrived at the same beach that he had been at last Wednesday when he had met Bailey for the first time. The small wedding they had today was here. Chase looked all over for Bailey, trying to be as inconspicuous as possible, but he didn't see her anywhere.

"She's not here yet," Mandy said, startling Chase from behind.

"Damn, Mandy, how about giving me some warning next time? About dropped my camera equipment."

"So, you do like her, don't you?" Mandy asked with a very knowing smile.

"Who?"

Mandy started laughing. Chase guessed he wasn't so good at hiding his feelings.

"Her name starts with a 'B'? Goodness, Chase, just admit you like the girl. She's sweet and a hard worker. These past four days have been wonderful. She's not even complaining about working the weekend. I don't think I've ever had an employee like that, not even when I was working with my mom."

"I think Bailey is nice. I'm glad she is working out for you."

"Seriously? Just nice? Chase, you have to remember. I can read body language well, and yours is giving you away. You like Bailey, and that's OK. You know, not everyone breaks hearts. Just take it slow. But I will say that as long as we have been working together, I've never seen you act the way you do when she is around."

"Mandy, I have no clue what you are talking about. I just wanted to tell her 'hello'. It's nice to work with someone who is so conscientious about their work."

Mandy started laughing so hard that Chase just rolled his eyes. He might as well admit that Bailey did seem to always be on his mind.

"When you decide to tell me that you like the girl, I'm all ears. But a little advice: just go ahead and ask her out. Don't wait around because she has only been to a few of my weddings, and I've seen the way the men of the wedding parties have looked at her. She might just slip right out of your hands. That would be a hell of a shame because I really like you, Chase. You have a good heart and good looks to match. That's mighty hard for a girl to find these days." Mandy patted him on the back and started to walk away. "And by the way, she's coming this way."

Chase's head jerked up quickly. Mandy was right. Bailey was walking toward them, and she looked beautiful. Today, she had her hair pulled back into a ponytail that fell down the center of her back. Her blue sundress with dressy sandals showed off her creamy, velvet skin and beautiful legs. Chase didn't think he could get enough of just watching her.

"Mandy, I got the napkins. Just gave them to the caterer," Bailey called out quickly to her boss, then turned to Chase. "Hi, there! You about ready to start taking some pics?" Bailey asked as Chase fumbled with his equipment.

"Just about. Mandy about made me drop my camera a minute ago, so I'm trying to get things back in order. How are you doing today? Get some rest last night?" At those words, Chase began to wonder just exactly what Bailey had done during the evening before. His mind wandered to places that made him feel hot all over, and the heat wasn't coming from the Florida sun.

"Yes, I did, after I had my dinner. I tried to read some of my book, but was so tired, I fell asleep."

"Maybe your book was boring," Chase said, wanting to talk to her more.

"No, it's really cute. It's a romantic comedy called *Camping in High Heels*. The main character has to go camping around the United States and has no clue what she is doing. I like it, but I guess I was busier at that wedding yesterday than I thought because I think my eyes shut the minute my head hit the pillow. Had to be the extra stress of the potential for a non-existent groom. How about you? Still sunburned?"

"Bailey, I need you over here," Mandy called out.

"We will talk later. Maybe after the wedding," Chase said.

"Sounds good," Bailey responded as she walked away, but not before giving Chase a glance over her shoulder.

9

The Sunday afternoon wedding went off without a hitch. Once again, another happy bride and groom and their families got to enjoy their time in the Florida Keys.

During the entire wedding, Bailey looked for Chase every chance she could. He had even found her a time or two and smiled her way. After the wedding and once everyone was gone, they had chatted for a few minutes, but she told him she needed to get back to her room to do some work.

Bailey felt this desire to be with Chase, but a part of her also told her to back away. She still needed to find out who she was. Bailey knew in her heart that she couldn't become involved with a man until she knew about her past. That wouldn't be fair to him, Bailey told herself. But Chase Cartwright was making it awfully hard to stick to this self-imposed rule.

Since there were no more weddings till the following weekend, Mandy gave Bailey the first two days of the week off. This would be the perfect time for her to look for a new place to stay. Plus, she wanted to visit some of the places around Key Largo and Islamorada to see if maybe any memories might magically appear in her mind.

Bailey used the first part of her morning scouring ads for apartments. She made a list of those to call to set up times to go and see the buildings, but it wouldn't be till the following week. During the afternoon, she took a drive to the Seven Mile Bridge just to sit and think.

Once she got to the old bridge, Bailey made her way to the park below, near the stunning, aqua water. She had brought a picnic dinner, so she could stay and watch the sunset, something she had enjoyed since she had come to the Keys. And she had also brought her journal.

As she looked at the book in her hands, it was showing some wear on the edges. This was Bailey's third journal since her accident, and she had been keeping copious notes, anything that might be even a glimmer into her past.

As she watched people stroll by her blanket and, at times, glancing up to watch a passing boat, she first wrote her list of to-do's now that she had a job in Islamorada. One of those items was to find a new therapist, though she wished that she could make the trip to Key West to the wonderful woman that was helping her there. But right now, the thought of going back to Key West frightened her because of the man who was looking for her. Bailey knew she could find someone here that would continue to help her along in this journey of finding herself.

Next, she just wrote her thoughts and the one thing that constantly came up was Chase. She had known him less than a week, and she couldn't get him out of her mind. Just the thought of him sent her heart racing, and she caught herself giggling even while she wrote words on the page. He brought feelings to her that she hadn't experienced since her memory had been erased, and she loved the way they felt.

Bailey only wished she didn't have these conflicting emotions inside about whether to let him into her world or to try to forget about him. Part of her screamed, "No!" but her heart was saying a big, fat, "Yes!" She knew deep down that there was no way she would be able to forget Chase. All these emotions were so new to her. It was as though she was experiencing what she was sure her therapist would call infatuation. Bailey had to have experienced these feeling before, but as of right now, she knew of none.

Bailey put the journal away in her bag and took out her dinner. The sunset would be starting in about thirty minutes, and even though she had seen so many Florida Keys sunsets since she had been here, they were all unique and beautiful. She wanted to soak in every minute of the light show. As she sat and ate, she watched the different people walk by. There were families and others were just couples, some holding hands. Then there were the singles like her. But when one man passed by her, she felt a coldness sweep through her.

From where Bailey was sitting, he didn't see her, and suddenly she felt good that she had chosen the spot she did. She continued to watch him as he walked toward the parking lot at the start of the bridge. There was something about him that gave Bailey a feeling of unease and, what she thought, was a bit of anger. The day had been so perfect, and now she was feeling something that had totally caught her off guard. She didn't recognize this person at all so why would she feel angry? The confusion of thoughts in her head brought about panicky feelings that suddenly felt like water being poured over her head.

Bailey took some deep breaths and practiced the relaxation exercises she had been taught by the therapists and doctors. As she sat there, staring at the sun making its descent into the horizon, she felt her body start to calm down. Her heartbeat slowed to a normal pace, and she started to feel more like herself again.

If she could only figure out why just the sight of the man had caused such a reaction. Maybe it would be another clue as to why she felt so driven to come to the Florida Keys. Did she know him? Was he someone bad and to be left alone? Or was this just her imagination running wild? Bailey really didn't know what to think, and suddenly, she wished she could talk to Chase. She hadn't known him long, but she felt like he would be the perfect person to talk to. She had a feeling that somehow, he would protect her.

Stop it! she wanted to cry out to herself. *You have to handle this on your own, not bring anyone else into this mess that is your life*, Bailey told herself sternly. But she wanted a confidant, someone who would be there for her always, no matter what.

Was Chase that person? Bailey had to admit that she hoped he could be.

■ ■ ■

Even though Bailey got to the office fifteen minutes earlier than her appointed time, Mandy was already at work. And from the looks of it, she had been there a while.

"Good morning," Bailey said once she sat her tote and handbag on her desk.

"Hey, there. I'm happy to see you. Hope you had a nice few days off because this next week is going to be a doozy. I left a list of items on your desk to do for the now-four different weddings. We already had two scheduled for this weekend, but I had a bride-to-be call me yesterday, practically begging us to handle the details of her wedding for Saturday morning. Since we don't have a wedding till that evening and hers is supposed to be rather small, I figured we could squeeze it in. Now, I wish I hadn't," Mandy said, tucking a strand of hair behind her ear.

"I think we will be able to do it. It will just be a long day," Bailey said, realizing the whole weekend was going to be busy.

"Well, then I received another call wanting us to handle another small wedding next Tuesday evening. I was hoping that I could just start giving you every Monday and Tuesday off, but I think we are going to have to plan your time off around the weddings. Really sorry about that, but for right now, that's the best I can do."

"It's no problem," Bailey assured her. She didn't mind the work. The only problem she could see was the chance to go and look at the apartments she had found, but she would take that up with Mandy as the need arose.

"Let me know if you have any questions about the lists. And please make sure Chase can work the weddings. If not, call Todd next. He's on the list of vendors I gave you. I always call Chase first because I like his pics better. Plus, for the flowers, try Floral Fantasy and Gifts. All the caterers are good, but that's the one area I'm not worried about. At least the two add-on weddings are just hors d'oeuvres. That should be easy." Mandy was talking and typing at the same time, and Bailey couldn't see how she was keeping all her thoughts aligned. But Mandy looked very stressed out.

"Mandy, don't worry. I'll get it done. If you need anything else, just let me know."

"Then I'll let you get the phone."

Bailey's day was busy, handling all the details for each wedding. She took the project sheets and ticked off each item one at a time. But the first thing she had done was to call Chase and leave a message since he didn't answer, leaving her a slight bit disappointed. She hoped his calendar was free for these extra events.

Before she knew it, the clock read after five o'clock. The day had sped by, and Bailey couldn't remember if she had even eaten lunch. The one thing she did remember was that Chase hadn't returned her call. Though she had worked all day and secured the major details for the two new weddings, she had secretly hoped each time the phone rang that he would be on the other end of the line, but each time, it wasn't him.

"So, the venues, florist, caterer, transportation – the major stuff – is secure for the weddings. Working on the small details now. Didn't hear from Chase, so I'll call him again tomorrow. But I'm going to take off now, if that is OK. I'm going to drive by a couple of places I called about renting. I'm very ready to move out of the hotel I'm staying in, so you might receive a call about my employment," Bailey said as she went and sat by Mandy's desk. They had barely talked to each other all day, even though they were only feet apart.

"Oh, I forgot you were staying in that hotel. I don't blame you, and whatever references you need, let me know. Even a personal one." Mandy paused for a minute. "Wait a minute. Did you say Chase didn't call back? He must be on the boat or doing a wedding for Rachel near Key West. I forgot that he had mentioned it a few weeks ago."

"I thought he only did weddings around here," Bailey said, hoping to get more information from Mandy.

"No, he goes about anywhere in the Keys. His work is very popular with all the wedding planners here. He always promises to work me with me first, but I know he can't always do that. It's just that I gave him his first wedding gig when he moved here, so he's been a sweetheart to keep me first in line ever since. I think the other planners here are jealous, but they do wrangle him every now and then. He'll probably call tomorrow, and then we will know what to do. Anyway, hope you find something you like. I can't imagine living for an extended time in a hotel. How do you cook?" Mandy said, suddenly looking concerned.

"Good ol' microwave," Bailey said with a laugh. "And then there is always take-out. Not to mention that I think I've tried just about all the restaurants around here. It will be very nice to have my own kitchen. And a separate room for a bed. Even a tiny yard to take care of if I find a small house. Just all depends on price."

"And location. You should ask Chase to help you. He used to be in real estate, and his family still is in Miami. They own one of the largest real estate firms in south Florida and have for years. They are like Miami socialites. Chase has never told me the full story of why he moved here for photography. Maybe you can ask him one day."

Bailey knew about Chase's family but didn't want Mandy to know she had been snooping on the Internet, finding out what she could about Chase. But she watched as Mandy raised her eyebrows as if to indicate that she was suggesting something.

"What's that for?" Bailey asked.

"Oh, come on. I've watched you two over the last week. Anyone with eyes can see there is something between both of you."

"Mandy, we just met. I've only seen him at the weddings." As soon as the words were out of her mouth, she knew that wasn't true. They had met at the bar and grill, and then Bailey had almost run him over with her shopping cart at the grocery store!

"It doesn't matter. There is something there if you would just let yourself admit it. And Bailey, he is one of the good guys. He is polite, sweet, and damn good-looking. I know he's been burned before in relationships, but I don't know the story, and even if I did, it's not mine to tell. But I know that if I was younger, I wouldn't let him go."

"Well, there is that whole cougar thing, you know," Bailey said, laughing.

"No way! I'm too busy, and I'm enjoying being divorced. This gal is staying single for a while."

"And with that, I'm out of here." Bailey walked out the door, but not before telling Mandy, "Goodnight."

She drove past two of the places she had written down on her list of potential homes. One was an apartment on the second floor, so she couldn't see much, and the other was a very tiny home in an area that didn't look too promising. Even though it didn't feel like she had done much, Bailey had at least started her search for her new place to live.

As she drove back to the hotel, she began to think about Chase again, and a smile just naturally came to her face. It had been days since Bailey had seen or talked to him, and she realized she missed him. How could she miss someone she had known for such a short time? It didn't make sense to her, but there was a lot in her life at the moment that didn't fit the way it should.

After Bailey took a shower and ate her baked potato and broccoli, she went out and sat on the porch balcony. The one benefit of staying here was that she could see the Atlantic

Ocean from her room. She would miss the view, but it was time to have her own place. Maybe she would ask Chase for help. He could help her find a nice home, and she would be able to spend time with him. A win-win in her book.

10

The last two days had been a blur of activity, and now Chase was just glad to be home. He was sitting on the dock with Moose, and no one else was around. He kept waiting for Maria to show up, as usual, but all his thoughts were on Bailey.

He didn't see the message she had left until today. After the late wedding yesterday, he crashed on his friends' couch in Key West. Abbey and Zach always welcomed him whenever he was in town. They usually let him use the spare room, but it was now being renovated into a nursery. Their first child was due soon, and from what Chase could tell, Abbey had Zach busy finishing all the little details. He had met Abbey and Zach through Garrett when he married his sister and since then, Abbey and Zach had become good friends of his. And he always appreciated the place to stay, even if this time, it had been the couch.

As he watched the sunset, he wondered what Bailey was doing. He had thought about her often over the last few days. He had wanted to call her as soon as he got on the road to head for home, but he didn't have his calendar in front of him. He was sure the extra weddings would be no problem, but he wanted to make sure before he made the commitment. Chase almost called just so he could hear her voice, but he wanted to appear professional and that they were only friends, even though he knew he already wanted more from her.

As soon as the sun had set, Chase and Moose walked back to his house. This time, Maria was out front, watering her plants. Chase was surprised that she didn't quickly run over to see him like she usually did, but only waved and said, "Hi." *Maybe,* Chase thought, *I made my point clear last time we talked.* It would certainly be nice to be able to walk the street without having to worry about her ambushing him, like she had done so many times in the past.

When he went to bed, he turned on the TV. As much as Chase tried to turn his attention to the show, he couldn't. He even turned everything off, hoping he would fall asleep, but that didn't help either. Bailey was the only thing he could see in his mind.

The next morning, he was up early, having finally fallen asleep. This was essentially a day off for him, as was tomorrow. Then a string of weddings were taking place. Plus, Skylar had asked for his help with pictures on the boat one day next week. He loved that his business was finally showing a profit, something that proved to his family that he had been right in making this move.

But most of all, it mattered to him. He was happy here in the Keys, doing what he loved. He was able to truly follow in Skylar's footsteps and make a go of his dream, just like she had. Now Chase had other things on his mind – a beautiful redhead, to be exact.

Chase paced back and forth, trying to decide whether to call Bailey at work or just drop by. He was always going by Mandy's office before, but now that Bailey was there, things were different. He was nervous, something Chase wasn't accustomed to. Finally, he decided to go by the office not only because he was returning Bailey's message, but because he wanted to see her.

As he walked through the door, Bailey was on the phone, but turned to see it was him. She smiled, holding up her finger, motioning him to wait a second. He looked over and couldn't see Mandy at her desk, so Bailey appeared to be all by herself.

"Hi, there! I was just getting ready to call another photographer – I think his name is Todd – to ask about the weddings. How are you doing? Did you get my message?"

Bailey looked stunning and almost as though she had been kissed by the sun. Her freckles were a little more prominent, making her look as sweet as ever.

"I'm really sorry I'm just now getting back to you. I had a late-night wedding, then spent the night in Key West before heading back late yesterday. A business in town wanted some photos for a new brochure. By the time I got home, it was too late to call. I knew the office would be closed," Chase said, taking a seat by her desk. "Where is Mandy?"

"Off to do some errands, so I'm holding down the fort." Her smile sent his heart racing just a bit. It felt so weird for him to feel this way about a girl. This was more intense than what he had ever felt for anyone in the past, and that was what had him confused and thinking about Bailey all the time.

"Then you are doing a very good job. I've worked with Mandy enough to know that she is usually here all the time, sending her assistants to do all the errands. She must really have some trust in you."

"Thanks. That makes me feel good because I really like it here. Have to admit these last few days have been a bit chaotic with all the weddings going on, but so far, so good. That is, if you can fit them into your schedule. Mandy said I had to get a 'no' from you first before I called anyone else, but I was starting to sweat here. So, are you free?"

"You can put me down as your photographer. Todd will just have to wait, but he is nice and a good back-up if I'm not around. He just doesn't have my skills," Chase boasted with a smile.

"Wonderful! Now I can check that off my list." Bailey grabbed a piece of paper and paused. "I was going to write down the dates and times, but would you rather me text them to you?"

"A text would be great. I guess that would also give me your phone number." Chase took a deep breath as he knew what he wanted to say next.

"I guess it would."

"Then may I call you sometime? Maybe we can go to dinner."

"I would really like that. How about tonight since we are going to be quite busy over the next week? Plus, I was hoping that I could ask you some questions about houses and apartments in the area. Mandy told me your family is in the real estate business." Once again, Bailey acted as though Mandy had given her his information because she certainly didn't want Chase to think she was stalking him on the Internet.

"Tonight would be great. Have you ever been to the Shrimp Shack?" Chase asked.

"Yes, and I love their food."

"I'll pick you up at six-thirty? But where, exactly?"

"It's a date and I'll text you the address," Bailey said, trying to conceal her excitement and act as casually as she could.

"See you then," Chase said before walking out the door.

Bailey sat at her desk, riveted to the seat for a few minutes. She had just agreed to go on a date. An actual date, and she wasn't sure what to do. She hadn't been on one since her accident. Her therapist had always told her that she would know when the time was right, but she didn't know what to do. She had been out with friends when she was living in Key West and a few had set her up with blind dates, but this was different in her book. The panic was beginning to set in just as Mandy walked through the front door.

"Are you OK? You are white as a sheet," Mandy said, setting her handbag down and coming to sit by Bailey. "Did someone cancel? Are the weddings still on? I knew that girl sounded a bit off even when she gave me the deposit. I bet she backed out of the wedding." Mandy got up and started pacing the floor.

"Mandy, everything is OK, at least with the weddings. Everything is on schedule, and as a matter of fact, Chase came by and has agreed to do the weddings."

"Thank goodness. I was beginning to get a bit worried. So, what is the matter? I can see you hyperventilating from here."

"He asked me out on a date, and I said 'yes'."

"Oh. But that is a good thing, right?" Now Mandy was sitting by her desk again, looking more relax and a bit hopeful.

"I guess, but it's tonight, and I've never been on a real date."

"Are you kidding?"

"At least not one that I can remember." Bailey said the words, then wished that she could take then back quickly. But it was already out there.

"What do you mean 'can remember'?"

Bailey took a deep breath and sighed. It was now or never to tell her boss about her past.

"Four years ago, I was living in San Diego, or least I think so. I was in an accident and lost my memory." Bailey went on to tell Mandy everything: her memory loss, her trip to the East coast, and her vague feeling that the Florida Keys was where she was supposed to be, possibly even to help her restore her past. The one thing she left out of her story was about the man who was asking for her in Key West.

"Bailey... my gosh, girl. Why didn't you tell me this?"

"Are you going to let me go?" Bailey couldn't help it now. The tears started to flow, even though she tried hard to hold them back.

"Why would I do that?"

"I don't know. Maybe because I don't know who I am. For all I know I could be some bad person."

Mandy sat back down and took Bailey's hands into her own. "Now that, I don't believe. You are Bailey Parker, one of the best employees I've ever had. You are sweet, intelligent, and very thoughtful. How could you ever think you were an awful person? Even with memory loss, I think the original personality traits are still there. You need to listen to those doctors and keep going to your therapist. Now that you have told me, whenever you need to go, you don't even need to ask."

"I don't have a therapist or doctor here yet, but I was going to find someone first chance I got. I haven't had anyone to talk to in a while, so thanks for listening. Honestly, I wasn't going to tell anyone." The tears were finally stopping, and Bailey felt a release. "Mandy, please don't say anything to anyone. Please."

"Do you plan on telling Chase?"

This was a question that Bailey had been contemplating since she agreed to go out with him. "Right now, I just have to find the courage to go on this date. From there, I have no clue what I'm doing."

"He is picking you up, right?"

"Yes."

"Then what you do is get home, freshen up, put your favorite outfit on, and then wait for him to come. Pretend that you are with other people. That might make you feel better. But Bailey," Mandy said, pausing just to look at her, "you are going to do just fine. You need to have some confidence in yourself. I have no clue what you're feeling because I can't imagine what you've been through or what it would be like to lose my memories from the past, but just live in the moment. Collect some new memories now. Make friends. Have fun. Don't always be trying to fix yourself. If the memories come back, that will be a blessing. If not, you're making new ones."

Mandy reached over and hugged Bailey so tight. Bailey wondered if this was what it felt like to be loved by a mother since she had no recollection of her own. If it was, she liked the feeling.

"Thanks, Mandy." Bailey swiveled to sit back at her desk. Mandy got up, squeezed Bailey's shoulder once more for reassurance, and then went to her own work spot. Bailey smiled and secretly thanked the older woman because now Bailey couldn't wait to see Chase this evening. And she would just let the conversation lead where it may.

11

Chase checked his reflection in the mirror by his front door once more before he stepped out. He had dressed casually for the evening, but he still wanted to look his best. He hadn't felt this excited about a date in so long. No, he was looking forward to going out with Bailey more than any other date he had been on that he could remember.

After talking to her earlier, when they made plans, Chase had left Bailey's office and went straight to the car wash. The car had been a wreck from his recent trip to Key West, with snack papers and drink cups on the floor. There was even sand in the seats and his diving equipment in the back. But in no time, the car looked presentable. It looked better than it had in quite a long time.

Once Chase was home, he cleaned up his house as best he could in the little time he had left. He didn't know if they would come back here, but if the possibility existed, he wanted to make sure his place looked nice and clean. He wasn't the best housekeeper because he never worried about anyone coming over. That could all change now.

As he pulled up to the hotel a little before six thirty, Bailey was already outside, waiting for him. The sight of her took his breath away, as she looked every bit the island girl. She was dressed in a colorful tank top with white, loose pants that gently moved with the subtle breeze. She waved to him as he pulled up.

Chase wanted to get out and open her door, but Bailey was there before he barely got out of the car.

"I was going to get that for you."

"Thanks, but I got it," Bailey said as she sat in the seat beside him.

"You look beautiful," Chase said as he glanced over at her, mesmerized.

"Thank you. You seem to clean up pretty good yourself." The blush on her cheeks wasn't from the small amount of make-up she wore, but from Chase's compliment.

"Are you hungry?" Chase asked as they pulled onto Highway 1.

"Actually, starving. Didn't eat much of a lunch, and we were quite busy this afternoon. I promised myself next time I went to this restaurant, I was going to try their shrimp tacos. Heard they were the best."

"And you heard right. But I kinda like all the food, and I'm pretty hungry myself. But the one thing I get every time I come here is the key lime pie. Maybe we can share a piece?" Chase asked as he glanced over at her.

"What do you mean 'share'? I might just want my own slice," Bailey laughed.

"Now that's my girl," Chase said with a laugh.

My girl? Bailey thought. And it brought a bright smile to her face.

"What are you grinning about?"

"That you thought we were going to share some food." There was no way Bailey was going to tell him the real reason.

"Well, sometimes, women eat such small amounts. Seems like they take most of their food home."

"So, you are the expert on women and dining?" Bailey said this as a tease, but she wondered just how much he did date. Was he seeing other women right now? Or was she the only one?

Stop, Bailey said to herself. *Remember what Mandy said: stay present and make memories right now.* Worrying about Chase's dating habits wouldn't help her enjoy this evening.

Soon, they were pulling into the parking lot in front of the Shrimp Shack. The popular restaurant was crowded, as usual, but they found out the wait would only be fifteen minutes or so. Chase took the menu out and they started discussing the food, leading to a discussion about what they each liked to eat. For Bailey, the conversation with this man just seemed to flow. She felt as though she was talking to an old friend, and that helped so much to take the strain away from trying to be perfect on this first date since her accident. Her therapist would be proud of her, she thought.

The food and the company were perfect. Chase told her more about his business, and she discussed working with

Mandy. They talked about the weddings they had done together so far and laughed over some of the things the bride, groom, and their wedding party had done. It felt so good to laugh with someone she truly enjoyed being with.

"Now for the key lime pie. So, are we sharing, or do you want your own?" Chase asked, eyebrows raised.

"I think I'll share with you. I'm just a bit full right now, but I can't say 'no' to the pie."

As they waited for the dessert to be brought to the table, Chase asked the question that sent Bailey into a panic. "So, tell me about yourself. Where are you from? What about your parents?"

The only thing she knew to say came suddenly to her. "Why don't you go first? I hear from Mandy that you might be able to help me find a place to live. Still have your real estate license?" Bailey sighed in relief as Chase took the bait.

"I do, but I need to update it. As a matter of fact, my sister, Skylar, and I both do. My family owns a rather large firm in Miami. My grandparents actually started the business about sixty years ago."

"I also heard that your family is considered like royalty in the Miami social circles."

Chase rolled his eyes as he sat back in the booth. "You've obviously been talking to Mandy. Yes, my family has a bit of money. My dad wanted me and Skylar to work in the business with my other sister, Mara, and my older brother, Harris. I happen to be the baby of the family."

"So, why did you come to the Keys to be a photographer instead?" Bailey asked, now interested in Chase's story.

"I have always wanted to be a photographer. Especially wildlife. But when you are born into the family I was, it was expected of me to follow in the footsteps of everyone else working at the real estate office. I was good at selling property, but didn't enjoy it at all. I ended up going and taking pictures of all our properties instead. Now that, I really liked.

"Then, one day, Skylar had enough guts to just strike out on her own. She has loved boats since we were kids. So, she saved enough money, then got her own bank loan to start a boat charter business in Key Largo. To say my parents weren't happy is putting it mildly. Then, on top of that, she met Garrett. My parents didn't think he met the family standards and let Skylar know real quickly. Plus, he is ten years older than her, so that was a sore spot. But she didn't care."

"Wow. She sounds like one tough lady," Bailey said, already liking Chase's big sister.

"That she is. Now she has a very successful business here in Key Largo, and she just opened another in Marathon. She and Garrett married, and they have a little girl, my niece, Taylor. They actually live a street over from me," Chase said. "And that is my little tale. Now about you."

Before Bailey could utter a word, the waitress sat the pie in front of them with two forks and they both dug in. Bailey was happy for yet again another distraction because she still hadn't quite figured out what she would tell him about her past.

"Now where would you like to go?" Chase asked as they both secured their seatbelts, back in the car.

"I don't know. You're more familiar with this area than me," Bailey said nervously. She was able to handle herself with no problem in the restaurant, but now she was in uncharted waters.

"I would love to take you to my house. But please don't get the wrong idea. As corny as this may sound, I want to show you a little spot that I love that is at the end of my street. Sound OK? I promise to be the perfect gentleman," Chase said, placing a hand over his heart.

"OK," Bailey said softly, tension and excitement all rolled into one. She wanted to spend more time with him, that was for sure. As for going to his home, she just didn't want to make a fool of herself.

She wanted everything to be perfect, but unable to remember anything about dating, she felt so lost. Though, Bailey could tell that Chase was doing everything he could to make her comfortable and feel at ease. This helped with the nervousness she was feeling inside - unless these jitters were because of being so close to him. If that was the reason for the way she felt, she would take the way she was feeling any time.

As they rode toward Chase's house, he explained how the property had first been a rental home that belonged to his family. Then, when he decided to move here after Skylar, his father relented and sold him the house. Bailey was just amazed that he owned his own place. It was something she wanted to do, but until she could uncover her past, it was like she was just a four-year-old. No one would take a chance on her with a mortgage, even though she had saved up plenty of money. Maybe Chase would be able to help her, but how would she explain her situation?

"Hey, are you OK?" Chase asked. "If this makes you uncomfortable, we can turn around and do something else. We can even go back to the bar where we met that night and sit by the water."

"No, I'm OK. What made you ask that?"

"You didn't answer my question."

"I'm sorry. What was it?" Bailey asked tentatively.

"Doesn't matter. Here we are."

Bailey looked at the little home in front of her. It was small with a beautiful front porch where hanging plants graced the edges. The blue-grey siding with white trim looked lovely, and it was like a little cottage out of a magazine.

"Oh, Chase, this is wonderful. It's so cute, and it looks like you are so close to the water."

"A canal is behind the house where I could take a boat out, but I don't have one of those right now. Even if I did, I don't really have the time. Anyway, there is always Skylar and her boats."

"I hope I get to meet her one day. She sounds fascinating with everything she has accomplished."

"I would love for you to meet her. Do you want to come in, or do you want to go ahead and take a walk down to the bench?"

"That's what you call it? The bench?"

"Well, that's what I call it. It's at the end of the street, right on the water. Moose and I go there as often as we can."

"Moose?" Bailey asked, giving him a weird expression.

"My rescue dog. He kinda goes everywhere with me when I'm not working. Except, I did take him with me to the Keys.

Abbey and Zach had a great place for him to stay, and he loved it there."

"Do you want to take Moose with us? I would love to see him."

"Sure. Come on in the house for a minute."

Bailey followed him into the little house, and it was just as nice inside as out. The décor was typical for Florida, but it certainly had a masculine flare. But the little dog that greeted Chase is the main thing that caught Bailey's eye.

"Bailey, meet Moose," Chase said, holding up the small dog that looked like he only weighed around ten pounds before putting him back on the floor.

"When you said 'Moose', I expected a large dog, like a Lab or something," Bailey said. She knelt, and Moose went straight to her, licking her hand and then her cheek.

"Moose, stop that. I haven't even been able to do that yet," Chase said, and Bailey couldn't help but look up and give him a sheepish grin.

"OK, Moose, let's go show Bailey the bench."

Chase only had to say the words and the little dog bounded out the door, looking back at his master as if to say, "Hurry up!"

"I guess he knows the way, huh?" Bailey asked, watching the little dog jump up and down with enthusiasm about the upcoming walk.

"That he does. You ready?"

"Sounds good to me."

Bailey and Chase began their walk toward the water, watching Moose explore as they walked.

"You said Moose went with you to Key West and stayed with someone named Zach and Abbey. Just good friends of yours?"

Chase told Bailey all about Abbey, how one day, she came to her best friend's mother's wedding here in the Keys and went back home, packed up her stuff, and moved back to Key West. She was Garrett's neighbor when he was living in the city, before he moved to Key Largo, where he met Skylar.

"They have a room they usually let me stay in while I'm down there, but now they are converting it into a nursery."

"They're having a baby! How sweet," Bailey said, happy for the couple, even though she didn't know them.

"I've actually been invited to a baby shower at their friend's house in Marathon, another neighbor at the time when Abbey was still single and Garrett lived next door. The lady that lived downstairs, Josie, married and moved to Marathon. Now there is a woman with a very interesting story, but it will have to wait till later because we are here."

Bailey looked around. The scene was so peaceful. Even though the sun had set, the full moon above gave them plenty of light, along with the small security light right down the street. With the moonlight reflecting off the water, it was beautiful. And Moose had already found his little spot, in front of the bench, closer to the water.

"Come sit with me," Chase said softly, holding out his hand to her, and she placed her hand in his. They walked to the bench and sat down, neither of them saying a word.

The bench wasn't too small, but Bailey sat close to Chase. She could feel the heat coming off of him, and just being this close to him felt like an electric current running between the two of them. It felt so amazing, and she didn't want Chase to move an inch.

"It's beautiful here," Bailey said as she looked around then back over the water. "This must be a favorite spot for everyone to come to and get away from it all."

"It is. I call it 'my spot' because I seem to be the one that uses it the most. I think over the years, people just get busy with their lives and forget it's here. I've even painted the bench a couple of times and replaced a few boards on the dock."

Chase pointed to the wooden structure about fifty feet away. It jutted out into the dark waters, but Bailey could see a small light in the darkness, signaling the end of the dock.

"Bailey, I need to ask you something."

With Chase's words, the hair stood up on the back of Bailey's neck. It was like alarm bells went off, and she didn't know how such a peaceful feeling only seconds ago could be long gone.

"Tonight, I've had a wonderful time. It's nice to spend time with you outside of work. But each time I've asked you about you, you've changed the subject. Is everything OK? Have I done anything to offend you?"

Bailey glanced over at Chase and could see genuine warmth in his eyes. He wasn't prying or trying to get anything out of her, but sincerely just wanted to get to know her. She could read all this in his eyes and through his body language. This was it, she told herself. Bailey knew that Chase was a safe harbor for her story.

"Well, hello again, Chase." Maria came around and stood in front of the couple.

Damn, Chase said to himself. He was trying to be nice, but now Maria was just getting on his nerves. He wanted this time with Bailey, and he figured that this time in the evening, no one would be out here.

"Hi, Maria. How are you?" Chase said as nicely as he could.

"I'm fine. This is the perfect night for a little evening stroll. So, aren't you going to introduce me to your friend?" Maria's voice was sweet, but Chase could hear the undertones of distaste mixed in.

"Maria, this is Bailey Parker. We've been working together on a few projects. Bailey, this is one of my neighbors, Maria Monroe."

Chase watched as Bailey shook Maria's hand. Bailey was so polite and nice that it even made Chase like her more.

"Nice to meet you. And it is lovely out tonight. Chase was just showing me this little spot, and it's perfect. A great place to unwind."

"He needs to bring you down here when there is a great sunset. We've watched many a sunset from here, haven't we, Chase?" Maria said, going to stand in front of him, eyeing him and giving him a fake smile.

"Yes, we've watched a few." *Under duress*, Chase wanted to add. "Well, it was good to see you, Maria. I think we are going to walk down the dock. Have a nice evening." Chase took hold of Bailey's hand and gently tugged in the direction of the dock, leaving Maria standing, watching the couple, but only for a few minutes. By the time Chase looked back, Maria was making her way back up the road to her home.

"Sorry about that. If I hadn't told her we were going for a walk, she would have joined us for the rest of the evening."

"She seems pretty nice," Bailey remarked, but she had also seen how the woman practically drooled over Chase. Her eyes left him only once: when Bailey shook her hand. Maria definitely had it bad for Chase, and from Bailey's vantage point, Maria didn't care who knew it. Plus, it was pretty clear that she wasn't happy seeing Bailey and Chase together.

"She is, but she wants to date, and I only want to be friends. I keep thinking that she will get the message, but she is, shall I say, persistent."

"She just knows a good guy when she sees him," Bailey said, looking up at Chase as they continued to walk toward the little light at the end of the dock.

12

Soon, Bailey once again found herself sitting close to Chase on the edge of the dock as their legs dangled over the dark water below. The moonlight was still bright and created a very pretty, romantic setting. It was something that Bailey had always dreamed about, but as far as she knew, had never experienced before in her life.

"Now, you never answered my question. Tell me about yourself, about your life in Key West. Have you always lived in the Keys? Your parents? Tell me about you. If that's OK," Chase said, scooting a bit closer to her.

Bailey took a deep breath. She really liked this man. And for her, it was becoming a feeling that they could be more than friends. She remembered Mandy's words from their earlier conversation and decided to take a chance.

"Well, there honestly isn't much to tell. I moved here from San Diego about four years ago. Just packed up all my stuff and headed to Florida. Something was drawing me to the Keys, but I honestly can't say why."

"What did you do back in California?"

Bailey sighed. How did she begin to tell him what happened?

"I don't know."

"What do you mean?" Chase asked, puzzled.

"I really don't know." Bailey looked toward the sky, then back to Chase. She could see the look of confusion on his face.

"Chase, I have amnesia. I was in a bad accident and ended up in a coma. When I woke, I had no memory of my life." Bailey waited for a moment to let it sink in.

"Nothing at all?"

Bailey shook her head. "Just some vague feelings, but that is about it."

"Bailey, I'm so sorry."

"I'm coming to grips with it. I've been lucky in some ways. The woman that saved my life became a friend. She helped me get back on my feet and helped me leave for Florida when I insisted I had to go."

"How did she save your life? What about your family?"

"Dena kept me from stepping out in front of a big delivery truck. When she did, I fell to the pavement and took a bad blow to the back of my head. My cell phone went flying into the street, being crushed by the truck. At least it was the phone instead of me." Bailey laughed lightly.

"My handbag had no identification, and no one reported anyone as missing. With my phone destroyed, there weren't any clues. When I was well enough, Dena even helped me pick out a new name. As far as I know, I'm Bailey Parker, but I honestly don't know my real name. My real family. If anyone even cares that I'm gone."

Chase sat quietly, looking out toward the water. He was so quiet that Bailey suddenly had reservations. Should she have told him so soon? What if he didn't want anything to do with her? Her heart started to race, and she could feel a sense of dread setting in.

It was like she had feared. Most people couldn't handle someone else's baggage when they don't even know who they are. She had a hard time dealing with the life events that had occurred. How could Bailey expect someone else to even begin to understand?

Chase put his arm around her, then took his other hand and lifted her chin. Though it was dark outside, Bailey could still see the welcoming blue eyes in the handsome man sitting so close to her.

"Bailey, there is no doubt in my mind that there is someone, a family, maybe even a significant other who is wondering what happened to you. You are too special to forget."

His words were soft and so meaningful that Bailey felt all the nervous emotions sweep out of her body. "Sure you don't want to run away from me? I'm still searching, trying to find who I am. I've built a life for myself, but I don't know who I really am. Was I a good person? What about my Mom and Dad? I don't even know if I had anyone special, but if I did, I wouldn't even know them." Those last words she spoke were said quietly because if there was someone, she didn't know how she could love them, not when she was most certainly developing feelings for the man that sat next to her.

"I've been to several therapists. I've talked to doctors and the police in San Diego. No one reported a missing person. No one that matches my description. I have no earthly clue about my background."

"What have the doctors said about the possibility of you regaining your memory?" Chase asked.

"I have a fifty-fifty chance. I write down everything that feels or seems familiar to me. I'm on my third journal of notes. One of the biggest things that I couldn't shake – and still can't – is that I'm supposed to be here, in the Keys. That's why my friend and her husband helped me. I had no money, car – anything! But they were so generous and gave me what I needed so I could travel here."

"Wow, that's a good friend."

"They are. And what is amazing is that they aren't wealthy people. They just do it because they feel led to help others. But if she hadn't pulled me back from the road, I wouldn't be here today. I could repay the money and the car they gave me, but there is no way I'll ever be able to thank her for saving my life that day."

"Do you keep in touch with them now?"

"Not really. It's been so long now. I should have contacted them more, but once I arrived in Florida, I just felt like I was on my own, and I was. So, we basically lost touch. I'm really all by myself. No family. A few people in Key West that I can call a friend, and now the people I work with like you and Mandy. Except I do think someone is looking for me now."

Bailey hadn't meant to let that last bit of information slip out, but there it was.

"How do you know?" Chase asked immediately.

"Please don't tell anyone. I wasn't going to say anything. That fact just kinda slipped out."

"I won't, but why the secrecy?"

"I'm not sure. All I know is that one day, when I was at work at the restaurant in Key West, I was in my office when I heard a man ask for me. Not that asking for the manager is unusual, but there was something about his voice and the way he asked the question. It gave me chills. I peeked out, and when I saw him, something inside of me just said 'don't go out there'. So, I stayed in my office till I knew he was gone down the street. I packed up the things out of my office that day and wrote a note to the owner, apologizing for leaving so abruptly. When I got home, I packed up my stuff in my apartment, which wasn't much, and left Key West. I thought for a moment to leave Florida altogether, but I really think my past is tied to these islands in some way. I keep hoping I'll see something or someone that will trigger a memory or two."

"Have you remembered anything yet?" Chase asked encouragingly.

"I just get vague feelings, except the other day, when I was at the Seven Mile Bridge." Bailey explained what happened and saw a distinct look of concern on his face.

"Maybe you should talk to the police here. Just in case. If you suspect someone is looking for you."

"They would think I'm a nut job. And sometimes, I feel that way," Bailey said discouragingly. "These were two separate men, people I've never seen before but I have these weird feelings? Scared? Angry? I can't even understand what is going on."

"Have you ever thought about hiring a private investigator?"

"Yeah, but I don't have the funds. I mean, I have money to live on, but the one investigator I did talk to told me that this could turn into a very long-term arrangement, more than likely, and could be very expensive. So, I just decided to do what I could on my own."

Chase sat there, wanting to hug her and tell Bailey that everything would be OK. He could not begin to understand truly what she had been through. Even what Bailey was going through now. "You know, I knew you were special from the moment I laid eyes on you that very first day, but now," Chase said, "I know it."

Bailey rested her head on his shoulder. "Thanks for listening. It feels so good to be able to talk about it again. I haven't had anyone here. Sometimes, I think that I'm OK with my life the way it is now, but then I start thinking. Why didn't anyone ask about me right after the accident? Maybe I was some hateful person. Maybe I don't have any family left. I can come up with hundreds of reasons, and if I dwell on them, I feel like I'm falling into a hole. But then I met you. Every time I saw you, you were so happy. And I couldn't help but smile. You're a gentleman, a great listener, and very cute, too." Bailey looked up at him with a mischievous smile.

But it didn't last long. It was only a few seconds before Chase leaned down toward her and softly, but gently kissed her lips. Her eyes closed automatically, and Bailey didn't fight the feelings flooding through her body or the way his lips moved upon hers. The sensations had a mind of their own, taking control of her body from head to toe. She loved every second.

As their lips parted, Bailey once again looked up into his eyes. "That was nice."

"I kinda liked it myself. Do you mind if I do it again?" Chase asked in a husky voice.

"Not one bit, but I have to ask you something first."

"What's that?"

"My story doesn't bother you? That I'm on a quest to basically find myself?"

Chase moved, causing Bailey to sit upright and turn to face him. But it was only seconds before Chase placed both hands on each side of her face, cradling her gently. "Bailey, I would love to be with you every step of the way, to help in any way I can. You are special to me, more now than before."

Bailey told him "thank you" in the only way she could at that moment. She leaned over and kissed him this time, but Chase took control. It was a kiss so deep and passionate that she forgot that she had any problems at all. For Bailey, it was only her and Chase under the light of a full moon. And it couldn't be more perfect.

But they weren't alone. Another pair of eyes watched every move the couple made.

13

"So, I need your help with something," Bailey said as she sat across the table from Chase. Bailey had a small break between appointments and they took every advantage of time, spending it together, since the next week would be so busy.

"You name it," Chase said before taking a big bite of his burger.

"Since you are a real estate agent..."

"Was a real estate agent," Chase corrected her.

"Well, you still know more than me. Can you help me find a place to live? Apartment or house – either would be great, though I think after seeing your home, a house would be nice. I just have to stay under budget. That's the only way I've been able to save money and take care of myself since the accident."

"That shouldn't be a problem. Harris can email me a list of properties down here for rent, and we'll go check them out."

"Harris is your older brother, right?" Bailey asked, trying to keep the members of Chase's family in correct order.

"You remember well," Chase said and gave her a wink. "Now I have something to ask you."

"Fire away."

"Let me hire a private investigator for you."

"No way. I couldn't let you do that," Bailey said shaking her head.

"Why not?"

"Because I don't have that kind of money. At least not yet."

"I'm paying for it."

"Again, I can't let you do that."

"Bailey, please. I know someone in Miami who is really good. He is a friend of mine, and once I tell him your story, he will be like a dog with a bone. And if you won't let me pay for it, we'll call it a loan," Chase said, reaching across the table to take her hand for reassurance.

Bailey wanted to say "no" again, but just the look on his face was so endearing. He truly wanted to help. It made her feel so good to know that she finally had someone on her side, someone that cared, and that it didn't matter what she had been through.

She had thought all this time that if someone knew of her past, they wouldn't want to have anything to do with her with things being so complicated, but with Chase, it had been just the opposite. He wanted to get involved in her life, to help her, and the thought of that made her feel elated inside.

"I tell you what," Bailey said. "I'll think about it, and we'll talk again after all these weddings. We've got too many other things going on right now to worry about an investigator."

"But wouldn't it be nice to have someone working for you instead of trying to figure all this out by yourself?" Chase asked between bites.

"I guess," Bailey said slowly, but Chase noticed the hesitation.

"There's more to it than money, isn't there?" he asked.

"I'm scared."

"Of what?"

"Of finding out who I was."

"Why?"

"Like I said before – what if I was some bad person? What if my past is horrible? What if it's sad or lonely or...." Bailey wanted to continue, but she couldn't form the words.

Chase sat back and looked at her for a moment. He could see where this would be a problem, and that it could come back and bite him, too. He was falling for Bailey, and maybe she had a husband, though they had both talked about that and the possibility was almost none. A husband or boyfriend would have moved mountains to find someone they lost. At least Chase knew he would.

"Even if those things were true – and I doubt that is the case – that is not who you are now," Chase said.

"And I don't want to change my name either," Bailey said, knowing that a name change was a silly thing to worry about.

"I don't think you would have to change your name. Anyway, I like Bailey Parker. It suits you just fine." He took her hand and kissed the back of it, sending tiny shockwaves up Bailey's arm.

"So, what about the home hunt for me? Are you in?" Bailey asked cheerfully.

"Definitely. I'll talk to Harris today, get a list, and after these weddings are done, we'll start checking them out. And we'll talk about the investigator. Deal?"

"Deal," Bailey said, grabbing the last French fry on her plate.

The next week or so was a blur of activity. For Bailey and Mandy, it seemed like it was one wedding after another. Sometimes, two in one day, but Bailey found it exhilarating. Now that two people she was becoming close to knew her secret, she almost felt like she could take deep breaths again. Though, she still couldn't help analyzing almost everyone she saw, everything she felt or even said, Bailey felt like her body and her mind were starting to relax just a little.

It also helped that Chase was the photographer at every wedding. Though they didn't get to talk very much, stealing a look here and there, a short conversation, and even a small kiss was enough to make Bailey look forward to work every day. They had even had dinner a few times after a long day, and once so far, they had even gone back to the bench just to relax after some of the more active weddings they did.

Sitting at her desk, looking over the calendar, Bailey knew they finally had a small break between events. This would be the perfect time to look for a more permanent place to live.

The hotel was eating up her money a little faster than she was comfortable with, so finding a house or apartment had become a top priority.

"Mandy, if it is OK with you, I need to go look at some apartments. Chase has the list and is going to help me, so I don't end up in some shady place. Our calendar is not so busy right now. Will it be OK if I slip out every now and then? I'll let you know, for sure. And I promise my work will always be done," Bailey said, her nerves in knots, even though she had become so close to her employer.

"You do whatever you need to. And hell, I'm not worried about your work. You move circles around me, but then again, that's not hard to do these days." Mandy laughed. "I'm just glad that Chase is helping you. You two are seeing a lot of each other, aren't you?"

"He's been at every wedding," Bailey said shyly.

Mandy laughed. "I may be older than you, but my eyesight is super fine. I've seen the way you two look at each other, and I even walked by at the Patterson wedding to see him kissing you by the kitchen. And believe me, if I had a man kissing me like that, he would be seeing all of me!"

"Mandy!"

"It's true," Mandy said with a giant smile on her face. "I'm happy for you two. I'm just glad you took my advice."

Bailey relented, knowing that she couldn't keep anything from this woman. "Thanks," was all Bailey could say.

The hunt for an apartment began the next morning. Bailey had two days off in a row, and she wanted to take advantage of them. Chase was off at least for one day, and they were going to get as much done as they could. The next day for him would be time spent out on his sister's boat charter.

One by one, they went to see apartments and small homes along Islamorada and Key Largo. Bailey took pictures and made notes, but nothing was right. The places were either too small or too big, with large monthly rental prices to go with them. After only one day of hunting, Bailey was about to give up. She wasn't sure what to do.

"You'll have to give me the list, so I can go looking tomorrow," Bailey said as they walked hand in hand to the little bench once again. It was becoming one of her favorite places to come and spend time with Chase. Being so close to the water, watching brilliant sunsets and just listening to the lapping water were pure relaxation for both of them.

"I have a better idea. Why don't you take a break and come out on the boat with me tomorrow?" Chase said, kissing her lightly on the top of her head.

"No, I have too much to do."

"That's the whole reason for taking a break."

"You aren't making any sense."

"Bailey, you have been non-stop since I met you. Don't get me wrong, there is nothing wrong with that, but you never give yourself some time for a break. Going out on the boat will be fun. You can talk to the tourists, and if it will make you feel better, you can be my assistant."

"Your assistant?" Bailey laughed.

"You're Mandy's assistant, right? I think I could use one, too, but I can't pay you right now. Hope that's not a problem." Chase laughed.

Bailey thought about it, and the idea did sound exciting.

"OK, Mr. Cartwright, you have yourself an assistant for the day. And no need to pay me. Being with you is enough," Bailey said, squeezing his hand. "But just to let you know, I don't scuba, and I've only snorkeled once. So, I'll probably have to stay on the boat."

"Never went diving? We'll have to change that," Chase said, pulling her closer to him.

"Hey, you two. Come join me. Looks like it's going to be a wonderful sunset." Maria sat on the bench and had brought a bottle of wine with glasses.

"Great," Chase mumbled under his breath. "You want to go back to the house?"

"No. We can share the bench or go down on the dock." Bailey didn't want this woman coming between her and Chase, so she was going to see if she could make a friend out of her instead.

As soon as they reached the bench, Chase saw that Maria had three glasses. She had planned this, and he wondered what was to come next.

14

"Here is a glass for each of you. Hope you like red," Maria said before pouring a little into each of their glasses.

Chase wouldn't have taken the drink had he not seen Maria pop the cork. This woman, whom he had before just considered a nosy neighbor, was suddenly giving him bad vibes. He only wished he could figure out why.

"Thanks," Bailey said quickly, not giving Chase any time for a sarcastic remark. "How are you doing tonight?"

"Good. Long day at work, but that's normal. How about you two?" Maria asked with eyebrows raised.

"Same here. Real busy." Chase kept his words short and to the point. He had wanted this time with just Bailey, even though they had been together all day. Most of all, he guessed, he just didn't want to the spend any time with Maria.

"So, Bailey, what do you do?" Maria asked as she sat back on the bench. Bailey took the seat beside her and Chase sat on a stone table someone had left in the little seating area.

"I work for one of the local wedding planners."

"Now I know where you met Chase. So, how do like the Florida Keys?"

"I love it here. Islamorada is a bit more laid back than Key West."

"You already visited the city?"

"I lived there for a while. I managed a restaurant there before moving here," Bailey said, trying to be polite, but she was sensing some bad vibes from Maria.

"Wow, I work at a restaurant here in town. I'm the assistant manager. You should come by sometime. You might be able to give me some tips. You know us girls need to stick together." Maria took a sip of her wine and winked at Chase.

Bailey couldn't help but notice the smile Maria gave Chase, as though she could eat him alive. This girl certainly had not received the hint that Bailey was with Chase. She could tell that Maria wanted him, and she would probably do just about anything to push Bailey out of the picture. Suddenly, Bailey knew that she and this woman would never be friends.

"Maybe one day, but things have been really hectic at the office. So many people getting married around here. I didn't realize it was such a destination spot till I started working with Mandy."

Chase cringed. He had hoped that Bailey wouldn't give away where she was working. Maria had only known that Chase worked with most of the wedding planners in the area.

"Mandy? Oh, yes, I think I know her. We have catered for her before, but it's been a while. Really nice lady and a great planner."

"She is, and I've enjoyed the work so far. But like Chase said, it's been so busy lately. How is the restaurant business here?" Bailey asked, trying to deflect the attention from her.

"Just the usual. Chase, you haven't been by in a while. You should bring Bailey sometime. Call ahead, and I'll make sure you guys get the VIP treatment," Maria said, once again sipping her wine and having eyes only for Chase.

"Maybe we'll do that," Chase said hesitantly. "Bailey, ready for a walk on the dock?"

Bailey looked at Chase, then back to Maria, who just sat there with an malicious smile on her face. "Sounds good. Thanks, Maria, for the drink. Have a nice evening."

"Oh, Chase, don't forget that the Alstons are having their monthly block party this Sunday."

"Will probably be working, but we might see you there. Bye, Maria." Chase took Bailey's hand in his and led her toward the dock. He only hoped that Maria would leave the little area, so they didn't feel like every move they made was being observed.

"She seems nice, but there is something about her that is a little unnerving," Bailey said as they sat on the dock.

"I don't mean this to sound like I'm boasting or anything, but she's had some type of crush on me for a while. Always coming down here when I want to be alone. She has even shown up at a wedding or two. Inviting me to dinner or out to events. She is nice, I think, but I'm not into her." Chase glanced over his shoulder and could see Maria still sitting on the bench, watching them.

"Well, I'm glad to hear that last part." Bailey looked over at him and couldn't help but lean over and kiss him softly on the lips.

"You keep that up, and we'll be giving her a show she might not like," Chase said with a snicker. "But then maybe she might leave us alone." His smile just about melted Bailey's heart, and she forgot about Maria. This time, it was she who looked back, but saw the dark-haired woman walking forcefully down the road.

"I think she might be just a little upset," Bailey said, and Chase looked back to see what Bailey was talking about. Chase saw Maria walking fast, and there was no mistake that she was not happy. Her body language spoke volumes.

"Now I have you all to myself," Chase said, pulling Bailey into his lap. He wrapped his arms around her waist, and she couldn't help but snuggle closer, laying her head against his with her arms curled around his neck.

"I love being with you. You know, you are the first man I've spent so much time with since my accident. I really didn't think anyone would want me, damaged and all. I'm not being a martyr; it just seems that most people want you to be perfect. Happy all the time. No problems. I haven't dated since the accident because I just didn't know how. I went out with groups of people, maybe a few blind dates with other people around, but I could never get a good read on the whole dating thing. I talked to my therapist, and she said I would know when it was the right time."

"Is this the right time?" Chase asked slowly in a deep voice.

"I think so. You are the right time, the right man. I'm glad I didn't rush anything. I hope this was the kind of person I was before the accident. Or I was just the opposite, and my mind is telling me to learn from my mistakes. I might never know."

"Does it matter? I think you are perfect just the way you are, Bailey," Chase said. He held her closer and kissed her, so sensuously that Bailey almost forgot where they were. Her hands seemed to have a mind of their own as they wove themselves through his hair, caressed his neck, and then cradled his face.

Chase couldn't help but slide his hands down Bailey's back and then envelop his arms around her waist. The feel of her body next to his was sending his senses reeling. He was falling in love, and he knew it. But he would say nothing to Bailey, not yet. He had to be sure, but in his heart, he already knew. Bailey was winning him, body and soul, with every second that ticked by.

It had happened so quickly that it all took Chase by surprise. He wanted to tell her how he was feeling, but he didn't want to scare her. But Chase knew that this was the woman for him. In his eyes, she was perfect in every way. She fit with him, and he could only hope that Bailey felt the same way.

15

"You do have sunscreen, right?" Chase said as Bailey put a towel into her beach bag. It was the first time Chase had been in Bailey's room, and could tell she had it fixed up nicely as she could for such a tiny place.

"Yes, I do. I can't but feel like I should be apartment hunting instead of going out on the boat." Bailey exhaled heavily. She wanted to go with Chase, and the boat trip sounded divine, but she also wanted out of this hotel. She had been here long enough, and she was so ready to have a home of her own, even if she didn't own it. Renting was fine with her; at least it would be her own space here on the island.

"OK, we have been over this already. You have got to relax. Plus, you get to spend the day with me," Chase said, kissing her expertly on the lips.

"I see you at work all the time, and now it seems all my free time is taken up by you." She touched her finger to his nose and winked at him.

"I hope you think that is a good thing."

"Oh, it most certainly is, but I really, really, *really* need to find my own place. What if I miss the perfect spot by going out in the boat instead of apartment hunting today?"

"I can promise you that won't happen. You're going to find it. We still have a lot of places to check. And if you are so desperate to get out of here, come stay with me." Chase said the words without thinking, and one look at Bailey's face made him wonder if he had messed up for good.

"Are you asking me to move in with you?" Bailey said quietly.

Chase was stunned, trying to make sure he said the right thing. "Not exactly move in, but stay with me until you find a place. That way, you could save the nightly cost of staying here, and you would be living in a real house. I have two extra bedrooms so it wouldn't be a problem. But only till you find your own place. Definitely not living together."

Great, that didn't come out right either, Chase thought, running his fingers through his hair. "What I meant was...."

Bailey couldn't help but laugh as she watched him get so flustered by his statement. She knew what he meant, but couldn't help but continue to tease him. "You mean you don't want me to live with you?" She pouted and stuck out her bottom lip.

She went to stand in front of Chase, who was looking at the ceiling. She knew he was trying hard to choose his next words carefully, and she couldn't hold back the laughter.

"Chase, I knew what you meant. I don't think you are ready to give up your man cave, and I've wanted my own home for a while. Now that's not to say that we might have a hard time trying to decide whose house we spend time at. At least I hope that's the case."

Bailey watched as color came back to Chase's face.

"Honestly, Bailey, I'd have you move in with me right now, but I think you need a place of your own with everything you have been through. But I wished it was closer to me. A place where I could watch over you."

"I don't need a bodyguard."

"I know that, but I'm just protective of you. If there is someone looking for you, I would rather be with you if they ever came snooping around."

"It's been a while, so hopefully whoever it was is gone."

"Do you ever wonder if that man might have been able to help you?" Chase asked.

"I thought about that, but when I saw him, I just had a bad feeling. I can't really describe it. Then I saw that man at the park by the bridge. Another weird feeling like I knew him and there was all this anger. But it hasn't happened since."

"Well, we will discuss this all later, maybe when we get back home this evening. But for right now, we have to get going, or my sister is going to be a bit upset with me. I tend to get to the boat just a few minutes before she wants me there, and it looks like this morning isn't going to be any different," Chase said, picking up Bailey's bag for her.

"Are you sure it's OK for me to come?"

"I called Skylar last night and told her I was bringing a friend. Then it all began."

"What are you talking about?" Bailey asked, wondering what was wrong.

"Skylar has been trying to set me up for so long. It's like she is trying to marry me off. When she sees you walk on board with me, I think I'm going to have one happy sister," Chase said.

"She is just trying to take care of her baby brother," Bailey teased.

"She is a protective one, and now Garrett is getting in on it. He wants to know if I've met anyone new all the time. I keep trying to tell them I'm OK. I know how to date, and if I'm interested in anyone, I'll let them know when I'm ready."

"Well, if you need me to, I'll vouch for your dating skills. You have been nothing but a true gentleman. But I think I'll keep to myself the fact that your kisses and your touch seem to have a very appealing effect on me. "

Chase walked up to Bailey, and before she knew it, he had her in a hug that sent fire between them. Having her this close to him brought up thoughts of not going anywhere today, but staying home all day with her. But he quickly shook the thoughts out of his head. "OK, you little minx, let's go. You're making it difficult to go anywhere and not keep you all to myself the entire day."

According to the clock in Chase's car, they were about five minutes late. Hopefully, the sight of Bailey walking with him would keep Skylar from fussing at him. Chase carried his equipment with Bailey following behind.

"Well at least you got here before the snorkel group. You know we have to get your stuff on board before they get here," Skylar said, her voice a little heated.

"And good morning to you, too. By the way I'm only five minutes behind schedule," Chase said, then moved slightly to the side. "Skylar, this is my friend, Bailey. She's going to join us today."

Chase saw the smile on Skylar's face and knew his tardiness was all but forgotten.

"Hope it's OK. Chase has told me all about you, your business, and your family."

"I wish I could say the same thing because I haven't heard a peep about you," Skylar said with a sound of happiness to her voice, eyeing her brother directly. "We're more than happy to have you on board. It's going to be a beautiful day, and while Chase is taking all those lovely pictures of the snorkelers, maybe we can take time to get to know each other."

"I would like that," Bailey said and immediately liked Chase's big sister.

"She might go snorkeling. She has only gone once before."

"I think staying on board with your sister sounds a bit more fun. Maybe I can snorkel next time?" Bailey asked. She could see a bit of disappointment on Chase's face, but loved the fact that she could spend some time with Skylar. "Where can I put my things?"

"Put your stuff on the front seat near the cabin. Should be fine there. Garrett will be here in a minute with everyone. I came a little early after I dropped off Taylor at the babysitter."

No sooner had Skylar uttered the words than Bailey heard voices in the distance. She looked down the dock to see a tall, dark-haired, very handsome man escorting about ten people toward them. Bailey assumed this was Garrett and the tour group for this morning's excursion.

As the people came aboard the vessel, Bailey loved watching the excitement on everyone's faces. She especially enjoyed watching Chase and how he interacted with the tour group. Bailey had seen him work his charms with wedding groups, but this was something so different.

As they headed out to sea with Skylar at the helm, Bailey felt like she was an observer of this whole unique experience going on around her. Garrett giving lessons for the snorkelers, Chase making sure equipment was ready, and a young man whose name Bailey couldn't remember taking care of the other chores that needed done on the boat as they made their way out to sea. What fascinated her, too, was that this was all possible because Skylar had taken a bold step to strike out on her own and start a company. There was a part of Bailey that wanted to do the same thing, but what she would do, she wasn't sure.

There were things Bailey loved, and she was finding out the tasks that she was good at, like staying organized, interacting with people, handling unexpected problems fast and even planning weddings. But there was no way she could become a wedding planner and be in competition with Mandy. She had been too good to Bailey.

Soon, they were at what Chase had declared was the perfect spot for their ocean adventure, the boat gently bobbing on the sea. When Bailey looked over the side, the water was crystal-clear, and she swore that she could see to the very bottom. The weather was nice and clear, with bright blue skies above with the occasional puffy cloud passing by.

Pretty soon, the entire snorkeling group was in the water with Garrett as their guide. Bailey watched as flippers occasionally flapped against the water and little, black breathing tubes moved leisurely through the surface of the water.

"How are you doing?" Skylar said, coming to stand beside Bailey.

"I'm fine. It's so beautiful and peaceful out here. Chase told me how you started this business. You're definitely someone to be admired," Bailey said.

"Well, thank you for those very kind words, but I'm just following through on a dream. I'm glad that Chase is going after what he wants, too. So, how long have you two been dating?"

"Um, we're just friends," Bailey said, unsure of what Chase had said to his sister.

"Bailey, I know my baby brother really well. Since he brought you today, you are special to him. So, that means you're most certainly more than a friend."

"So, Chase has never done this before? Brought a girl with him on the boat?" Bailey asked.

"Maybe twice, but I don't know what he has told you about his past relationships."

"I know about Blair and someone that he dated right after her. Other than that, he said there was no one special."

"Wow, now I know things are heating up between you two. He never talks about Blair or Shari to anyone. I sure hope the feeling is mutual."

Bailey stood there in stunned silence. Was she ready to admit to Chase's sister that she had feelings for her brother? She was just beginning to feel comfortable with Chase.

"We enjoy spending time together."

"Bailey, I'm sorry. I put you on the spot, and I didn't mean to. When it comes to Chase, I just get overprotective. I want him to be happy. He's been through a lot with our family, and like I said earlier, some past relationships. I guess I should believe him when he says he's doing fine."

"Well, I think he is mighty lucky to have a sister like you."

"Do you have any brothers or sisters?" Skylar asked as she looked at the swimmers in the water.

"Uh, no," Bailey said. This sudden question confirmed that Chase had kept his word and hadn't said anything to Skylar about her memory loss.

"You are very lucky. Well, no. I love my siblings, and I'm closer to Chase than Mara or Harris, but there were times growing up I wanted to be the only child. That's why I would sit and watch the boats from an upstairs room in our family house in Key Biscayne. I learned everything I could about boats, to the point I was driving my parents and siblings crazy."

"That's where your passion came from. Chase told me you took a big chance leaving the family business to move here."

"It was definitely different, and I had a not-so-happy mom and dad, but things eventually worked out. And I met Garrett." Bailey watched as Skylar glanced out over the water, looking for her husband. There was a soft tonal switch in Skylar's voice indicating the love she had for her husband. It was almost palpable.

"Sounds like you have a beautiful love story just by the way you say his name."

Bailey saw the blush on Skylar's cheeks. "Yes, ours is an interesting story. I'll have to tell you all about it one day. Right now, though, I think we have some snorkelers that are ready for a break."

One by one, the swimmers climbed the ladder, took their equipment off, and sat on one of the cushioned seats for a rest. Bailey helped Skylar pass out water bottles and then listened as the tourists talked about what they had just seen below the surface of the water. With Garrett by their side, he was able to tell them about all kinds of interesting things below, especially the different species of fish. The tour group was even privileged to have been visited by not one, but *two* sea turtles, which delighted the three women that were visiting from New York.

Chase was the last to board. He had stayed in the water for just a bit longer, taking pictures, Bailey assumed. But finally, he came up the ladder. Even with his camera equipment on his shoulder and snorkeling gear on the other, Bailey swooned.

This was the first time she had seen him with only swimming trunks on, and he was *hot.* The muscles along his arms, chest, and down through his abdomen were taut and well-defined. Bailey had felt the firmness when they had embraced and kissed, but a shirt was always between them. Now she couldn't help but stare.

"Bailey, would you like to go?" She quickly looked over to Skylar, but had no idea what she was talking about. Bailey had been in her own little world for a few seconds, stunned by Chase's physique.

"We have about twenty minutes or so before we leave, so everyone goes swimming or snorkeling again if they like."

"Come on, let's go swimming. We'll save snorkeling for next time," Chase said, holding out his hand.

"OK." It was the only word that came to Bailey, still thinking about Chase as he stepped back aboard the boat, dripping with water. She went to her beach bag and took off the top and shorts she had been wearing, revealing a two-piece coral-colored bikini. One thing she did know was that she loved to swim. Even while in Key West, she would go swimming as much as possible, be it a pool or the beach. But snorkeling, only once.

By the time she was at Chase's side, everyone except Skylar and Garrett were in the water.

"So, we have to go down the ladder since there are others in the water. My preferred method is to jump off the side of the boat. Maybe next time, we can do that. Ready?" Chase said, looking so protectively into her eyes that Bailey could only nod.

She went down the ladder into the warm waters of the Atlantic Ocean. As Bailey swam away from the boat, it felt wonderful, like every muscle in her body relaxed all at once in the soothing water. Chase came down after her, and she was just as in awe of his backside as the front. Chase was a perfect male specimen, and hopefully, he was all hers.

As Chase swam toward Bailey, he loved the bright smile that lit up her face. *Man, she is beautiful,* Chase thought, moving closer to her. He almost forgot to breathe when she finally discarded her shirt and shorts, wearing nothing but the bikini that enhanced her incredible features. From its color and style, Bailey couldn't have chosen better. Chase tried not to stare, but her creamy skin and sexy curves had him riveted. And apparently, Skylar had seen his reaction because it was her hand that had slightly nudged him in the back when Bailey started walking toward him.

"The water feels amazing," Bailey said as Chase swam up to her.

"See, you should have come in with us earlier." He dove underwater, and Bailey looked from side to side to see where he would pop up. But in the crystal-clear water, she could see he was coming right up beside her.

"Hi, there." Chase's voice sounded so sexy, she couldn't help but put her arms around him. Even though they were both treading water to stay afloat, she couldn't help herself. She wanted to touch him, almost to reassure herself that this was all real, that what she was experiencing right now wasn't a dream. These feelings. This man.

"Believe it or not, Skylar is signaling for everyone to come back on board."

"Already?" Bailey couldn't believe that she had to get out of the water, but as she looked toward the boat, she saw the others climbing back on board.

"Yes, but I'm already planning a future date," Chase said with a teasing tone.

"And what is that?" Bailey asked.

"Anywhere we can go swimming and I can see that bikini again." He grinned at her.

Bailey was sure her cheeks were flushed at Chase's words. She also felt those same shivers again at his words, even though she was blanketed in warm waters.

"Sounds good to me. I think I could handle some time with you in nothing but a pair of shorts." Chase winked at her before they both swam back to the boat.

The ride back seemed so short compared to the ride out to the diving spot. Everyone chatted away about what they had seen, and Chase talked to each about the pictures that would be available for pick-up in about an hour once they were on land.

"How do you do that?" Bailey asked once he was seated beside of her.

"What?"

"The pictures. How do you do them so fast?"

"I have a printer and everything I need back at the office at the dock. I show them the pictures on my computer, they pick which ones they want, and I print them. Easy."

"Reminds me of Disneyland, when I got my picture made with one of the characters, but my dad wouldn't pay for the picture." Suddenly, Bailey felt like she was going to pass out. She started to hyperventilate, and it seemed she couldn't remember where she was.

"Bailey, look at me." She could hear Chase's words, and she slowly turned to him.

"You're OK. We are almost at the dock. Just take some slow, deep breaths." She did as he instructed her to but everything around felt surreal. She had remembered something, and it had felt like a bolt of lightning had hit her brain.

Bailey could see Disneyland in her mind, and someone was walking by her side. She remembered standing beside a character, but she couldn't see who it was, then begging someone, a man, to please buy the picture. But all she heard was, "Not right now." The worst thing was she couldn't make out the face.

"Bailey, look at me." It was Chase's voice and she turned to where she heard the sound.

"We're almost back at the dock. You're going to fine but you have to take some deep breaths."

Bailey looked at Chase, seeing a look of concern spreading across his face. "I think I'm OK, but Chase, I finally had a memory return. A memory!"

Bailey still felt shaky inside but she couldn't contain her excitement as a smile graced her face. But she leaned into Chase's arms, letting him cradle her until they were at the dock.

16

"That was a good trip," Skylar said, coming up to Bailey and Chase, who were still on board.

"What time is the next one?" Chase asked.

"In a few hours, but it's a scuba certification dive, so you don't have to go unless you just want to come along. Do you dive, Bailey?"

"Oh, no, not me. I get claustrophobic with a snorkel mask. I can't imagine what I'd feel like with a tank on my back, breathing through a tube, with water all around me. I think — no, I *know* I would panic." Bailey answered Skylar's question, but her mind was on the sliver of memory that had found her a little earlier.

"I don't dive much either, but I can. That's Garrett's expertise, and he swears our daughter will be right beside him one day. He keeps trying to teach her about all the fish, and she is trying to get him to remember the names of her dolls," Skylar laughed.

"She'll appreciate it when she is older," Garrett said, coming up to his wife and giving her a solid, loving kiss.

"And as you can see, open displays of affectionate are a part of this family," Chase said as a signal for his sister and brother-in-law to come up for air.

"Always keeping that love alive," Garrett said, hugging his wife.

"Well, since you won't be needing me this afternoon, we are going to go look at more apartments," Chase said.

"You guys are moving in together?" Skylar said the words so fast that they seemed to blur together.

"No," Bailey said quickly. "Chase is helping me find a place to live. I'm staying at a hotel right now, and it's getting to be a bit old. Need my own place, but everything I've seen or looked up seems to be in a place I'm not so sure of or out of my price range."

"Harris gave me a list, and we are just knocking them out one by one."

"What about our apartment downstairs?" Garrett said, looking at Skylar. "It's been empty for a while, except for my research papers and some odds and ends. We keep saying we are going to turn it into an entertainment room or something, but haven't."

"That's a great idea," Skylar said, "as long as you don't drink, party, or do drugs, which, from spending time with you today, I don't think you do." Skylar smiled broadly at Bailey, then over to Chase.

"Thanks for the offer, but I couldn't do that. It would be such an inconvenience to you," Bailey said.

"We talked about renting it out at one time, but when Taylor came along, we didn't want just anyone living so close to us. Plus, a baby crying probably wouldn't have brought in too many potential renters. The problem is that it's one big room with a small kitchen and a closed off bathroom. And it definitely needs to be cleaned up. Why don't you come by this evening, have a look and we'll have dinner? Already have beef stew in the crock pot at home."

Bailey looked at Chase and couldn't believe her luck. She smiled slightly, but was so excited inside. Having remembered something only a short time ago was huge, but now this? Maybe the apartment would work out, but she was reluctant to get her hopes up.

"Sounds like a plan. We'll see you tonight. And thanks for letting me come today and for the apartment offer. I really appreciate it," Bailey said as she and Chase got off the boat and walked down the dock.

That evening, when Chase picked her up, Bailey was a jumble of nerves. She wanted to make sure that she looked just right for the evening because Skylar and Garrett could become her potential landlords. Though they had spent the day together on the boat, tonight was different. This was Chase's family, and she wanted to make a good impression.

"Do I look all right?" asked Bailey as Chase walked into the room when she opened the door.

"I think you look perfect," Chase said, wrapping his arms around her. "I'm not sure why you're so worried. You already met everyone today."

"I know, but this is really important to me. I can't believe that they offered to let me live in the apartment at their house. I'm not sure how I feel about that."

"What do you mean? That would solve all your problems. You wouldn't have to look anymore, you'd be one street over from me, and by staying with my sister, I would feel better about you being on your own when I can't be with you."

Bailey loved the fact that Chase wanted to take care of her. It made her feel cherished and special, something that she could never remember feeling before in her life. But she didn't want to burden him.

"Well, I haven't seen anyone like those men again, and hopefully, after what happened today, maybe I'm getting my memory back!" Bailey said excitedly. "I've been wracking my brain since I got back here, trying to figure out who the man was that I recalled. I can't really see his face, but at least I know one thing."

"What's that?" Chase asked.

"That I went to Disneyland," Bailey laughed.

Chase looked at her and smiled. He loved seeing her this happy. It seemed that the more time that passed, she was becoming more relaxed and happy about her life despite her past circumstances.

The evening was just as nice as the morning had been. Skylar and Garrett had a lovely home, closer to Chase than

Bailey realized, though their home was further down the street making it closer to the ocean. They had a large dock on the canal behind their home, and one of their boats was moored along the side. The house stood three stories tall, but the family only lived on the second and third floor. The first floor was the apartment they had spoken about earlier.

"This was so good," Bailey said as she helped take plates to the kitchen. "Let me help you take care of these."

"Nope. You and Chase are going to go check out the room below. It really needs a lot of work, but if you are willing to fix it up, we are willing to rent it to you. Chase has vouched for you, but after spending the morning with you, there was no need," Skylar said, giving Bailey a welcoming smile.

"Thanks again, but how much would the monthly rental fee be?"

"Why don't you go see what you are getting yourself into before we talk money."

Chase and Bailey took the keys to the room and headed downstairs. The door opened to a very large room. Just like Skylar had told her earlier, there was a kitchen to her right as she entered the space and a closed-off room just beyond it, which she assumed was the bathroom. Other than that, it was just one big room.

As Bailey stepped around boxes and storage crates, she envisioned the possibilities of turning this space into a beautiful little apartment. Though she had said earlier that she wanted a separate bedroom, she could accomplish that by using bookshelves, a room divider, or crates to make that happen. The windows that were on three of the walls let in enough light, and she even had a beautiful view of the dock and canal out the back.

"Whatcha think?" Chase asked, coming up behind her, encircling his arms around her.

"Honestly, I think it is perfect. I can see so much potential." Bailey turned herself around in his arms, so she could look into those eyes she loved so much. "And I like that I would be living so close to you. This way, I can keep an eye on Maria and make sure she doesn't steal you away."

Chase laughed. "You've got to be kidding!"

"I feel the need to protect you, like you feel that for me."

Chase looked down into her loving face, which he swore he could never get enough of. He had to tell her.

"Bailey Parker, I think I'm falling in love with you."

Bailey looked at him, feeling an exhilaration like nothing she had felt before. Maybe even better than the way she felt after receiving the memory she regained this afternoon. This man really loved her.

"Chase, I have to say I feel the same way, too. I love you," and Bailey stood on her tip-toes, pressing her lips to his. The kiss was gentle at first, but heated into a fiery bliss that left them wanting much more.

"Um, hi, there," Garrett said, interrupting the couple. Bailey turned beet-red, and Chase just looked at him with a smile.

"Skylar wanted me to come down and make sure everything was OK. And to see what you thought."

"Tell my sister we'll be up in just a moment."

Garrett grinned at both of them. "Just take your time."

"How's that for timing?" Chase said, looking back to the girl in his arms. "I do love you, Bailey. Heart and soul."

"I love you, too."

"So, are you going to tell them you'll take the apartment?"

"I think so... on one condition."

"What's that?"

"Will you help me get this place livable and cleaned up?" Bailey asked in the sweetest voice she could muster.

"It would be my pleasure," Chase said, giving her one more kiss before they headed toward the door. But Bailey stopped suddenly.

"What's wrong?" Chase asked concerned.

"If I'm going to live here, I have to tell them about my past. I have to let them know about the man that's looking for me. They have a child, and I don't want to put anyone in danger."

"Bailey, if you were in danger, don't you think something might have happened before now? Maybe that man is the bearer of good news."

"I still can't shake that panicked feeling every time I think of him. But I know without a shadow of doubt that I belong here in the Keys. Sometimes, it gets so confusing. But the one thing that I am one hundred percent sure of is you. Thanks, Chase."

"I'm the one who should be thanking you." They couldn't help but kiss once more before heading up the stairs.

When Bailey found out the price of the monthly rental, she was shocked. She even offered to pay more, the fair asking price in the area, but neither Skylar nor Garrett would hear of it. Then Bailey told them her story, and they still had no problem renting the room to her. In fact, Skylar told her it would be better for her to be here, where people knew her, where the neighbors took care of each other and watched out for each other.

"And guess what?" Chase said quickly.

"What?" Bailey asked, puzzled.

"You now have your own little bench at the end of this street. That way, we can go sit by the water and not be bothered by Maria."

"Is that woman still pestering you?" Skylar asked suddenly. "I thought she would have realized that the ship had sailed as far as you are concerned."

"I guess you could say that. She was waiting at the bench the other night with wine and glasses for us to all sit and talk. Have to give Bailey credit. She talked to her and was real nice, but I just feel like Maria is up to no good."

"Well, at least she is living on your street," Skylar said.

"But it's your fault she still wants to date!" Chase exclaimed. "If you hadn't' tried to set us up, none of this would be happening."

"I told you not to do it," Garrett said.

"She was always so nice to me at the restaurant. I thought you guys would get along. I guess I should've gotten to know her a bit better before I set you up on that blind date."

"You two went out?" Bailey asked.

"Once!" Chase made clear.

Bailey couldn't help but giggle at Chase's loud declaration, and Skylar followed along.

"It's not funny, you two," Chase said. "I thought she was nice, but now she's just a bit creepy."

"Well, just spend more time over here, and you should be safe."

"That won't be a problem because I'm going to be helping Bailey clean up the apartment and get settled."

"The only problem is that my schedule is jam-packed over the next few days, so I might be coming and going. Is that a problem?" Bailey asked.

"That sounds like our life. Here is your key. You can move in whenever you like."

Bailey smiled and looked at Chase. Things were settling down. She even felt like her life was starting to follow a little routine. More importantly, Chase loved her, and that thought sent a shot of pure contentment coursing through her body.

17

Bailey was at the office the next morning before Mandy. She had woken earlier than her normal time, but had a hard time even falling asleep last night. Yesterday had been such a great day that she had relived it over and over, several times before she was finally able to close her eyes.

After dinner, she and Chase had walked down the short way to the bench beside the ocean's edge. The one on this street was much bigger, but there was no dock that jutted out over the water, only a large, sandy, man-made beach with a few palm trees, which Bailey actually liked. They sat like they had before, watching the ocean, but this time, wrapped up closer to each other.

Their declaration of love had solidified their relationship, and Bailey couldn't be happier. No matter what her past held, Chase told her he would be there for her. Plus, his own sister and her husband were not bothered about her past accident. If anything, they were concerned and accepted her just like she was. For the first time, Bailey truly felt that she could build a life from this point and let go of her past. She was Bailey Parker, after all. Whoever the person was before the accident was long gone.

After looking over the papers on her desk and then the calendar on the wall, Bailey got to work. She needed to get a lot done this morning, so she could take a break today to do a bit of shopping. There were a few things Bailey needed to purchase because she and Chase were starting work on her new apartment tonight. They figured they could have it ready by the weekend, or at least to the point she could move her own things in. She would have to buy a bed and a few chairs to get by, and that could be done tomorrow. She just wanted to move in as quickly as possible, but with such a full schedule, they would only be able to work on it here and there.

When Mandy arrived, Bailey filled her in on the details of the last few days, from remembering something from her past for the very first time to the fact that she now had a new home. And Bailey also shared the very personal fact that she was ready to let go of the past and move forward with Chase in her life.

"I knew it!" Mandy said loudly. "You two are little peas in a pod. Perfect for each other. I'm so happy for you both!"

To Bailey, it seemed like each day was busier than the next. The weekend brought three weddings, and it seemed as though she and Chase were in constant motion. The apartment was cleared out, cleaned and ready for Bailey to move her own things into the place. Her purchased bed was delivered the following Monday, before one of their scheduled weddings, and the next morning, before she had to be at work for another event, Bailey moved her things from the hotel to her new home.

Though she could only place the boxes and suitcases in the huge room before heading back out the door, she knew tonight, she would be in her own place instead of the hotel, and she beamed with excitement as she looked around the room.

Chase walked out the door before her, but Bailey glanced back one more time and couldn't help but feel giddy at the thought of coming home to this place.

When she woke the next morning, at first, she couldn't remember where she was, but then it dawned on her. Even though Bailey was greeted with boxes, bags, and suitcases, it felt wonderful. She went and fixed herself some coffee and peeked out the back window. Everything along the canal looked so peaceful and quiet. She would have never known that an excited three-year-old lived upstairs, but even if she heard anything, that wouldn't have bothered her.

She didn't have to be at the office till around noon because they had another evening wedding tonight, then a couple days off before the next round of weekend weddings. Then there was nothing on the calendar for five days in a row. Though Mandy loved every bit of business she could get, a small stretch of little activity would help them both because after this little break, there were more weddings coming up fast. But next week, Bailey told herself, she would take the time to find just the right items to make this little place all her own.

The ringing cell phone caught her attention, but try as she might, she couldn't find where she had placed it. Bailey could hear it ringing, but then it stopped. She lifted a couple of bags and looked through her purse before she heard it ringing again. The kitchen. Her tote bag was there, and she finally located the ringing device.

"Bailey?" It was Mandy's voice, but she sounded very different than usual.

"Hi, Mandy," Bailey said, suddenly concerned. "Are you OK?"

"Bailey, I'm so glad I got ahold of you." Mandy's words were a bit slow and slurred, as though she had been drinking.

"What's going on, Mandy?"

"I fell."

"Are you OK?"

"Oh, sure. This medicine is awesome," Mandy said, this time sounding much more animated.

"You fell? Are you hurt?" Bailey asked, a feeling of alarm rising inside of her.

"I was. Well, I guess I am. This medicine, though, just takes it all away. I told that nurse she better not go too far. This is the best stuff ever."

Nurse? Bailey now was officially worried.

"Mandy, where are you?"

"Hold on. Let me ask."

Bailey could only hear garbled words on the other end of the line until an unfamiliar voice took over.

"Hi, are you family?"

"This is Bailey Parker, Mandy's employee and friend. Is she OK?" Bailey asked quickly.

"Do you know of any way to contact her family?"

"As far as I know, she has no family living here, except an ex-husband in Key West whom she isn't too fond of."

Bailey could hear Mandy trying to talk in the background. The nurse responded with, "OK, that's fine."

"What's going on? Is Mandy OK?"

"Can you come down to Mariner's Hospital?"

The hospital? "I'll be right there."

Bailey dressed in a flash and was out the door. On the way, she called Chase, and he said he would be there as soon as he could. When Bailey walked in, she was escorted back to a room in the Emergency Department. Mandy was sleeping, her neck in a brace and her right leg completely immobilized from her thigh to her foot.

Before she could turn around to find a nurse, a tall man dressed in scrubs walked in.

"Hi, I'm Dr. Foster. Are you Ms. Thompson's daughter?"

"No, I'm her friend and employee, Bailey Parker. As far as I know, she doesn't have any family in the area, except her ex-husband, and I have no way to get a hold of him."

"I believe the nurse was finally able to contact him, but he won't be here for a couple of hours."

"I told her not to call him," Mandy said, her voice soft, as though she was speaking through a haze.

"Mandy, what in the world happened?"

"Doc, it's OK. This is my friend. I don't care if she knows what is going on."

"Well, it seems like your friend took a tumble down her stairs this morning. We've done scans, and right now, she is lucky. Only a broken leg, but it happens to be the femur, so we are going to have to do surgery to put a pin in the bone to stabilize it. She has already signed the papers, but we wanted to make sure she had someone with her. Plus, she will need help once she is able to go home."

Bailey looked back at her friend, who seemed to have fallen asleep once again.

"When will you do surgery?"

"This afternoon, if not sooner. Will you be here?" the doctor asked.

"Yes, it will be no problem."

"You have to do the wedding this evening." Though Mandy's eyes were closed, and she was certainly receiving pain medication through the IV drip, she still was thinking about work.

Bailey had completely forgotten the wedding after getting the call from Mandy.

"Don't worry. I have it all handled. Just go back to sleep."

"We are getting ready to move her to her room. We will prep her there before we take her to the operating room. If you have any more questions, just let me know."

"Thanks, Dr. Foster," Bailey said, her mind racing, wondering what to do next.

"Bailey, I'm fine. Really. This medicine is like so wonderful." Mandy chuckled as she talked slowly. "Can't believe I fell. I've walked those steps thousands of times and never a problem. And then today? I just tripped. Oh well." Then, as if her emotions took a sudden turn, she started to cry. "What about the weddings? What am I going to do?"

"That's what I'm here for. I'll be able to handle all the details. Maybe I'll get Chase to help me. He's in the waiting room and keeps texting me to know what's going on. Close your eyes, and I'll be right back." Bailey gently squeezed her friend's hand, but Mandy had already drifted back to into her medicine-induced sleep.

"How is she?" Chase asked nervously when Bailey walked through the emergency room doors into the waiting area.

"Very happy with the medicine they have her on, except she is worried about the business," Bailey said with a nervous laugh. "She fell down her steps this morning and broke her leg. She has to have surgery this afternoon, and her ex-husband is on his way from Key West. Apparently, he was her emergency contact."

Chase rolled his eyes and shook his head.

"Is there something I should know?" Bailey asked quickly.

"Mandy and her husband didn't quite part on friendly terms. From the little bit Mandy has said here and there, he is a party guy. She never said what exactly led to the divorce, but I guess it was maybe an affair on his part because one day, she just went totally ballistic, calling him every name in the book, and this was after the divorce. There is no telling what she'll do when he gets here," Chase explained.

"In the state she is in, she probably won't even remember," Bailey said, thinking of her friend's mood swings with the IV medication they were giving her for pain. "He is supposed to be here in a few hours. Hopefully, before they take her back for surgery."

"When this is all over, I have a feeling that Mandy is going to change the emergency contact quickly," Chase responded, looking concerned.

"I have a big favor to ask you." Bailey sat beside him and clasped his hand. "We – now I – have a bunch of weddings coming up, and there is no way I can do them by myself. You wouldn't want to be photographer *and* my assistant till Mandy gets better, would ya? I know you have other people you work for, but none of them have probably broken their leg, leaving their poor assistant alone to handle everything."

Chase watched Bailey, her nervousness showing as she bounced her leg up and down furiously. He gently placed his hand on her leg, and she slowed down its rapid pace.

"I don't think that will be any problem. We'll go over the calendar later. The problem I see now is that we need to get ready for the wedding this evening."

"I hate to leave her here by herself. Let me go talk to her and the doctor once more."

Bailey checked on Mandy, and she was still asleep. Whatever concoction was being administered straight into her veins was working miracles. Hopefully, after surgery, it would do the same job.

Bailey found the nurse since the doctor wasn't available, left her cellphone number, and asked them if they would have

Mandy's ex-husband call her after he arrived. Bailey also asked if they would let her know when Mandy was out of surgery.

Then she went back in Mandy's room, told her sleeping friend they were thinking of her, and headed back to Chase. They did have a lot to get done – and quickly.

18

Bailey and Chase wasted no time getting to work. Bailey's lists and the information that Mandy had on her desk for the wedding let them tie up all the loose ends fairly quickly. Chase went back to his house, grabbed the camera equipment, and was back to the office while Bailey made a few more phone calls about the weddings for the upcoming weekend.

Bailey said a silent prayer of thanks to Mandy for keeping such detailed notes and everything so organized. She didn't know what she would have done if things had been in disarray. But at the same time, as she glanced at the calendar and saw the file folders lining Mandy's desk for the weddings that were to take place over the next weeks, a sense of being overwhelmed came over Bailey. She was so looking forward to fixing up her apartment and the chance to spend more personal time with Chase. But now it seemed like all of that would be put on hold.

By the end of the night, the day had been successful. Bailey hadn't been able to go back to the hospital to check on Mandy because visiting hours were over by the time the wedding was finished. But she had heard from the nurse and Mandy's ex, Dennis, that the surgery was successful and that Mandy was resting comfortably. She promised Dennis that she would be at the hospital in the morning to check on her and asked if he needed anything, but he was fine.

Bailey didn't know what she would have done without Chase's help today. He had been there every step of the way, even making sure that she ate, which she had completely forgotten about in the rush to keep everything running smoothly for the bride and groom. How Mandy had done this on her own before, Bailey had no idea.

Though Bailey wanted to spend some time with Chase this evening, they both decided that it had been a long day and went their separate ways reluctantly. When Bailey parked her car in front of her new place, she looked up to see the lights still on upstairs. She had promised that she was not a night owl or party person, but there were going to be times like this when late-night homecomings would be the thing. She hoped Skylar and Garrett didn't regret their decision to rent her the space below.

Even with her things still stuffed in boxes and scattered everywhere, it felt so good when she entered the large room, then locking the door securely for the night. The bed was a mess from this morning, when she had rushed out the door, but Bailey didn't care. It looked so inviting right now because she was bone-tired.

She quickly took a bath, sent a text to Chase that said, "Thanks for today! You are the best" and slid between the sheets. And this night, she had no trouble at all falling asleep.

The next morning was a bit more peaceful and less chaotic. Bailey woke to the sound of her phone's built-in alarm and laid there for a few moments, looking around as sunlight streamed through the windows that had been covered with sheets temporarily. When her phone buzzed again, this time, it was Chase, and she immediately had a goofy smile across her face as she read the message:

"Good morning, sweetheart. Hope you got some rest last night. I can't wait to see you today. How does breakfast at Mangrove Mike's sound, then we will head to the hospital?"

Bailey quickly texted back, "Yes," and got up to get ready, keeping the smile plastered on her face as she thought about the man who was just one street over from her.

She just about had everything in her tote that she would need for the day when she heard the knock on the door. A quick glance out the side window and she saw the man that made her heart skip beats.

"I was just getting ready to call you to see if we were meeting at the restaurant or riding together. Wasn't sure what your schedule was today," Bailey said, but Chase didn't answer her.

Instead, he had his arms around her quickly, but gently, and his mouth descended on hers like a hungry lion.

Bailey didn't protest. Her hands snaked their way up to his shoulders and around his neck in no time, and the passionate kiss continued. But finally, Chase pulled away, leaving her breathless.

"Good morning. I've been wanting to do that since I opened my eyes this morning," Chase said, his breathing a little ragged as he locked eyes with her.

"I'm not complaining one bit. I think I could get used to morning greetings like this," Bailey said.

"My wedding shoot this afternoon in Marathon canceled on me. Seems the groom got cold feet last night and called things off."

"That's terrible! Poor girl must be devastated."

"From what I was told, she and her bridesmaids are on their way to Key West for a few days to live it up. Apparently, this is her way to 'forget the bastard' – the bride's words, not mine. Anyway, that means I'm free to help you completely for the next week and a half, unless I have to go out on the boat again. Skylar hasn't said anything, so right now my calendar is clear," Chase said, holding his hands out to her.

"Then I will take you up on the offer because I'm going to need it. There are four weddings from Thursday to Sunday. At least it's just one a day instead of two a day. That's brutal. Most everything is in place. Just the weddings are to be done. Then after that, it's five whole days of nothing," Bailey said with a smile.

"I know that between the two of us, we can do it," Chase said, hugging Bailey again, "especially when we get to look forward to much well deserved time away from work. What will we do?"

"I still have some work to do, but hopefully, we'll have a little more personal time," Bailey said, hugging him tightly. "I think we make a pretty good team, but right now, I'm starved. I did call and check on Mandy. She was sleeping. I guess it was her ex that answered. I thought he sounded nice."

"We'll get the whole story, hopefully, when we get to the hospital."

Mangrove Mike's Cafe was packed with both locals and tourists, but they soon were seated at a table and eating a full breakfast. Bailey loved the local restaurant and the relaxed atmosphere that surrounded them. She had been here several times, never leaving disappointed. And it was always a pleasure to sit across from Chase and share a meal.

As they talked, Bailey felt so happy, so normal. She didn't know that she could feel this way, her life having been one big anxiety show since the day of her accident. But now it seemed her life was becoming more like she had imagined. She had friends, a job she loved, and now a man she adored. So many firsts for her – new memories to replace the ones she couldn't reach in her mind. And each day, she could feel that she was letting go of the past and embracing her present and future. It all felt so right.

"Ready to go? I'm a little anxious to meet Dennis. Like I said, Mandy hasn't mentioned much about him, except to use his name with a cuss word here and there. Last thing she needs right now is more stress after this surgery. Plus, she isn't going to be too happy about being out of commission for a while," Chase said as he laid the tip on the table and they walked out the door.

19

It was only a few minutes and they were walking into the hospital. Once they had Mandy's room number, soon they were quietly knocking on her door.

"Come in," the weak voice said.

Bailey opened the door to a partially lit room with the TV playing softly in the background. Mandy was laying in the bed, her head elevated just a bit and her leg completely surrounded in thick medical bandages, leaving her unable to move.

"Hey, there," Bailey said in a low voice. "We came to check on you."

"How did the wedding go last night?"

"It was fine, but that's not for you to worry about right now," Bailey said, shaking her head at her friend, who seemed to have a one-track mind.

"We want to know about you. When are you getting out of this place?" Chase asked quietly, trying to lighten the mood.

"Not soon enough." Mandy's voice was feeble, and Bailey assumed that it was from the medicine. "The doctor came in this morning and said that everything went well yesterday, just took them a bit longer than they expected. I guess I'm going to be in the hospital for about a week. I have to do some rehab, but he said it was a good thing the bone broke closer to the knee instead of higher. All I know is that it hurts like a son of a bitch."

"What about pain medicine?" Bailey asked.

"It's doing a pretty good job, but I wish they would give me something for my nerves, too. Dennis being here is not helping the situation at all." Even though Mandy was under the influence of pain medication, it hadn't stifled her disdain for her ex-husband.

"Where is he?"

"Went to get some food. Thought he was going to sneak some food back for me, but he hasn't shown up yet. Probably left the hospital. He can't handle stuff like this. Why I didn't change my emergency contact, I have no clue. I thought after my divorce, I had taken care of everything, down to the last detail. Wouldn't you know, I forgot something like this. Ugh."

"Well, at least he came. Did he spend the night here? Where is he staying?"

"Oh, hell no. I made him leave about eleven o'clock last night. He didn't want to stay with me when we were married, and I wasn't about to have him spend the night in the hospital with me. He is staying down the street at the hotel nearby. But he did show up real early this morning, so he was here when the doctor came by. He asked all kinds of questions. Shocked me."

"Can I come in?" the male voice behind Bailey and Chase came through the small crack in the door.

"It's OK, Dennis. You can open the door."

An older, nice-looking man stepped into the room. He had salt-and-pepper hair with a mustache. He was a bit shorter than Chase and fit and trim. As soon as Bailey saw him, she had this feeling like she had seen him before, but she couldn't figure out where.

"Hi, I'm Dennis Thompson, Mandy's husband." Dennis extended his hand out to Bailey, then Chase.

"Ex-husband," Mandy said very plainly.

"Nice to meet you," Bailey said. "Glad you were able to come."

"Definitely. Anything for Mandy," Dennis said.

"Are you kidding?" Mandy remarked, her voice now sounding a bit more animated. "That's not what things were like when you were living here. Anything for me, my ass!"

"Mandy, let's not do this right now. Just concentrate on getting well, OK?" Dennis said nicely, but Bailey could tell that he was holding his tongue, trying not to react to Mandy's outburst. Then he proceeded to look at Bailey intently.

"Do we know each other? I swear I've seen you before," Dennis asked.

Bailey's nerves went into high gear. This wasn't the man she had seen in Key West the day she left the restaurant or the one from the park. Was someone else looking for her, too? Did he know her from her past? So many questions crowded her mind that she almost forgot to answer him.

"I don't think so, but when you first stepped into the room, I thought that I recognized you."

"Have you ever been to Key West? Been on a city tour?"

"I lived in Key West for several years."

"Where did you work?"

Bailey's body was tensing with every question Dennis asked her. She felt Chase slip an arm around her waist and give her a squeeze. Just knowing he was by her side gave her courage to answer Dennis's questions.

"It was a little restaurant near Mallory Square. I was…" but Bailey didn't get to finish her sentence.

"That's it!" Dennis exclaimed. "You were the manager. I go there all the time to eat. Wow! How did you end up here?"

"Damn, Dennis, you sure are nosey," Mandy said, her medicine starting to kick in again. Her eyelids looked heavy.

"And you have quite a mouth on you when you're on drugs," Dennis retorted.

"I'm not on drugs, you nitwit. It's medicine," Mandy said. Now with her eyes closed, her speech was getting slower by the second.

"I think we better go and let her rest. Are you staying here with her?" Bailey asked quickly, wanting to leave the little room. She could feel panic rising within her.

"Yeah, unless she makes me leave. Think her and I have some talking to do. Don't like the way things ended between us, and this just made me realize that anything can happen in an instant."

Bailey wasn't sure why, but in that second, the panic she was feeling slowly faded. She liked Dennis. She didn't know the full story between the two people across from her, but for some reason, she hoped that they could at least talk and work out their differences. But there was almost something more to their relationship, and she couldn't figure out what it was. It was just a feeling she had that she couldn't explain. But these kinds of feelings were happening to her lately with lightning speed, so Bailey tried to dismiss the thought.

Noticing that Mandy was softly snoring, Bailey once again turned to Dennis. "When she wakes up, let her know that Chase and I have everything under control with the weddings. She will know what we are talking about."

"She is an excellent wedding planner. The best, as far as I'm concerned. Glad she has you to help her. You like working with brides instead of managing a restaurant?"

"Actually, yes. The pace is about as fast, but there is a bit more breathing room. Plus, even though brides and grooms can be a bit contrary, I saw more problems at the restaurant than this. I also enjoy watching two people in love starting their new lives together. It feels good to be a part of something like that."

"Glad you are happy, and it was good to see you. Nice to meet you, Chase. Mandy is lucky to have you two."

"Let me know if anything changes in her care and how she is doing. Mandy has my number in her phone. And tell her if she needs me, to call anytime."

"We'll check on her later," Chase said as they both walked to the door and left the room.

"Wow," Chase said as he reached for her hand and they walked out of the hospital.

"What?" Bailey asked.

"I don't think I've ever seen you give that much information about yourself to a person you just met. I didn't think you would say anything since he lives in Key West, and that is where that man was looking for you."

"You are going think I'm really weird when I say this, but there was something about Dennis. I can't really explain it, but it was as though I know him."

"Well, according to him, you do – or did."

"No, it's more than him coming to the restaurant in Key West, but something else."

"Are you remembering something again?" Chase said hopefully.

"I don't know. All I can say is that it didn't bother me to talk to him. I panicked at first, but then I didn't feel any hesitation."

As they got in the car to go to the office, Bailey sat quietly, thinking about the two people they had just left and why they felt so familiar to her.

20

As they sat in the sand by the water at the end of the street, Bailey felt so relaxed as she dug her toes into the little granules that surrounded them. The last couple of days had been long as she and Chase prepared for the four weddings that would begin tomorrow. Plus, they had been working on her little apartment, and it was starting to look like a beach cottage, which delighted her.

Except for Mandy breaking her leg, Bailey was enjoying every minute. She loved working alongside Chase, and the two of them worked so well together. He was quickly becoming the most important person in her life, and Bailey felt that she was finally ready to just move forward in her life, with her past memories or none at all. If they ever surfaced, she would face them, and hopefully, if things continued as they were, she would have Chase by her side.

"What are you thinking about?" Chase moved closer to her and began to softly kiss her neck.

"Well, I was thinking about my life. How I'm ready to let go of my past and move forward. But when you do things like that," Bailey said, grinning, "it's very hard for me to concentrate."

"Well, I'm glad to hear that, but you made me a promise."

"What are you talking about?" Bailey asked, turning to look at him.

"I helped you find an apartment, and now it's time to hire the private investigator."

"But Chase, I'm serious. I don't think I need to know who I was before the accident. I'm Bailey, and I live in the Keys. I have a wonderful job, a beautiful place to live, and most of all, I have you. What more could I ask for?"

"Thank you for that wonderful compliment, but," Chase said, bringing his hand up to her face, slowly caressing it.

"But what?"

"Bailey, I think that you will feel better knowing about your past. You might never remember, but I truly believe that if you at least know who you were, your parents, any family – whatever, then you can put this behind you once and for all. And I don't believe for one second that someone isn't looking for you, even if it's been four years. I know that I would never stop looking. Plus, we know that someone did ask for you in Key West. Whether it was just a customer wanting to talk to you about bad food, which you have told me you were sure it wasn't, wouldn't it be nice to have it all cleared up? To know?

Then you can truly move forward with your life, doing anything you want to do."

Bailey stared out toward the ocean, the sky growing darker by the minute. It was only a minute ago she had decided to forget about what had happened to her, and within a few minutes, Chase had changed all that. She knew in her heart that Chase was right, but now just wasn't the best time. With Mandy in the hospital, there was no time to meet with a private investigator. Plus, she just didn't want to ruin how things were right now. Everything felt so perfect to her.

"I just can't right now."

"So, you are going back on your promise?" Chase said with eyebrows raised.

Bailey leaned into Chase's chest, put her head against his shoulder and sighed. "No, I'll talk to someone. But can it wait till after this slew of weddings?"

"Most definitely. I wouldn't do that to you. Or me!" Chase exclaimed. They did have a lot of work these next few days, but then they had almost a whole week free of events.

"I'm going to call my friend, and hopefully, next Friday, we'll ride up to Miami. I'll get him to meet us at my parent's house. That way, you can meet them and see where I'm from."

"Meet your parents, too? Talk about a stress-filled day," Bailey said with wide eyes.

"Bailey," Chase said, pulling away from her slightly so he could see her eyes, "you mean more to me than I can say. I don't think I've ever loved someone the way I love you. I know it's been fast, and you might think I'm crazy. I wonder sometimes if I'm putting myself out there to be hurt again, but I don't care. I love you, and I want you to be happy and free from all this wondering about who you are. I know you, but deep down, I think there is still a part of you who wants to know your story.

"As for my parents, I want them to meet you. With all my siblings married and having families, they think I'm doomed. But that's not why I want you there. I want to introduce them to someone whom I think is one of the best persons I know. And I feel so privileged that you want me in your life."

Bailey was speechless. The way Chase was looking at her and the words he had just declared made her eyes water with tears of joy. She felt so in love with this man, but questioned herself since for her, this was her first love. Her therapist had warned her to be careful because she might experience just infatuation with someone, like a teenager with their first crush. But Bailey knew what was between her and Chase was more than that. This was genuine love, and she could feel it with every fiber of her being.

Bailey leaned in and first kissed Chase on the lips, teasing him by pulling away, only to kiss him on that sensitive part of his earlobe, then down his neck. Her hands explored his chest, feeling the firmness underneath the shirt he was wearing.

For Chase, the sensation of Bailey's lips on him was about to send him over the edge. He gently lowered her to the sand and found her lips. He couldn't keep his hand from moving up her arm, to the soft skin of her neck and wanting to explore even further, though he held back. The sand seemed to cradle their bodies as they lay there together, lost in their own little world.

"Well, there you two are. Haven't seen you for a while, so I thought I might find you over here." Maria's voice rang through the air, causing both Bailey and Chase to sit up abruptly, with sand flying everywhere.

"Hi, Maria. How are you?" Bailey said as nicely as she could. Such a romantic moment in her life, and this woman had ruined it. She was beginning to understand Chase's frustration with her.

"I'm fine, but I think you two are probably feeling a little better than me. You know, there are rooms that are better suited for, um, these little escapades." The tone of the woman's voice set Bailey's teeth on edge. Had she always been this way with Chase?

"Don't know what you are talking about, Maria. We were just relaxing after a long day," Chase remarked, trying to keep his voice from showing the irritation he was feeling at her intrusion.

"Well, if that's relaxing, I'd love a little bit myself."

With that, Bailey stood up quickly, brushing the sand from her. Chase followed suit. "I need to get home. Busy day tomorrow."

"Home? You have a place nearby or are you staying with Chase?" Maria asked, her voice sounding sickeningly sweet.

"Maria, it's really none of your business." Chase was through with being polite. He had had his fill of Maria, and this had to stop.

"So rude. I've never known you to be like this, Chase."

"Maria, we just want to be left alone. And enough with the questions. I've tried to be polite, and so has Bailey. Please just let this, whatever it is, go. Have a nice evening." Chase took Bailey's hand, and they walked up the street.

"Do you think she is watching us?" Bailey asked.

"It doesn't matter."

"Yes, it does. I don't want her to know where I live."

"You have a point there. Let's walk over to my house. We can actually cut through here, and you can hang out with me for a while," Chase said, leading her along a little pathway. With the trees forming a canopy and the tropical flowers on each side, Bailey felt like she was walking through a garden at dusk.

Once inside the house, they both sat on the couch, each not saying a word. But Chase couldn't help himself. He leaned over to Bailey, and with a kiss, he began what he started down at the little beach.

Bailey loved his every touch, but wondered if things were progressing a little faster than they should. Though she never wanted him to stop, Bailey pushed back gently.

"What's wrong?" Chase asked, his voice sounding breathless.

Bailey hesitated. "Chase, you know I love you. You mean the world to me, but I'm not sure I'm ready to take that next step. For me, this is like my first relationship, and I want to take things slow. Except I have to admit that when you touch me, it's hard to resist these feelings I have. Feelings I'm sure I had before, but everything is so new to me."

"I'm sorry, Bailey," he said. "I wasn't thinking. You kinda do that to me every time we are together." He kissed her again, then sat back against the couch, gathering her into his arms like a warm blanket. "I will follow your lead. I'll say that it probably won't be easy, but I know that it will be worth it. But I think it would be best if you stayed here tonight. I'll even sleep on the couch, and you can have my bed."

"Oh, no, I couldn't do that to you."

"Then what if we just lay with each other and get some sleep. Promise I'll be on my best behavior." Chase wanted her by his side, and if this was how it had to be right now, that was OK.

"That's sounds perfect."

■ ■ ■

Waking up in Chase's arms was like a dream come true. Chase had stayed true to his word and had only held Bailey through the night. But for her, it was the first time she had slept with someone, having someone so close by and feeling so protected. Bailey could only imagine what it would be like to be with him in a more intimate way, but now was not the time. But she was sure she would know when it would be right.

Chase had slept against her the entire night, enveloping her in his arms. Bailey felt even more cherished than she had before. The warmth of his body next to hers was so comforting.

"Good morning," Chase said soothingly, close to her ear.

"Good morning." Bailey twisted around to face him and laid her head on his chest.

"I'm sorry again for last night, but sleeping with you – I think it's the first time I felt so relaxed since my accident."

"I'm glad. You deserve so much more, Bailey, and I plan to be the guy who gets to show you the world."

"Now I like the sound of that."

Bailey slowly sat up, not wanting to move from his arms, but she knew that she needed to go back to her apartment.

"I think I better go and change clothes. Then I need to go to the office for a while and visit Mandy while I'm out, especially since we will be in Miami tomorrow."

Chase sat up in bed quickly. "Seriously?"

"You're right, Chase. I just didn't want to admit it. I need to know, if possible, about my past. But it's just that – my past. This," she said, placing her hand on his chest, near his heart, "is my present. And hopefully, my future."

21

The drive to Miami was beautiful. The sky was a bright blue, with puffy, white clouds here and there. With the temperatures in the low eighties, the car windows were down, and classic rock music played as Chase and Bailey made their way into the city. It seemed like they each knew every song that played as they sang along, and Bailey even tried her hand at playing the air guitar, giving Chase a serious laugh. It was as though Bailey was finally letting down the walls that she had surrounded herself with all these years.

Bailey made sure that all her work was up to date and ready for the weddings that would be coming up in a little over a week. Everything was in place. She checked on Mandy at the hospital, and her recovery was coming along fine. The thing that astonished her even more was that Mandy and Dennis were talking, even having civil conversations with each other in her presence.

After the way Mandy had talked about her ex-husband and how she treated him when he first arrived after her accident, Bailey wasn't sure why the two ever got together. But watching them together made her happy. They felt like old friends to her, like a part of her ever-growing Florida Keys family. And who knew? Maybe the couple would reconcile their differences and find love again. Bailey was learning that anything could happen.

When Chase pulled the car into the driveway of the large home on Key Biscayne, Bailey was in awe. She couldn't believe that Chase had grown up here. When Skylar had found out about their plans for the day, she gave Bailey some useful information about what to expect today, filling in small gaps of information that Chase had left out about the dynamics of his family. But seeing the house let Bailey know that Chase's family was extremely wealthy.

"This is it," Chase said as the car came to a stop in the driveway.

"Totally not what I expected," Bailey said as they sat in the car. "I have to admit something,"

"What?"

"Right after I met you, I looked you up on the internet. That's how I knew that your family was like Miami royalty or something. You were pictured at all kinds of social events and such. But I never expected this."

"You were stalking me on the internet?"

"No, I just wanted to find out more about your photography," Bailey said. "Well, that and more."

Chase laughed. "I assure you that we are most definitely not royalty. Too many little skeletons in our closets. We are very far from the perfect family, that is for certain. But even with those ups and downs, I think we are just like most families, except my parents do have a bit of money. One thing we all learned as we grew up was how to take care of any money we made. My dad drilled as many money facts as he could into us, like investments and such. I think that is why Skylar has done so well outside the family business. She had houses to rent before she even decided to start her business and defy the family tradition."

"So, do you have anything else to tell me before we walk in there?"

"I've really shared most of my life with you. Except I will say that I have a sizeable investment portfolio. While Skylar fell in love with boats, I was always fascinated with photography and the stock market. Two things that are completely different. Before I had any money, I would play paper stocks on the internet."

"Paper stocks?"

"No money involved. It was like pretend money, and I was good at it. So, when I started to make a little money of my own, I invested a bit here and there, and things just grew. My friend keeps telling me that I need to go into financial planning, but it holds no interest to me whatsoever. But I do still play the market, and I call it my 'back-up plan' if the photography doesn't pan out."

"Well, your photography is working out just fine, so I guess if you ever get tired of it, you could be a man of leisure."

"No, my investments are just that – investments for the future. I act as though they don't exist and live off my business in the Keys. And even if I did want to dip into my funds, I would find something else to do. Sitting around or being lazy out on some yacht – things like that have never been a part of our family. That's another thing I have to say about my dad. He instilled in us a very strong work ethic. Now my mom has had her ups and downs. She is the perfect Miami socialite, even with a few scandals thrown in, but we all survived."

"Scandals?" Bailey asked, intrigued.

"I think I'll leave that tale to Skylar. She's better at that than me. Are you ready to go in? Travis should be here any minute."

"The private investigator, right?"

"Yep. Talk about someone who loves his job, it's Travis. I've known him since we were kids, and he has always been fascinated by mysteries, unsolved cases, and conspiracy theories. He got his degree in political science, but that was just to satisfy his dad. The whole time we were in school, he was already doing some investigating on the side and even worked for free with a private investigator. Almost like an intern. Again, another kid that bucked family tradition and didn't go to work for his father."

"Your world is very interesting, Chase. And when you talk about it like that, I makes me want to know about the time before my accident," Bailey said, realizing that Chase had been right all along. She was glad that he had gently pushed her toward this meeting.

The door they entered led them to the large, spacious kitchen, where an older lady stirred something in a pot that smelled absolutely delicious. There were several other pans on the stove and bowls scattered across the island in the center of the kitchen.

"Hey, Maggie," Chase said, going around the counter and giving the petite woman a hug.

"My sweet boy. How are you?" Maggie held one hand up to Chase's face so tenderly that Bailey knew this woman loved him. But who was she?

"Maggie, I would like for you to meet Bailey. Bailey, this is Maggie, my second mom, as far as I'm concerned."

"So, this is the young lady that has caught your attention. She is very pretty, Chase," Maggie said, coming up to Bailey and taking her hand. "It is so nice to meet you. Make sure to take good care of my Chase."

"She already does, Maggie," Chase said, smiling at Bailey.

"I've watched this young man grow up, and what a fine man he has turned into. It's my cooking that has helped along the way."

"And that you are a very good listener. You've always been there for all of us kids," Chase said before turning back to Bailey. "Maggie has cooked for us for as long as I can remember, and her food is wonderful. I'm surprised we aren't all overweight in this family."

"Never. I cook healthy. You know that, boy. How many times did I have to throw away those snacks before I got you to eat real food?" Maggie's grin was infectious, and Bailey took an instant liking to the woman, but Bailey was also stunned.

Their own cook? Chase had grown up with a personal cook? What else was in store for today?

"Since I knew you were coming today, I cooked your favorite dinner," Maggie said.

"But it's lunchtime."

"I don't care. I don't see you as much as I would like, so this is a special day for me."

"Where are Mom and Dad?"

"In the family room, waiting for you. They seemed very eager to meet Miss Bailey." Maggie grinned at her to give her encouragement, which Bailey desperately needed.

"Then we will see you in a bit. Travis will be here shortly, and I'm not sure which door he will come in. Just giving you a heads up."

Chase went around the counter and took Bailey's hand.

"You ready? Don't be scared. I promise they don't bite. You are going to be fine," Chase said, giving her a kiss on the cheek. He led her down the small hallway, into a large room.

The space was beautiful, decorated in the Florida beach style, giving the whole place a laid-back but polished look. It featured beautiful wooden floors, bamboo furniture with big, soft cushions, and rugs in muted colors of the Caribbean. And at the sound of their footsteps, Bailey saw the woman and man sitting in the room turn to them.

"It's about time you got here," the man said, standing and giving Chase a hug. "Good to see you, son."

"Good to see you, too. Mom and Dad, I would like you to meet Bailey."

Bailey shook Chase's parents' hands, then she took a seat beside Chase on the large sofa that faced his parents. Sadie Cartwright was dressed in a tailored dress that gave her the look of being at the office, rather than relaxing at home. She was nice, but quiet. Jonathan, Chase's dad, seemed to be just the opposite of his prim and proper wife. Dressed in a pair of relaxed jeans, a polo shirt, and a pair of boat loafers, he seemed right at home and had a bright smile for Bailey.

"I'm so glad to meet you both," Bailey said, mustering up as much confidence as she could. "Chase has told me so much about you and his sisters and brother."

"Hope it is all positive," Sadie said, taking a sip of her tea.

"Oh, absolutely." Bailey wanted to engage in more conversation, but it was as if her mind went instantly blank. She knew that Chase had told his parents part of the reason for their visit today was to meet with the private investigator. Bailey was reluctant at first to share this with them, but if she was going to date their son, they might as well know the real her, or at least what she knew of herself.

"Chase told us your story, and I'm really sorry to hear about what happened to you. That had to be an awful experience to go through," Jonathan said just as Maggie brought Chase and Bailey two glasses of sweet tea.

"It has been a challenge, but things seem to be getting better each day, especially since I moved to Islamorada."

"Chase says that you work for one of the wedding planners he works for, too," Sadie said. "At times, it is still hard for me to believe that our son takes pictures of brides and grooms."

"I love it, and I make very good money," Chase said. "So, let's not broach that subject today, OK?"

Sadie sighed very quietly and didn't answer her son's question.

"So, how is business in the Keys?" Jonathan asked.

"We've been working together a lot because Mandy, Bailey's boss and owner of the company, broke her leg and is still recovering. So, the two of us have been running the business for her while she recuperates."

"My goodness, I hope that you are being well compensated for your time." Once again, it was Chase's mom who seemed to find a wrinkle in what they were doing. Bailey interjected this time.

"Mandy has been good to both of us, especially me. Even when she found out about my accident, there was no judgment about who I was, my skills, or anything. I'm grateful for that. Chase and Skylar have been there for me, too, and I finally feel like I have people around me that, if I never regain my memory, I can still be happy with."

"I see you have a very positive outlook on your situation. That's admirable." Sadie looked at Bailey and gave her a subtle smile. After all the talk previously, Bailey felt intuitively that this was a good sign. Maybe Chase's mom might be warming up to the new woman in her son's life.

"Hey, you guys." A man's voice boomed through the room, and Bailey turned to see a man Chase's age come bounding into the room.

"Good to see you, Mr. and Mrs. Cartwright. Sure has been awhile." Bailey had to assume that this was Chase's friend,

Travis. He was shorter than Chase and a bit heavier. His cheerful face made him likeable immediately, and Bailey hoped that he was as good as Chase said he was.

"Man, Chase, it's been a year or so. Do you ever come up here anymore?" Travis said, giving his friend a hug.

"You just need to come visit me in the Keys. It's more relaxed and fun than Miami, but probably not so much for you. I'm sure things keep you hopping up here."

"You got that right. I have two other investigators working with me now, so things are growing. Was hard to do that because you know how particular I am about things." Travis stopped and looked at Bailey.

"I'm assuming that you are Bailey Parker," Travis said, holding out his hand, which Bailey shook formally.

"That I am. It's nice to meet you."

"Mom, Dad – if you don't mind, we are going to go out on the back porch to talk."

"No problem," Jonathan said. "Just remember that Maggie is fixing dinner for us before you head back to Islamorada. I'm already hungry."

"Well, if you can't wait, go ahead and eat. I'm not sure how long this will take."

"Take your time."

Chase lead the way through the French doors, which led onto a stunning back porch that overlooked the lovely waterway, with large yachts on each dock that jutted out into the water. With each step Bailey took in Chase's family home, she couldn't believe the grandeur of it all. She pictured in her mind what it must have been like to grow up in a place like this.

"So, Travis, how does this work?" Chase asked as they each took a seat around the glass patio table.

"First of all, Bailey, I need you to give me every detail you can remember: your accident, the hospital, any friends, people – absolutely anything that you can recall. Even something that you don't think would be of significance can be huge for me when I'm looking at your case." Travis paused and took a notebook, pen, a few papers, and a cell phone out of his messenger bag.

"I'll be recording this whole conversation. I need you to sign here that you agree to this." Travis handed the pen and paper to Bailey to sign.

As Bailey looked at the paper and knew what she was about to do, her hands started to shake.

Chase noticed her hesitancy. "It's OK. We've talked about this, and I'm right here with you. I'm not going anywhere, and we are in this together. Just remember that." Chase looked at her, his eyes so full of hope that it gave Bailey courage to sign along the dotted line, even though small tears were starting to form in her eyes. Reliving this all over and in detail was going to be much harder than she originally thought.

Bailey seemed to travel back in time, answering question after question to the point she started to get a headache. There were times when she couldn't answer something that Travis asked her about just because she was getting tired and stressed. It was like her brain was a blank slate sometimes. Then other items Travis would question her about brought back painful memories of that time right after the accident that she had tried to put out of her mind so long ago.

"I think that is enough information for me to get started," Travis said, putting his notebook and pen away slowly. "I want to say first how sorry I am, for what happened to you and for asking so much of you today. I know retelling me things over and over is tiring, but it helps me do my job for you.

"So, I can promise you this. I will do everything in my power to find out what I can. Since you said you think someone is looking for you, that might help this case. But why no one has looked for you before now or the police weren't able to help is a mystery. With that being said, I feel like I'm going to be able to find out what happened. I've been doing this for quite a while, and even though it might take time, I'm hopeful."

"How long do you think it will take?" Bailey worried. She knew that the longer it took, the more money it would cost.

"It doesn't matter," Chase said. "Travis is good – the best."

"But traveling to San Diego and, well, the money," Bailey said softly, trying to find the right words.

"We already talked about that."

"Listen, we will work something out. Chase and I have been friends since we were eight years old. He's always had my back when I needed it, and I've got his. Now you are part of the circle, too. So, let's just see what I can find out first."

Bailey shook her head, and the trio walked back into the family room after spending over an hour on the sunny back porch.

"You guys ready for dinner?" Jonathan asked.

"Thank you, Mr. Cartwright, but I've got to go," Travis said, heading toward the door.

"When are you going to start calling me Jonathan?"

"Old habits are hard to break. Take care, and tell Mrs. Cartwright I said 'bye'."

Bailey stood fixed by Chase's side as she watched Travis walk out the door. She felt emotionally drained and really wanted to go somewhere and just sleep. She felt like she had run a marathon, and the headache that had begun during the long conversation was still there along with the fatigue.

This was the first time since the accident that she had divulged so much information to someone in one sitting – except for her therapists, and they didn't even talk about the whole tale at once. And now she would have to sit through dinner. Bailey could only hope that they didn't stay long, even though she wanted to make a good impression on Chase's parents.

In no time, the table was set, and they sat down to Chase's favorite dinner: taco salads. But Sadie told Bailey that these were no ordinary salads. Maggie made everything, including the taco shell bowls, by hand. And with the first bite, Bailey could understand why Chase loved them so much. Everything tasted exquisite. Plus, she was starving after the hour-long session of discussing her trauma.

The conversation around the table was pleasant, but both parents wanted to know a bit more about Bailey and her accident. Since she had just rehashed everything only moments ago, it was hard to tell again, so she kept it short and to the point. They didn't need all the details that she had shared with Travis and Chase.

Sadie and Jonathan were sympathetic to her plight and offered encouragement, letting her know, as Chase had, that

Travis was the best. He had even done some work for their real estate company that had helped them tremendously.

Now that her stomach was full, the fatigue hit Bailey with more intensity. She was so tired and just wanted to head home.

"Bailey, are you OK?" Sadie asked cautiously.

"I'm sorry. Is something wrong?" Bailey said quickly.

"You just seem like you were about to pass out."

"I'm so sorry. I think I'm just really tired."

"It's probably time we head back to the Keys. It's been a pretty long day," Chase said, worried about Bailey because he could see how tired she was.

"Next time, why don't you guys come to the Sunday dinner? That way, Bailey, you can meet everyone: Harris and Tracey, Mara and Paul, and the grandbabies," Jonathan suggested as they got up to leave.

"That sounds wonderful. I would love to come back."

"Then it's a plan. Chase, we will let you know when, and make sure Skylar comes with you. I'm ready to see Taylor again."

"Dad, you and Mom could always come to Islamorada to visit us, you know. Highway 1 works both ways."

"I know, but kids should come see their parents. That is the proper thing to do."

Chase rolled his eyes, but gave both of his parents a smile. "Love you guys."

"Thanks again, Mr. and Mrs. Cartwright. It was so nice to meet you," Bailey said before making her way to the car that looked like a safe haven from everything that had happened only a few hours ago.

Once they were in the car and pulling onto the highway, Bailey leaned back in her seat.

"I'm really sorry, Bailey," Chase said apologetically.

"What for? I'm the one that about fell asleep at the table during dinner."

"For that. I should have known that going over all the information with Travis would be taxing on you."

"It's OK, really. I just hope I didn't embarrass you with the way I was in front of your parents. I felt tongue-tied walking into their mansion."

Chase laughed. "Come on now. It isn't that big."

"Chase, really? Our house had-"

Bailey stopped herself. Another memory had popped to the surface.

22

"Bailey, are you remembering something?"

Bailey only sat there, looking at the cars coming toward them as they drove down the highway. It was like her mind gave her a glimpse of a house. It was big, but not like the home they had just left. It had a round driveway in the front, with huge plants on the front porch. It was some sort of cream-colored brick, with chocolate-brown trim. But this was all she could see.

"Bailey, are you OK?"

She looked over to see Chase almost in a panic.

"I'm fine," Bailey said slowly. "It's just that I remembered a house." Then she proceeded to tell him what she could see in her mind.

"As soon as we get home, just write it down. Travis gave you his cell number for things like this." He reached over and took her hand, giving her a hopeful squeeze.

"This is good, right? But I know you're tired, so why don't you lay the seat back now and try to take a nap. You've had such a long day, and I know you are exhausted. And since we have some time on our hands tomorrow, you are going to sleep in and take the morning off."

"But what about the weddings? I need to check on-" but Bailey wasn't able to finish her sentence.

"After you sleep in, you can call from home. You have everything with you and can work from there. I almost wish Mandy would work out of her home, meeting clients there. She insists that a storefront is more professional, but hardly anyone meets her there."

Chase waited for a response from the girl in the seat beside him, but as he looked over, Bailey was fast asleep.

■ ■ ■

When they arrived at Bailey's house, she still was asleep. Chase got the house keys from her handbag, then scooped her up out of the passenger seat. As he walked to her door, he saw Skylar coming down the stairs, about to say something, but Chase shook his head wildly. Instead, Skylar grabbed the keys, opened the door, and helped Chase put Bailey in her bed, then they both slipped out the door.

"What happened today? Is she OK?" Skylar asked as soon as the door closed.

"She's fine, but exhausted. I should have known better than for her to meet Mom and Dad and talk to Travis."

"Why? Did they do something?"

"Actually, they were pretty nice today, and Maggie made homemade taco salads."

"Oh, that sounds good right now. We were so tired, it was sandwich night. But what happened?

Chase took a seat on the stairs and sighed. "Skylar, I knew about Bailey's accident, but until today I had no idea what she has really been through. I can't imagine losing my memory of you, my childhood – I mean, everything. She has no recollection at all before the accident. I just felt so bad for her. It made me want to protect her so much, even more than I did before."

"Well, I don't think she is looking for pity, or she would be telling everyone she knows. I have to admire her for that. But I'm glad she has you. I know that you will take care of her. You love her, don't you?" Skylar asked softly, putting her arm on her baby brother's shoulders as she took a seat beside him.

"I do. I mean, this is nothing like I had with Blair or Shari. Now that I know how it feels to really love and care for someone, those relationships don't even compare." Chase sat silently for a moment, staring at the swaying palms trees.

"I'm not just saying this because you are my brother, but you're a special guy. That's why I've wanted you to have someone in your life for so long. I thought you were lonely. I guess you were just biding your time till Bailey came along. So, you knew better than me in this instance, but don't let it go to your head," Skylar laughed. "I'm still your big sister."

"Thanks, Skylar," Chase said in almost a whisper.

"For what?"

"For just being you. And helping Bailey out. Renting her this apartment was huge. It just means a lot to me."

"You're welcome."

"I'm going to head home. I told Bailey to sleep late in the morning, but I doubt that she will. We need to check on Mandy, and we have some work to do. But today was stressful for her, so I hope she listens to me."

"We'll see. Bailey seems pretty headstrong, so don't be surprised if she wakes you up because you look a bit tired yourself. Go home and get some rest. Love ya!" Skylar said as she gave Chase a hug and went back upstairs. He walked to his car, but not before looking at the little place where his love was sleeping soundly.

■ ■ ■

Chase's cell phone rang loudly. He looked at the phone, and it was Bailey, just as Skylar had predicted. A glance at his clock showed why she was calling him: it was already nine o'clock in the morning.

"Hey, there, beautiful," Chase said, his voice a little gravelly from just waking up.

"Hi, yourself. I guess I owe you thanks for last night. I woke about midnight to being tucked into bed. I can't believe I don't even remember getting into the house," Bailey said, sounding surprised.

"Because I carried you in."

"You did?"

"And Skylar helped open the door, so I could put you in bed. You were out. I mean, like someone had given you a sleeping pill or something. I was worried at first, but you seemed fine. How are you feeling this morning?"

"Kinda weird to describe. I feel like I got some sleep, but still very tired."

"You went through a lot yesterday."

"Yeah, it was pretty intense. I hope I made a good impression on your parents."

"Don't worry about it. Ask Skylar what happened when Garrett met the family."

"That' s the second time you've said something about that. I take it that Skylar and Garrett's relationship wasn't well received?"

"Oh, that's putting it mildly." Chase chuckled. "Like I said before, just ask her about it one day."

"I'll have to remember to do that. So, I was thinking about going to see Mandy, then off to the office. I need to make sure everything is still on schedule for the weddings next week. I know we have some time, but I'm sure there are some messages I need to take care of, too."

"I need to check with Skylar about any boat trips since I have a few days off. Why don't I meet you at the office later for lunch?"

"That sounds good."

"Tell Mandy I said 'hi'."

"I will. And Chase?"

"Yes?"

"Thanks for yesterday... and one more thing."

"What's that?"

"I love you."

"I love you, too."

23

Bailey clicked the phone off and just sat there for a few moments. Even though yesterday had been hard, it had been cathartic, too. But she had no idea how tired she had been from the ordeal till she woke in the middle of the night, still in her clothes, under the blankets on her bed. She had gotten up, changed in to pajamas, and immediately crawled back under the covers, only to wake at seven o'clock this morning.

Chase had told her to sleep in, and this was past her usual six o'clock wake-up time. So, she took her time getting ready this morning, fixing herself a nice breakfast and going over her planner to see what needed to be done today. She had wanted to call Chase earlier, but thought he was probably sleeping in, too, seeing how much he had done for her last night.

Bailey headed to Mandy's house now that she was finally home from the hospital. She had been so busy that she hadn't been able to see Mandy in person, but knew that Dennis was taking care of her. She only hoped that the arrangement was working out. And she was just about to find out since she was pulling into Mandy's driveway.

Bailey knocked on the door, not hearing any activity coming from the house. She hoped that she wasn't too early and regretted not calling first. But it was only a few minutes before Dennis answered the door.

"Good morning," Bailey said. "How is the patient?"

"Not patient. She thinks she should be able to start walking without the walker and a bunch of other things, too. But come on in, and by the way, good morning to you, too."

Dennis stood back and let Bailey in. The house smelled so fresh and clean, with a flower scent wafting through the air.

"Bailey, is that you?" Mandy asked, her voice seeming to come from the kitchen.

"Yes, it is. Hope I'm not too early." Bailey followed Dennis to the spacious kitchen that was situated with a view of the water. It seemed like everyone she knew in Islamorada had water in their backyard.

"Are you kidding? Been up since five o'clock."

"You look good and sitting at the table. Looks like you are making progress."

"Yeah, Dennis helps me, so I don't have to lay in bed or stay in the living room all the time. Starting to get a bit of cabin fever," Mandy said, sounding irritated.

"Since Bailey is here, I'm going to go to the grocery store. Won't be gone long. Anything else you want to add to the list?" Dennis asked, holding the sheet of paper that Bailey could tell was one of Mandy's famous lists.

"No, I don't think so," Mandy said, her voice completely changed to one of calm.

"Then I shouldn't be gone long." Dennis came over, kissed Mandy on the top of her head, and strode out the front door.

"Wow," Bailey said, looking at Mandy with wide eyes.

"What?" Now Mandy sounded like her normal self.

"Looks like you two are getting along fine."

"Believe it or not, he's been a big help," Mandy said, knowing that she was eating some of the words she had used to describe Dennis not long ago. "It's probably just these pain meds. Not as good as the ones at the hospital, but at least they are helping the pain and probably my mood."

"It's just nice to see you two being civil. And even though you're recovering, there is something different about you."

"Yes, I have a broken leg!"

"No, not that. You seem like maybe you are in love?" Bailey said the words very carefully, not sure of the reaction she would receive from her friend.

"Ha! You've got to be kidding," Mandy said as fast as she could. "Though, I'll admit it's been nice to have him here. He's been really helpful, but that's all."

"Mandy, you don't have to answer this question if you don't want to, but I have to ask. Dennis seems so nice. Why did you two get a divorce?"

Mandy leaned back in her chair. "We are just two completely different people. I'm more of a homebody, and Dennis likes crowds, parties, being where the action is."

"Doesn't seem that way to me."

"And you've not known him very long either."

"There has to be more to it." Bailey was probing because she saw a faraway look in Mandy's eyes, as though she was remembering something.

"There was." Mandy took a deep breath before she could continue. "Dennis and I met during our first year in college back in Texas. It was at a frat party, and I swear from the moment we met, we were inseparable.

"During our Christmas break, we had a big, serious argument. And I never went back to college. I didn't even let him come and see me. It hurt like hell because I wanted to see him so bad, but I knew I couldn't." Mandy's voice had softened considerably, and Bailey wondered what could have happened that would cause her to leave school, never wanting to see him again.

"Then about four years later, I ran into Dennis at a bar in Austin, Texas. I was there with some friends, and I couldn't believe it was him. He looked mighty good. We caught up with what was going on in our lives, and we agreed to go out to dinner the next night. And that was it. I was hooked all over again. It was like fate had brought us back together. Once again, just like in college, we were together all the time. Within three months, we had decided to get married. I knew back then that he liked to be part of the crowd, go out whenever he could, but I was determined I wasn't going to let him go this time. So, we went to the justice of the peace and got married. Man, my parents were livid, and so were his. But we didn't care.

"So, since everyone was upset, we decided to move. Get this! We put a map on the wall of the United States, closed our eyes and made ourselves promise that wherever I put my finger that was where we were going to live. My finger landed on Key West."

"Seriously? That sounds like something out of a movie," Bailey said, fascinated by Mandy's story.

"Yep. We packed and moved in a little over a week. We didn't tell anyone till the day before we left. My mom was hysterical and begged us not to go, but we did. Anyway, we got to Key West and found a little house. We both got jobs within a week of being there; his with the power company and me working as an assistant to the president at an accounting firm. We barely made it paycheck to paycheck, but Dennis loved it here. It seemed we were always out on Mallory Square or at a bar on Duval Street. I wanted to be home more, and he wanted to party.

"Over the years, I just started staying home, but not Dennis. We grew further and further apart, till one day, a friend of ours told me that she saw Dennis with another woman. I confronted him, and he said they were just friends and he was with a group of people, but that didn't matter to me. He was spending more time with his friends than me, so I decided to leave. That's how I ended up here on Islamorada."

"But I thought you said you were working for your mother, right?"

"She moved here about ten years after we left for the Keys. My dad passed away, and about a month later, she said she was moving here to be near me. She was living off of investments and such that my dad had. When she got here, she just decided she wanted to be a wedding planner. She had corporate experience, but this was all new to her. But with time on her hands, she tackled it with a vengeance. Within a year, everyone here knew her, and the business grew so fast. So, when I left Dennis, I came to work with her."

"So, you and Dennis never talked anymore? Especially living so close to each other?" Bailey asked.

"Only here and there. I would still hear about his escapades through our mutual friends, which only made me feel better about my choice to get a divorce, but then the stories stopped. I heard how he had settled down. That he was dating some woman, and he didn't go out so much. But that didn't change the way I felt."

"Is he still with that woman?"

"Dennis said they broke up some time ago."

"So how do you feel about him now?" Bailey said.

Mandy took a deep breath and looked out the window, toward the water. "I don't know, Bailey. We've talked so much lately. About our mistakes. About our past. Things we wished we had done differently. It's almost as though we are different people now. He's been kind and helpful. I have to admit that this is the Dennis I met that first time in college."

"You two are talking about me, aren't ya?" Dennis walked in the door, arms full of grocery bags.

"I didn't even hear the door open," Mandy whispered. "Glad I didn't say anything too bad."

Bailey laughed because she hadn't heard him come in either, so wrapped up in Mandy's story.

"I think it's time for some more meds," Mandy said. "I can feel that pain getting stronger, plus I'm ready for the more comfortable chair in the living room."

"You be careful with that pain medicine. My mother had a terrible time with them after a surgery she had when I was a teenager," Bailey said casually, then realized what had happened. This time, she almost felt dizzy at the sensation of the memory recall.

"What did you say?"

Bailey sat at the table, unable to utter a word. Another memory had surfaced, but it wasn't something she could see. Only a thought about her family.

"It was another one. I remember something else, but I can't see anything like I did with the others."

"You've been remembering things?" Mandy asked incredulously.

"Only two others. They happened over the last week or so."

"That's fantastic!" Mandy practically screamed. "Right?"

Bailey didn't know what to think. After her emotional session with Travis yesterday and now another memory, more questions swirled through her mind.

"It is, but why now? What am I doing differently that would cause memories to surface, even if it's just bits and pieces?"

"Does it matter? Maybe soon, you will have enough to know more about your life."

"Well, hopefully, I won't have to wait on my brain. Chase and I went to Miami yesterday to talk to his friend, who is a private investigator. He is going to take my case. Chase insisted on it, even though I told him it was too expensive. But his friend is going to help out, and I told Chase that I would agree to it only if he consented that he is loaning me the money."

"Oh, honey, that is wonderful. You're regaining your memory, and you have Chase. I just knew that boy was going to be good for you. You really like him, don't you?"

I love him, Bailey thought to herself, but she wasn't ready to tell anyone about that just yet. "I do, Mandy. He's helped me find a place, helped out at the office..."

"Oh, by the way, how are the weddings coming along?"

Bailey had to suppress a laugh because Mandy's mind didn't stay in one place too long. She gave Mandy a rundown of everything and how things were progressing. Bailey even asked if it would be OK to work a bit from her home, and Mandy agreed as long as the door to the office had a professional sign and contact numbers because Mandy didn't want to lose any business. Bailey wanted to tell her that most of the time, a client never even came into the office, but she decided to leave that for later, once Mandy was well and not on any medication. The office had just been a place to help Mandy feel like she was in a business. From Bailey's point of view, it helped Mandy feel more professional.

"Argh, I feel so helpless like this. I want to work or do something. I can't even really go anywhere. I have a checkup at the end of the week, and I'm dreading that. Just getting home was a pain in the ass – literally!"

"There are phone calls and such if you really want something to do, but if you are still on pain medicine, it might not be time to go back to work just yet."

Bailey watched Mandy's face practically glow with excitement and turned to see Dennis entering the room with a familiar box.

"A treat for my lady." Dennis walked toward Mandy, who now had a goofy grin on her face. Bailey watched the exchange between the two people, and it was so different from what she witnessed not too long ago, when Mandy found out Dennis was even coming to town.

"Donuts," Dennis said, handing Mandy the box. She quickly opened it, looking at the delightful treats, and was quick to have a first taste.

"Oh, these are delicious." Mandy shut her eyes, relaxing, as though the treat had magical powers.

"Bailey, you want one? If he keeps this up, and since I can't exercise much right now, I'm going to be as big as this chair I'm sitting in."

"I don't think that is going to happen, but even so, you will still be beautiful." Dennis came to sit beside her and took one of the donuts for himself.

As Bailey sat across from them, it made her feel good. They did seem so right for each other, and she wondered what that first big argument was that kept them apart for so long. Maybe this time spent together might bring them back together again. In a way, Bailey really hoped so because she had this strange feeling that they were meant to be together.

24

The wedding venue was ready. As Bailey looked around, the area was beautiful. She had to say that this was one of her favorite weddings so far. The couple, in their fifties, were saying "I do" for the second time, and they had spared no expense.

The chairs were lined up in the sand, facing the ocean and toward the seashell decorated arched trellis that had the light blue water as the backdrop. Plus, they had timed the wedding to make sure the sunset would be part of the ceremony.

This was a rather large wedding. The tent for the reception festivities was to the left of the ceremony area. A steel drum soloist would play music for the bride to walk the sandy, flower-strewn aisle that would lead to her groom. The first chair of each row had white netting with starfish dangling on the outside edge.

For the reception, under the tent, round tables were centered around a dance area. Each chair at the tables had a wedding favor bag full of beach-themed gifts for every guest. Bailey knew because she and Chase had filled all those bags the night before while eating pizza and watching TV at her house.

"So, everything's ready?" Chase said giving her a quick kiss before she could respond.

"Seems so. The Island Time Trolley is picking up both the bridal and the groom's parties but in separate vehicles arriving fifteen minutes apart. The caterer is all set, too. That has been the hardest part about this wedding," Bailey said, looking over to the little building where the restaurant workers had been coming and going.

Maria was here tonight, and thankfully, she wasn't in charge, but she was assisting the manager, who happened to be her father. Bailey only hoped that she didn't put a wrinkle in tonight's festivities. She wasn't too happy with Bailey or Chase last time she saw them, but that had been some time ago. Bailey only hoped that Maria was past her obsession with Chase.

"I'm sure Maria wants to keep her job. Her father isn't going to let something happen. This has to be one of his biggest events. This couple has done it all. They even told me they wanted every picture that I thought was great. They didn't even give me any specifics, just left it all in my hands. I can't remember the last time a couple did that. I usually get a list of dos and don'ts." Chase smiled, still holding Bailey around the waist.

"Well, looks like people are starting to arrive. I guess it's time to get this show on the road."

Bailey handled each part of the wedding like it was second nature to her. The trolley brought both parties at just the right time, ensuring the bride and groom didn't see each other. The steel drum musician played a soft melody as the stunning bride made her way toward her groom. And as the couple had hoped, the sunset was spectacular just after they said, "I do."

Everything proceeded as planned, from the sit-down dinner, first dance, cutting of the cake, and even the bridal bouquet toss. Bailey loved that the wedding had been so happy, with everyone just enjoying the moment. Whether it had to do with the age of the couple or not, she wasn't sure, but it was just a wonderful evening from the start.

Bailey had run into Maria several times as dinner was served, but they only nodded to each other, not saying anything. Bailey had even seen Chase stumble upon her. She had seen them talking, but she had no idea what was said and wasn't worried. Bailey knew how Chase felt about the girl, and more importantly, she knew how he felt about her.

All the normal festivities were done, and the dance floor was popping. The steel drum band had packed up for the night, and a DJ had taken their place. The bride and groom requested music from the '70s and '80s, and it seemed like everyone, young and old, knew each song, singing along. At least twenty-five or thirty people were still having fun on the floor, along with the happy couple.

"Now this has been a fun wedding," Chase said as he and Bailey looked on. "They're having a blast, and no one is even drunk. Kinda unusual for a wedding, don't you think?"

"I guess these weddings do happen occasionally. But there's something about tonight that was really special. Done with the pictures?"

"Yeah, finished a while ago. How about you? Is everything wrapped up?"

"Sure is. The caterer is about to leave, and the tent and lighting people are just waiting. I think they are playing cards around the corner, which is fine. The DJ said there are just a few more songs, and he is packing up, so I guess that is when the wedding party will leave."

"Well, if there are only a few more dances, may I have this one, Bailey Parker?" Chase extended his hand out to her just as the one of the slow, romantic songs from the '70s began to play: "Biggest Part of Me" by Ambrosia.

Chase took her on the dance floor, pulled her close to him, and they both began to sway with the music.

"Listen to the words of the song. This is just for you," Chase whispered in her ear.

Bailey knew the song, but wasn't as familiar with the lyrics, so she listened intently as Chase drew her closer, both of them moving in sync. It seemed each word touched her heart. *Wash away the past. Start anew.* Chase even sang a bit of the song to her, causing that familiar tingling sensation she loved that seemed to happen every time they were together.

"I love you, Bailey. You are the best part of me," Chase said and brought his lips to hers.

For Bailey, there was no one else on the dance floor at that moment, even though there were many couples near them. It felt so magical, and when their lips parted, she looked into Chase's deep blue eyes.

"I wonder how I got this lucky," Bailey said softly.

"We are lucky. I'm so glad I found you."

Bailey snuggled her head next to Chase's shoulder, opening her eyes only for a second. But it was long enough to see the stare of a woman in the distance: Maria. Her stone-cold look sent a chill through Bailey.

"Maria is staring at us," Bailey said.

"I don't mean to be mean, but she will have to get used to seeing us together."

"I know, but I just have a weird feeling about her. Like she is up to no good. You know her best. Is she the kind of person that would do something, I don't know, bad?" Bailey asked anxiously.

"I don't think so, but I guess you never know. You don't have to worry. I'm here with you. Always, if you will let me."

"Sounds wonderful to me." As Bailey laid back against Chase, she looked over to the same place where Maria had been standing, but this time, she was gone. But now a tall man walked toward her, and a feeling a dread washed over her. She recognized him: it was the man from Key West.

"Are you Bailey Parker?" the man asked as he came up to stand by the dancing couple.

"Who are you?" Chase asked. He could feel Bailey shaking in his arms.

"My name is Gregory Randall. I'm a private investigator from California." He looked at Bailey once more. "Are you Bailey Parker?"

"Yes," Bailey said timidly, not sure whether to answer the man or not. Her heart was beating so fast, she had to take deep breaths to calm down, but it wasn't working.

"I was wondering if we could talk."

"She is working, so…"

"Chase, I can do this," Bailey said. "Mr. Randall, I don't mind talking to you, but not here. As you can see, this is my job, and this is a wedding. If you leave me your card, I'll contact you."

Mr. Randall looked at her suspiciously. "It's very important that I talk to you. It has to do with your accident and amnesia. I have information for you."

Bailey stood, dumbfounded at the man's words.

"Like she said, not here. How did you know where to find her, anyway?" Chase asked, mad that the man stood his ground and hadn't left.

"I just asked around. Sooner or later, you find what you are looking for. Your guy will be calling soon, too, I suspect. Give me a call, Miss Parker."

Gregory Randall turned and walked away. In the background, Bailey saw Maria was back with a big smile on her face.

25

"I wish I knew what to do," Bailey said once they were seated in her car. "What if he knows where I live? And it had to be Maria who told him who I was. You should have seen the look on her face."

"Not that I'm defending Maria, but how would she even know him?"

"If he was asking around, maybe she just got lucky. I wonder if he told her anything about me."

"Hey, we don't even know if he talked to her." Chase reached over and stroked her shoulder, hoping that his touch would help her to relax, but Bailey's body was set to alarm mode.

So many thoughts were coming to her mind that Bailey couldn't keep up with them. The overwhelming feeling threatened to send her into a panic attack, and she felt like she needed to just run. Like she had that day in Key West, when Mr. Randall had said her name.

"I need to go," Bailey said quickly.

"I'll follow you home. Or better yet, you need to stay at my house tonight. Maybe he doesn't know where you live, but he will probably follow you now. If Maria did give out your information, she will have hell to pay from me."

Chase was angry and not sure what to do. He had placed a called to Travis since the man had told them that their "guy" would be contacting them soon. Apparently, he knew about Travis, so something had come to the surface. But his first priority was making sure Bailey was safe.

"I need to go to my place. I can't always hide at your house. But then I don't want to put your family in danger. I just need to go."

"Bailey what are talking about?"

"Leave the Keys. Get out of here tonight, before he can find me again."

"No way!"

"Chase, you don't understand."

"Bailey, I don't think *you* understand. You confirmed tonight who you were. You think he isn't going to stay as close to you as he can? What if he has good news? What if he wants to reunite you with your family? If the news is negative, we'll handle it together. You can't run. It will find you. Most of all, you can't leave me. I just found you, and I'm not letting you go."

The tears that had threatened Bailey's eyes from the moment Mr. Randall had left the wedding finally made their way down her cheeks.

"Hey," Chase said, making another attempt to help her clear her thoughts, "please just follow me home, or I'll follow you. I'll come stay with you at your place. I just would feel better if someone was with you all the time till we find out what is going on."

Bailey nodded because no words would form. She felt like she was trapped, and now it was turning into paranoia, similar to the feeling she had when she woke from her coma. The feeling of disorientation was so consuming, Bailey thought she was going crazy.

"I'm going to follow you, OK?" Chase asked as he gently stroked her shoulder.

"OK."

Chase walked with Bailey to her car, looking around to see if he saw the man anywhere, but the only people nearby were members of the wedding party and the event staff taking down the venue. But Chase had been around Travis enough to know that investigators could hide just about anywhere, so he was sure that Gregory Randall was close by.

He followed Bailey to her house, calling Skylar to let her know what was going on. She told him that she hadn't seen anything out of the ordinary, but she and Garrett would keep an eye out. Also, she was glad that Bailey wouldn't be alone.

Once they were inside Bailey's apartment, Chase secured all windows and doors while Bailey took a shower. He wanted her to feel as safe as possible, but the happy life she was finally building after all these years seemed to be crumbling before her. Chase was determined to help her keep everything in place.

When Chase's cell phone rang and he saw the caller ID, he sighed with relief. It was Travis.

"Travis, man, I'm glad you called."

"I got your message. I can't believe that son of bitch got to you before me."

"You talked to him?"

"For only a moment. Just enough to let me know that I confirmed his suspicion that Bailey was in the Florida Keys. But there is much to tell, and it's late. You staying with Bailey at her place?" Travis asked.

"Yeah. Talking to him tonight really upset her, and there was just something about the guy I don't trust. I just don't know what this guy is capable of or what is going on."

"I don't think you have anything to worry about from him. It's complicated, but I'll be there in the morning to talk to Bailey. Will that be OK? Any weddings going on?"

"Actually, tomorrow would be good. We have a day off. I'll let her know. Thanks again, Travis."

"You're talking to Travis?" Bailey asked.

Chase turned around to see her walk out of the bathroom with only a towel wrapped around her. She was beautiful, but looked so fragile right now. He just wanted to hold her and tell her it would all be all right.

"I was. He is going to be here in the morning to talk to you. He says there is lots to tell you, and he knows about Mr. Randall."

"How?" Bailey didn't know what to think.

"He didn't say much. But for now, it's late, and you need some rest. I've already made sure everything is locked up and secure."

"What about Skylar and Garrett? They need to know. I don't want them to be in any danger."

"From what Travis said, he doesn't think Mr. Randall poses a threat, but I called Skylar on the way here. But Bailey, I think everything will be OK. If Randall meant to do you harm, I don't think he would've approached you at a wedding. At least I don't think so."

"Everything just feels like it did after the accident. Like jumbles of messages flooding my brain." Bailey was holding both sides of her head in her hands, trying to shake off the bad feelings.

"That's why you need sleep. It's a good thing tomorrow is a day off."

"But I need to check in with Mandy. I told her I would stop by."

"And you will, but let's talk to Travis first."

"I'm going to go get dressed."

"And I'm going to need a pillow and blanket for the couch."

"Will you sleep with me? I just want you near me. I'm sorry if that sounds so needy."

"It's not needy. It's called love, Bailey." Chase caressed the side of her face, and she smiled.

Bailey slipped into her pajamas, then under the sheet and coverlet on her bed. Chase crawled in beside her and wrapped her in his arms. And even though she was nervous and jittery, Chase soon felt her body relax, and she was in an exhausted sleep.

He lay there, watching her and realizing how much love he felt for this woman. But part of him was scared, too. When they talked to Travis in the morning, Chase's whole world could change.

26

Bailey peered out the window once more, looking for a car that wasn't there yet. Travis had called to say he was almost here, but for Bailey, he couldn't get to her house soon enough.

She had fallen asleep in Chase's arms last night, but her rest had been fitful. She was exhausted by the night's events, and the anticipation of what Travis had to tell her today had her in knots. When she finally had a routine, a new place to call home, wonderful friends – all of it could suddenly be taken away or changed forever.

When Bailey saw the car pull up and park, she felt her breathing speed up. This was what she had waited for since waking this morning, but now that he was here, she suddenly wanted him to leave.

"Is that Travis?" Chase said, coming to stand behind her.

"Yes."

"Bailey," Chase said, turning her to look at him, "it's going to be fine. You've got this, and I'm right here with you. Do you want me to stay in the room while he talks? I could always go outside."

"No!" Bailey exclaimed. "You said you would stay with me."

Chase hugged her tight. "I'm right here."

With the knock on the door, Bailey let Travis in, and they all took a seat in the area Bailey had designated as a living room, with a couch and two small chairs.

"Hi, guys. First of all, I want to apologize for not being able to talk to you before Greg showed up."

"Do you know him?" Bailey asked quickly.

"Met him in San Diego when I went out there to do some checking on your case. It seemed that we kept running into each other in the same areas. He introduced himself and we had coffee. I didn't know that he had been hired to find you, but he figured that I was working for you. Did some checking on him, and he has broken some really big cases in California. Anyway, like I told Chase last night, I think I might be the reason he found you."

"Why?" Bailey asked.

"I didn't give him any names, but I just told him where I was from, that I was doing a friend a favor because she had amnesia. That's it. But when I talked to your mom, I found out he was working for her and had been for quite a long time."

Bailey didn't hear anything except the word "mom".

"You found my mom?" Bailey's voice was barely above a whisper.

"Bailey, I found out a lot about what happened. There is much to tell you, and some things I promised that I wouldn't. So, let me just start at the beginning.

"After you gave me all the information you had, I did my normal Internet searching, which didn't leave me with much. I had to finish up a few things I was working on, then I flew to San Diego. I checked everything from talking to the police, looking at newspaper articles, and so much more. I eventually talked to your friend, Dena, the one that saved your life. She said that a man, whom we now know as Gregory Randall, had come by her house and asked if she knew Hailey Palmer. She swears that the music was turned up, and she told him she knew Bailey Parker and asked him what he wanted with you. That's how he found out your name."

The light bulb went off for Bailey. "You mean my real name is Hailey Palmer?" she said quietly.

"Yes."

"What about my mom?"

"First of all, when I finally found her and told her who I was, I about had to catch her from falling! Thought she was going to pass out but she started crying instead with a smile on her face. Greg hadn't confirmed your identity yet because he went to Key West after getting some information from your mom. Then he had your name and came looking for you. Then I showed up and confirmed everything for her."

"Tell me about her."

"I can't," Travis said.

Bailey sat up straight and scooted to the edge of the couch. "But why not?"

"She made me promise not to. She actually told me to convince you to come to California to see her."

"I can't do that!"

"Bailey, why not?" Chase said. "This is your mom. The family you've always wondered about all these years."

"I know, but this is all happening too fast. I finally felt like I was putting my life together. Things were starting to make sense, and now..."

"Bailey, I know it will be hard, but Mrs. Palmer has plane tickets for you and anyone you want to bring with you to California. And I think that by going back to where everything happened, you might get some closure. Your mother really wants to see you. At first, she was going to fly here, but after we talked, she thought that for you to come back to where you once lived might be best. Plus, she can show you things like pictures and places that might help your memory. I know this is traumatic, but I really think you can do it."

"I'll go with you," Chase said quickly.

"But I can't go. Mandy can't even run the business yet. She is still healing from her accident."

"Then let's put a plan in place to make it happen. We'll look at the calendar and go talk to Mandy. I know another photographer that would be more than happy to help out. Just know that we can make this work. And once you have the facts, you can decide how you want to live your life. The past can be just that: the past. But at least you'll know." Chase looked at her, seeing fear and doubt in her eyes, but then she slowly nodded.

"I'm really sorry that I can't give you more details, but Mrs. Palmer was pretty adamant about you hearing everything from her. And after learning only part of the story, I think that is the best thing. And if Chase is going with you, I know you can do this."

"Thanks, Travis. I really didn't think you would find anything, or if you did, it would take years."

"I told you he was good," Chase said with a laugh, trying to ease the tension that had filled the room.

"Let me know when you decide to go. I have information to give you, but not before the day you leave for California. Then we'll talk again when you get back home," Travis said.

"Sounds like my mother likes a bit of intrigue herself," Bailey said thoughtfully.

"I think she just wants to protect you."

"From what?"

"Bailey, you have been though what most of us can never imagine. And she knows that."

"But Travis, you haven't said anything about a father. Do I have one?" Bailey asked curiously.

"Once again, that is for your mom to tell you. I really hope you will go see her as soon as you can." Travis stood up, shook their hands, and soon was walking out the door.

"Do you feel any better?"

"What I feel is confused. Gregory Randall being all-cryptic and scaring me to pieces. A mother that has sworn my investigator to secrecy. By the way, do we still have to pay him since he isn't giving us all the information?" Bailey said with a nervous laugh. "I have to go back to the place that I said I would never return to. Plus, I've got to talk to Mandy and get these weddings taken care of." Bailey sighed heavily trying to digest everything that had just happened.

"Can we just run away? Maybe to some little island in the Bahamas and live off the grid? They've got the best beaches, and we can just sell t-shirts and live off love," Bailey said, plopping back on the couch and closing her eyes.

"As tempting as that sounds – you living in a bikini almost all year round – I think we'd better be making plans for a California vacation."

27

As the plane sat on the tarmac at the Miami Airport, getting ready for take-off, Bailey looked out the window and almost wished they had never hired Travis. Then none of this would be taking place.

But then again, it might. Her mother's investigator had found her, so she would probably still be going to California. The only thing that was keeping her calm and sane was that Chase was by her side.

Travis had met them at the airport this morning with a letter from her mother. He said that it would explain everything about the trip. She wanted to rip it open and read it right then and there, but she decided that she would wait till they were in the air, on their way west.

It had taken almost two weeks to arrange everything, so Bailey and Chase could make the trip. After talking to Travis that day, they went straight to Mandy's house to explain everything. Mandy was more than thrilled that Bailey had the chance to finally meet her family and was willing to do whatever it took, even hiring someone temporarily and still guaranteeing Bailey her job while she was gone.

Since Mandy was now walking with crutches and getting around better, she was more than willing to go back to work. Even excited to have an excuse to go back to the office. Dennis offered to help her with the upcoming weddings, which, surprisingly, Mandy said she would accept. Bailey loved seeing these two together, and though Mandy hadn't said anything, it looked as though the pair were getting cozier each time she saw them together.

Bailey went through the plans for each wedding that would take place while she was gone, checking and double-checking that all venues, caterers, photographers, and other details were all in place. Though there were things that had to be done the day of the weddings, with everything booked and deposits made, Bailey felt better about leaving everything in Mandy's care.

She even made lists for her boss to make it easier, but it felt so weird. It reminded her of her first day in the office when Mandy had handed her a stack of papers with several lists on top. This is where both women were alike, even though they were thirty years apart in age. Mandy had become like a mom to her. Bailey felt like she could talk to her about anything, at any time. They worked so well together, and Bailey hated to leave her with so much just as she was getting better. But Mandy insisted that she could do it so now there was no excuse for Bailey not to make the trip to see the family she had forgotten.

"Are you OK?" Chase asked, holding her hand and stroking the back of it for reassurance.

"I am. Just feels strange, and I'm nervous. Chase, I don't know if I'm ready to go back to where this nightmare began. I honestly never wanted to go back to California. I remember when I was driving toward Florida that it felt so good to be leaving the West coast. Now I'm walking back right into the middle of what I left behind."

"You know, that's probably a good thing," Chase said softly. "Hopefully, you are going to be able to close this chapter in your life and move on from here."

"But I've already done that. With you, my job, my friends, a new place to live."

"But your past was still haunting you."

Bailey swore this morning that she was not going to cry, but she couldn't help the tears that were forming in her eyes.

"It's OK," Chase said as his finger brushed away one of the drops of water that slid down her cheek.

"I know."

"When are you going to open the letter?"

"Once we are in the air."

The take-off was smooth, and in no time, the pilot was turning off the seatbelt sign and some passengers began to move about the cabin. Chase adjusted his seat for more comfort, but Bailey looked at the envelope in her lap.

Her mother had paid for first class tickets for their cross-country voyage, which Bailey was grateful for. With the way she was feeling, she wasn't sure that sitting in tight quarters for hours would have been good for her peace of mind. Since she was already on edge, she was sure claustrophobia would plague her.

"Would you like something to drink?" the flight attendant asked, breaking Bailey's concentration.

"Just water. Thanks," Bailey said.

"Same for me." Chase looked back at Bailey as the attendant disappeared behind them. "So, are we going to watch a movie, talk, sleep? Whatcha wanna do?" Chase said with his sexy smile.

"I think it's time to see what my mother has to say."

"Then I'll leave you alone."

Bailey took the envelope and very carefully opened the seal. The note was handwritten and two pages long.

> *My dearest Hailey,*
>
> *You don't know how long I have dreamed of writing this letter to you.*
>
> *Or better yet, to see you once again in person. So many people told me you were gone, probably passed away, but your father and I always believed that you were still somewhere, waiting for us to find you. And now you are on your way here.*

Before you arrive, there are a few things I would like to share with you. Of course, I would much rather tell you this in person, but I don't want you to be shocked when you arrive. Since we now know about the accident and your memory loss, I wanted to make sure you had some information before arriving back home.

First of all, your father is no longer with us. He passed away two years ago after a biking accident one morning. It was a sudden loss, and after your disappearance, his passing was even harder for me. I do want you to know that he loved you so much and never gave up on finding you. But I can tell you more once you are here.

You also have an older sister, Heather. You were best friends before your move to San Diego. Then, once you disappeared, she was heartbroken, just like the rest of us. She lives nearby, here in Carlsbad, and I can't wait for you to meet her, her husband, and their son, your nephew.

I have plenty of space in the house for you and anyone that you have decided to bring with you. But I can also make arrangements with a beautiful spa close by if you don't feel comfortable staying at the house. I want you to feel relaxed while you are here.

I know that all this is probably a bit of a shock, and I'm hoping that I'm able to help you with any questions you have about your family and your past. I'm so sorry this happened to you and that you have been lost to us for so many years.

If you decide to visit the scene of the accident or your friend that saved you that fateful day, all that can be arranged.

Looking forward to seeing you soon.
With Love,
Mom

Bailey read the letter twice before she sat back in her seat, looking out the window.

"Everything OK?" Chase asked.

"I think so. I had a dad, but he passed away two years ago. I also have a sister, brother-in-law, and nephew. I have a family, but I don't know them. I have no idea who they are. This all feels so foreign. My life is back in the Keys, not in California."

"And we will be going back there, but this trip is just for closure, Bailey. That's all. Plus, some of your memories might return being in the place where you lived most of your life, and if they don't, it will be OK. You do have a life. A wonderful, full life. Friends and people who love you. Especially me." Chase took her hand and brought it to his lips, gently kissing the back of it.

Bailey folded the letter and put it back in its envelope, then into her tote. In just a short time, she would be meeting the family that she had thought she needed to know, so desperate to find out who she was. But as she sat on the plane and rested her head on Chase's shoulder, she wondered why she hadn't just dropped everything and went on living her life as she wanted to in Florida.

But that nudging in the back of her mind reminded her that as much as she wanted to just let the past lie, her desire to know who she was before her accident was greater. She needed to know who Hailey Palmer was, but in her heart, she was Bailey Parker.

■ ■ ■

As the pilot came across the speaker and made the announcement to prepare for their descent into San Diego, Bailey felt her body begin to tense. She had calmed after reading the note from her mom and in the hours they had spent in the air, talking, taking a nap, and even watching part of a movie. But now they were getting ready to land.

Bailey knew there would be transportation waiting for them, but didn't know where. Chase kidded with her that there would probably be someone with a sign that bore her name, and she hoped he was right. She had the address they would be going to in Carlsbad, about thirty-five minutes north of the city. With the difference in time zones, it was still early in the day, and now that they were here, Bailey was anxious to find out more about her mother and sister. To even see the spot where her life changed forever and the woman who had been her guardian angel.

"I'm shaking so bad," Bailey said as they exited the plane. "What if no one is here?"

"Then we'll find a car and drive. You have the address. No big deal," Chase said casually.

"You're right. I guess I just can't think straight right now. I'm a bundle of nerves."

"Hey, there you go," Chase said, almost laughing.

Bailey looked to where Chase was pointing, and she saw a man holding a board that did, indeed, have her last name, Parker, written across it.

"Do you think that might be our ride?"

They walked up to the man, who was smiling from ear to ear. "You are Miss Parker, aren't you?" he said.

"Yes, but how did you know?"

"Ms. Sharon gave me your picture." The man held out a picture of Bailey that had been taken from a distance. Bailey immediately assumed that this was taken by Gregory Randall. That could be the only way her mother would have a recent picture of her.

"So, are you our ride to Carlsbad?" Chase asked, smiling at the little man who had such a bubbly personality that it was hard not to be happy in his presence.

"I sure am. Name is George. I've been helping Mrs. Palmer since Mr. Palmer died. Sweet lady she is, and so generous. So, follow me, and we'll get your luggage and be on our way."

Bailey could only smile and shake her head at George, then follow him to baggage claim. But in no time at all, they were sitting in the back seat of a limo and riding along the freeway.

"Ms. Sharon told me to cut over and go up Highway 101 because it was a favorite of yours. Sound OK to you?" George asked, looking at Bailey through the rearview mirror.

"Sounds fine." Bailey had no idea if it was fine or not, but as soon as she saw the beautiful Pacific Ocean, she was glad they had taken the road.

"Oh, it's gorgeous," Bailey said, feeling a smile on her face for probably the first time today.

"It is. Always thought the beaches here were pretty, if not a bit rocky. Though, the water isn't as warm as Florida. I'd probably be in a wet suit all the time here," Chase said.

"George, can we pull over to the beach. Just for a few minutes?" Bailey asked.

"No problem."

Before Bailey knew it, she was standing in the sand at the Seaside State Beach. It was beautiful. The sand between her toes and the cool water that came up in waves to her ankles felt so good. This time, she was by herself. For some reason, she needed this time alone and had asked Chase if he minded if she walked out by herself. She felt selfish, and if it had bothered Chase, he didn't say. He only kissed her softly and told her take her time.

As Bailey stared out at the ocean, she saw a man in her mind's eye, in a wetsuit, with a surfboard. She remembered hanging on a board, but was so scared. The man's face, though not clear, was a happy one. Whoever this man was – maybe her dad – he had tried to teach her to surf. At least that was how she interpreted the memory that came to her while standing at the ocean 's edge. Another memory had come to her but this time it didn't shock her as the ones before had.

Bailey squatted down to the ground and swished her fingers through the fine sand. How she wished she could just stay here for a few hours to collect her thoughts, but she knew her mother was waiting. And for her mother, it must have seemed like a lifetime of fear and doubt. To her mother, the daughter she lost was coming home.

For Bailey, she was entering the unknown, a frightening place. But she was so glad to have Chase as an anchor. And if it were not for Chase, she could almost say with utmost certainty she would not be here on the sandy beach of California, looking at the great ocean before her.

As she walked back to the car, Bailey watched as families played along the stunning beach. Children were making sand castles, parents nearby and relaxing. There were also couples soaking up the sun as they chatted or appeared to be napping. Then there were those by themselves who seemed to just be enjoying the California sun. The whole place was peaceful and, in a way, reminded her of the feeling she had in the Florida Keys. How she ached to be back there right now, but she was determined to see this through.

"How do you like it out there?" George asked when she was finally back in the car.

"It's wonderful. The water is a little cooler than I'm used to, but nice all the same."

"Unless you see somewhere else you would like to stop, we should be at the house shortly. Just let me know."

"Thanks, George," Bailey said, giving him a smile before looking over at Chase.

"Thank you for letting me go out there by myself. I know that was awfully selfish after all you have done for me."

"This is your trip, Bailey. I'm just along for support and to make sure that you are OK. I'm your great protector, your knight in shining armor."

Bailey grinned at his words. "To protect me?" she asked.

"That's what one does for those they love. And you are on the top of my priority list. Your happiness means everything to me, Bailey. I hope you know that."

"I do." She gave Chase a gentle kiss, then continued to watch more of the ocean pass by them as they traveled along the road.

"I had another memory."

"You did?" Chase asked excitedly.

"When I was standing out on the beach. It was a man teaching me how to surf, I think. It was very vague, but instead of jolting me like the others had, this one seemed to just slip into my mind. Do you think being here might make a difference?" Bailey asked with expectant eyes, like Chase would magically know the answers.

"I don't know, but at least you're here to see. If you had never come, you wouldn't know. Now you know that one day, you tried to surf. Too bad you can't try those skills back in Florida. Not enough wave action in the Keys."

"Not sure if I'd want to tackle that anyway. Remember – me and snorkeling is hard enough, and let's not even discuss scuba," Bailey laughed.

Chase was so happy to see her finally smile, talking casually and relaxing just a little. He knew it wouldn't be for very long, but at least he could see that Bailey was embracing being back here, where the trouble all began.

28

"This is the house I saw in one of my memories that came to me in Florida," Bailey said.

They parked in front of large, one-story, cream-colored house with a rust-colored, tile roof. The plants were on the porch, too, just like she had seen, but they were much smaller. And the driveway did, indeed, curve around to the front of the simple but large house.

"It's brick and stucco, just like I saw." A feeling of warmth enveloped her as she looked at the structure. This was her home. She was sure of it.

"Ready?" Chase asked and gave her an encouraging kiss on the lips. "I think someone is anxious to see you." Chase nodded his head in the other direction and Bailey looked to see.

It was an older woman standing just outside the front door. She stood about Bailey's height, with beautiful silver-gray hair that fell to her shoulders. She knew her mother was in her mid-sixties, but this woman did not look this age. Was this her, or a friend?

Bailey stepped out of the car with Chase right behind her. As she walked toward the door, it became apparent that the woman standing at the door was, indeed, her mother as she clasped her hands, then brought them to her face, trying to wipe away the tears that were streaming from her eyes. The woman behind the lady just smiled broadly.

"Hailey?" the older woman said.

"Hi."

"It's really you. You look so beautiful."

Bailey could tell that her mother wanted to touch her, but hesitated, not knowing what the exact protocol would be. So, she turned to Chase. "And this must be your friend, Chase. I'm Sharon, Hailey's mother." Sharon reached out her hand to Chase, but her eyes did not leave Bailey's face.

Then, as she came to stand in front of Bailey, she gingerly gave her a hug and Bailey embraced her back. And as she did, she felt like a wave of deja vu came over her, like this scene had already played out in another time.

"This is your sister, Heather," Sharon said as the tall, blonde-haired, blue-eyed woman stepped forward.

"Hi, Hailey," Heather said and gave her sister a small hug.

"Let's all go inside. George, if you don't mind, would you bring their bags in? Thank you so much," Sharon said, still staring at Bailey as if she might disappear.

The inside of the house was immaculate and stunning. The house might have been only one story, but it seemed huge and sprawled in many directions. Bailey looked around, hoping to see something she knew, but nothing seemed familiar to her.

"How was your flight?" Sharon asked as they all took a seat in the large family room in front of a floor-to-ceiling fireplace made of river stones.

"It was nice. Thank you for the tickets," Bailey said nervously, not knowing what to say or even ask.

"I want to say thank you for the first-class seats. Made the trip much more comfortable," Chase said with his smile.

"When we would travel, Nathaniel always insisted that we fly first class for that same reason. Especially when we went overseas."

"My dad's name is Nathaniel?" Bailey asked.

"Yes, it is. If he were here right now, he would be so over-joyed that you are here. You always had that same sense of adventure that he did. Your sister and I were – or should I say *are* – a bit more reserved."

"Mom and I would go shopping, while you and dad would go ziplining, hiking, rafting, or something like that," Heather said with a smile.

"I liked adventures?" Bailey asked.

"Hailey, there is so much to tell you, but I don't want to upset or overwhelm you. I want this time we have together to be as enjoyable as it can be. To make new memories to-gether. Just the fact that you are here is a miracle. I know that it might not feel like that to you, so we will go at your pace," Sharon said.

"Thank you." Bailey still was at a loss for words, which seemed to create an awkwardness that she was sure could be felt throughout the entire room. But she also felt like she had a million questions she wanted to ask right then and there.

"I know I had George bring your bags in, but I forgot to ask if you wanted to even stay here?"

Bailey didn't know how to respond. Part of her wanted to run, that same familiar feeling when she was in a situation that threw her a curve ball. But then the other part wanted to stay here, to find out who she was. So, she looked at Chase for help.

"Whatever you want to do is fine with me," Chase said softly.

Bailey looked back at her mother. "I guess we can stay here. I want to know more, but honestly, I feel like an intruder. Everything feels so odd. I'm sorry."

"There is nothing for you to apologize for," her mother said, reaching for her hand and placing it in hers. "It's hard for me to even begin to think what you've been through. I talked to several doctors before you came to make sure I didn't do anything to cause you any more trauma, but everyone said to just be myself. To let you ask the questions. And that's what I intend on doing. I asked you here because I want to help you, but more importantly, I had to see with my own two eyes that you were actually alive." Sharon had tears in her eyes once again.

"Everyone kept telling Nathaniel and I to give up on find- ing you. They even told us that we needed to have a memorial service, so we could have closure, but both of us knew that you were still alive. Even if we weren't your birth parents, the bond between this family has been strong, especially between you and your father."

"You're not my mom? I mean, my real mom?" Bailey asked, feeling like she had been punched in the gut by life once again.

"No, sweetheart, but I thought that you knew that from Travis, the young man that you hired to investigate what happened. I thought for sure he would have told you that."

"He said that I would have to talk to you. That you wanted to tell me the whole story and wouldn't give us many details. He said they were per your instructions." Bailey was feeling anxious now, another big piece in the puzzle that was her life. She was adopted. Another set of parents out there, maybe.

"Mom, remember, you did want to tell Hailey everything," Heather said gently, as though she might be talking to a small child. Bailey noticed this, and the way Heather looked at her that maybe something was wrong with their mother.

"Oh, Hailey, I'm sorry. That's right. Please forgive me." Sharon's eyes looked at her pleadingly, as though to beg her not to go away.

"It's OK. Just a bit of a shock. This whole time, I thought you were my mom."

"Oh, I am. We raised you as though I gave birth to you. And you and Heather were like best friends. You did practically everything together. You followed your big sister everywhere, even though there were times when Heather thought she was too old to have you tagging along."

"Well, I'm five years older than you, so you can imagine how it felt to have my eight-year-old sister want to go to the mall with me and friends when I was thirteen. So, instead, I would bring you home a surprise each time, which usually satisfied you," Heather said with a laughed that caused Bailey to smile.

"I have to ask you: do you want to be called Hailey or Bailey?" her mother asked.

Bailey looked down at her hands, trying to make sure she was saying the right thing. "I know that you know me as Hailey, but to me, I'm Bailey Parker. I've been Bailey Parker for four years now, and I don't remember Hailey."

"Then we'll call you Bailey. I remember when I found out your name, I couldn't believe how similar it was to your given name."

"I thought about that, too," Bailey said. "Was Hailey the name you gave me, or my birth mom?"

"She didn't give you a name. She told me she was afraid to because she didn't want to become anymore attached to you than she already was." Sharon paused, as if wondering if she should say anything, but continued.

"Bailey, she loved you so very much. I know because she and I spent the last two months of her pregnancy together. We became friends during that time, but knew that after your birth, we would never see each other again. She knew the day she put you in my arms that your father and I would give you the best home possible. And she loved the fact that you already had a big sister."

Bailey sat there, not knowing what to say, but was suddenly filled with more questions than when she had entered the house.

"I have a suggestion, "Chase said. "It's been quite a day for us, and we are still on east coast time. Let's get unpacked and rest a bit, if that is OK with you," Chase asked as he nodded toward Sharon.

"Of course. I should have thought of that when you two walked in the door. I think George put your suitcases in your rooms. You each have your own room and a bathroom nearby. Let me know if you need anything." Sharon got up quickly, taking Bailey's hand and leading her and Chase down the hallway.

"I think while you get settled, I might just take a nap of my own. It's been an exciting day, so I think I could use about thirty minutes myself."

The two rooms were right next to each other, but Bailey was hoping that Chase could stay with her. She wasn't sure what to expect in her mother's house. As she looked around the room, it felt familiar to her, but she wasn't sure if it actually did, or it was something she was wishing for.

Was this the room she lived in so long ago? If so, it didn't have the décor of a young child or even a teenager. But the room was beautiful, like the rest of house. The southwest decorating theme was evident throughout the room, and Bailey smiled. It was so homey and cozy.

A knock at the door brought her out of her thoughts.

"Can I come in?" Chase said, entering the room.

"Of course," Bailey said, going straight to him and encircling his waist with her arms. It felt so good to be held by him. He was like the rock she needed for this whole journey she was on.

"You are doing so good, babe," Chase said, kissing the top of her head. "Your mom and sister seem very compassionate.

I mean, I know we just met them and everything, but they're nice."

"I have a feeling that something is wrong with my mom."

"Why?"

"When Heather reminded her about something, it was though Heather was talking to a young child."

"I noticed that, too, but didn't want to say anything. I'm sure we'll find out everything over the next few days. At least there is only a wall that separates us," Chase said with a smile.

"I'm so glad you came with me."

"Where else would I be?" He hugged her more tightly, but then there was another knock at the door.

"Bailey?"

It was Heather's voice outside her door. Bailey's roller-coaster of nerves went into motion.

"Can I come in?" Heather asked as Bailey opened the door.

"Sure," Bailey said, stepping back. But she saw the hesitation in Heather's eyes as she realized that Chase was standing in the room.

"I'm sorry. I thought you were by yourself. Just wanted to talk to you for a minute about Mom."

"I'll just go to my room."

"Chase, you can stay. It's OK, right, Heather?"

Heather hesitated for just a second, but she relented. "Sure."

"Is everything OK?"

"Mom, is, um, OK, but has been diagnosed with possible early onset dementia. She swears that it is nothing, but the doctors say it could be serious. She still seems to have most of her memory intact, but her short-term memory suffers at times. Like not remembering that you didn't know you had been adopted. I'm so sorry about that. I hated to come in here and tell you this when you just got here, plus with everything you have been through, but I thought that you needed to know," Heather said softly.

"Thanks, Heather. Do you stay here to help her?"

"No, but my house is just down the street. George helps with house maintenance, and she has a housekeeper that comes in each day to help her. Dad made sure that if anything should happen to him, she – well, all of us – would be taken care of. But I promised her that I would let her tell you everything."

"Heather, was this my room at one time?"

"Yes, it was. Do you remember it?"

"I don't know. It was just a feeling. I know that sounds crazy."

"No, it doesn't," Heather said, putting her hand on Bailey's arm. "I hope that more of your memory will return. Maybe just being here will help."

"Thanks, Heather. Oh, one more thing. I don't think Mom would be able to tell me this."

"What's that?"

"About me and you. Before I leave to go home, can we sit and just talk, like sisters? I've never had that. I mean, I don't remember what it's like to have a sister."

Heather walked over and gave Bailey a hug. "We will most definitely have that talk. Except it will probably take more than one conversation. We were little hellions when we were younger, you more than me. Like Mom said earlier, you had this adventurous side to you."

"Did you know I was adopted?"

"I had just turned five when Mom and Dad brought you home. I never even thought about it, so I basically learned the truth when you disappeared."

"Why didn't they tell me earlier?"

"I think I should let Mom talk to you about that."

"I'm sorry. You're probably right."

"Do you need anything else right now?" Heather looked from Bailey to Chase.

"We're fine."

Heather shut the door. Now Bailey had even more questions for the family she couldn't remember.

29

Bailey woke from her nap and noticed that the room was slightly darker, indicating that it was close to sunset. One look at the clock let her know that she had slept for two hours! She wondered why no one had woke her.

As she stepped into the hallway, she heard voices coming from down the hall, and she followed the sounds. She turned the corner into the large kitchen, where Chase, her mother, and another woman she didn't know were talking and cooking food that smelled delicious.

"Hailey – I mean, Bailey, please come in. Do you feel more rested?" her mom asked.

"I do. I can't believe I slept that long. Someone should have woke me up."

"You needed to rest. A long flight mixed with stress is tiring. Rosita is making dinner. I hope you like spaghetti with meatballs. It used to be one of your favorites as a little girl," Sharon said.

"Actually it still is, and it smells wonderful. Didn't realize how hungry I was till I smelled the food." Bailey went and took the seat beside Chase and moved as close to him as she could. She needed that sense of security that only Chase could give her.

"When you and Heather were little, I'd sometimes come out here and find this kitchen a mess. You two loved to cook. Cookies were your specialty, though. But your dad loved the brownies you girls made. I'd just stand back and watch you all. I've never been much of a cook. I'm surprised any of you survived and were healthy," Sharon laughed.

"It was because your daughters would come and save the day." Heather now joined the group in the kitchen and came up to hug her mom. "I'm going to go get Davis and Tom, if that is OK with you, Bailey." Heather looked at her with expectant eyes, hoping for her approval.

"Maybe we should wait," Sharon said.

"No, it's fine," Bailey said. She suddenly felt like she was a burden on everyone. She didn't want them to feel like they were walking on eggshells while she was around. "The more, the merrier. I would like to meet my nephew and brother-in-law."

"Well, let me warn you in advance. Davis is all little boy. He may be two years old, but he thinks he is five or six. Wants to try everything, is into everything, and will ask you so many questions that you will probably want to scream at the end of the evening," Heather laughed.

Bailey laughed, too, and for the first time since learning about her family, she felt like she was a part of something bigger than she could have thought about only a few short months ago. This was the family she had wondered about for the last four years. If only her father was here.

"We'll be back for dinner," Heather said, grabbing her handbag and car keys, then was soon out the door.

"How long before dinner will be ready, Rosita?" Sharon asked.

"About an hour."

"Then, Bailey, if you feel up to it, how about a walk in my little garden out back?" Sharon asked.

"That sounds good."

"I'm actually going to get caught up on my email, so you two enjoy yourself," Chase said, knowing that Bailey needed this time to be with her mom, just the two of them.

Sharon led Bailey out the back door, into a beautiful sunroom. It was capturing the last rays of the sun for the day, but there was still enough light for a stroll outside.

"Your father built this room for me. As I said earlier, he loved the outdoors, and me? Well, I was the indoor girl. So, I would sit here while he was outside in the garden or playing with you girls."

The garden her mother had in the back yard was filled with ripe tomatoes, squash, zucchini, green beans, and several vines of grapes. A variety of herbs created boundaries on each side of the immaculate little space.

"This is wonderful," Bailey said as they strolled through the vegetables and fruit, with the herbs creating enticing scents. "I used to have a garden," but then Bailey's voice trailed off.

"You had a garden in the Keys?"

"No, it was here," Bailey said softly and looked at her mom, whose eyes lit up.

"You remember?"

"I think I do, but it wasn't like this."

"It wasn't when you were here. It was a bit bigger and not as organized as I keep this one. Your dad would plant things closer together. It was also much bigger because he planted just about every kind of vegetable he could find. For me, it was harder to harvest the plants, so when your dad passed away, I took over with a bit of help. I kept the vegetables and fruit I liked and changed things just a bit. But I wanted to keep the garden because it was so important to your father. And to you."

"To me?"

"You loved it out here. Always playing outside and me chasing you around, making sure you wore sunscreen. With your fair skin and red hair, you would burn easily. When I found out that you were in Florida, I remember wondering how you were taking care of your skin," Sharon laughed. "Can you believe that? I find out that the daughter I thought was long gone is alive, and I was worried about your skin!"

"Sharon... Mom, I'm so sorry."

"What are you sorry for?"

"For putting you through such heartache. I can't even begin to wonder what it was like to lose a child."

"But it wasn't your fault. You were just headstrong and wanted to follow your own dream."

"But why did I move to San Diego? Was I working here? What did I do?"

"Shh," Sharon said. "Let's take one thing at a time. And we have a few days to talk. This is when you remind me of your father."

"I wish so much I could have met him. I did remember something earlier on the way here."

"What was that?"

"I asked George to pull over to the beach. When I was out there, I remembered a man trying to teach me to surf."

Sharon shook her head and laughed. "That was your dad. Like I said, you would try just about anything. But when it came to surfing, you didn't like it too much. Though your dad was persistent, you eventually told him in no uncertain terms that surfing wasn't for you. Your love was ziplining."

"Ziplining?" Bailey asked, puzzled.

"Yes. Everywhere we traveled, you would find the closest place to zipline. Sometimes, your dad was even nervous at how high those lines were, but not you. You have ziplined all over the world."

"What do you mean, all over the world?"

"Bailey, we traveled every chance we could. At the time, we were by no means rich, but our spare time and some of the money we saved went toward travel. Since the time you girls were little, we traveled everywhere from London, Paris, Spain, Thailand, Australia – so many places. We would travel with your dad on business trips, mostly."

"What did he do?"

"He worked for one of the largest technology companies in the world and loved every minute of it. He started as a lowly assistant, and as he learned more, he moved up the corporate ladder. And instead of buying nice things, we just kept our same house – adding onto it, of course – and kept our older cars. Your dad invested money instead of saving, but always made sure we were taken care of. So, these travel adventures often centered around work, but we all loved it."

"Did we ever go to the Keys?"

Sharon smiled again. "We traveled to so many wild, wonderful, exotic places. But you and your father loved the Florida Keys more than any place we went. Don't get me wrong. Our adventures were terrific, and you were always the first one to say 'Let's go,' but every year, we went as a family to the Keys, staying in Marathon, mostly. We would rent a house for a week. Then there were trips where just you and your dad went there. As a matter of fact, just six months before you disappeared, you and your father bought a house on Marathon."

"We had a house there?"

"You have a house there. A realty company rents it out for me now. We went there a couple of times after you disappeared, but even for your father, it was hard to be there with you not around. After he passed away, I never had the desire to go back. When I found out that was where you were, I cried. It was like I should have known all along."

Bailey stopped walking, looking toward the darkening sky.

"What is it, Bailey?"

"The day I left California, Dena, the woman that saved my life, asked where I was going. I told her I wasn't sure, but there was this feeling inside of me that was pulling me toward Florida. I remember when I crossed the state line, just seeing the words 'Welcome to Florida' seemed so peaceful. And then

I just kept driving south. It was like I was on some sort of mission that I wasn't privy to. It makes sense now."

Sharon hugged her daughter, and Bailey didn't want to let go. Even though her memory wasn't there, things were feeling like they should for the first time in so long.

"Hey, you two, dinner is ready," Heather called out from the house.

"I know you are hungry. Let's go have some dinner."

30

Bailey entered the house to the sounds of a laughing child, but what surprised her most was that it was Chase on the floor, tickling a little boy. Bailey smiled and was most surprised at the sight.

"Bailey, this is my husband, Tom," Heather said. The man standing beside her was about her sister's same height, with graying hair and a more rounded frame. His smile was infectious, and for some reason, Bailey felt like she already knew him.

"Hi, Hailey. I'm sorry. *Bailey*. Heather has told me all about you, so I feel like we've already met." Tom shook Bailey's hand, then beamed back at his wife. As Bailey looked at the couple before them, they just didn't seem to go together, but the way they looked at each other, there was no denying that the love between them was strong.

"And this little handful," Heather said as she scooped up the child that was running in circles around their legs, "is

Davis." Heather turned the little boy toward Bailey. "Can you say 'hello'?"

"Play with him," the little boy said, pointing his finger straight at Chase.

"Hi, Davis," Bailey said, capturing small boy's attention. He gazed at her, a little red-cheeked boy that suddenly looked very shy. "I see you've made friends with my friend, Chase."

"He tickles."

"Are you ticklish?" Bailey asked, trying to engage the little boy, but she didn't know quite what to say. She hadn't been around a lot of children, so she was at a loss for words.

"Yes, he is," Tom said, taking the boy out of his mom's arms and placing him in the chair at the table.

"Are we ready to eat?" Sharon said, and everyone took a seat around the large dining table. Bailey took her place right beside Chase, still having those moments of wanting to flee.

"Haven't had spaghetti in a while," Sharon said. "Bailey, you will have to visit more often."

"Might be able to work that out," Bailey said quietly.

"What do you do in – which Key do you live on?" Tom asked.

"I live on Islamorada, and I'm the assistant to a wedding planner."

"Well, right now she is the wedding planner because her boss broke her leg very badly. We've been handling all the weddings," Chase said as bowls of food were passed from one person to another.

"Greg had told me that you were working for a wedding planner. Still following your dream," Sharon said.

"My dream?" Bailey had no idea what her mother was referring to.

"I'm sorry. That's the reason you moved to San Diego. To work for one of the largest event planning companies on the West coast. You were one of the best here locally, but they snatched you away."

"That's why I was in San Diego?"

"You had just moved there."

"But what happened?" Bailey said with a little more force in her voice that she meant. "I'm so sorry. I didn't mean for it to sound like that. Excuse me for just a moment." Bailey got up quickly, and Chase followed right behind her.

Before she knew it, she was outside in the cool air, looking up at an almost full moon.

"Hey, there," Chase said, coming up behind her, putting both hands on her shoulders. "Are you OK?"

"No, I'm not. Things are moving too slow. I want to know everything. I want to know now. I want to sit with my mom and have her tell me the whole story – everything. I feel like everyone is tiptoeing around me like I'm some china doll about to break. I feel like I am going to snap if someone doesn't tell me who I am, or at least who I was. Am I going crazy, Chase?"

Chase hugged her, gently rocking her as they stood in the moonlight.

"No, you're not, but I think your mom is trying to take it slow, so she can spend more time with you. Look at it from her perspective. She's trying to treat you like a person that she just met, when I think all she wants to do is just sit with you and marvel about how her daughter is alive and back in her life.

You both want the same things, in a way, but want to go about it differently. For me, it's hard to sit here and watch you two play this dance. But let's go back and eat. Maybe you can spend some more time with your mom after dinner."

Bailey shook her head. "OK, but I feel bad for leaving like I did."

"I'm sure they understand."

As they entered the dining room once more, everyone was quiet, except for Davis, who was giving them all the information on the little toy trains he loved so much.

"I'm sorry I left so quickly." Bailey sat back in her seat, trying to smile at everyone around her.

"You have nothing to apologize for. This is different for all of us, but you are the one who has had the most trauma," Sharon said trying to give her an encouraging look.

"She wasn't the only one that has had a hard time, Sharon. Look at what you and Nathaniel went through, even Heather. This has affected the whole family." Tom's words were blunt, and as Bailey looked at him, he suddenly didn't seem like the man she had met earlier.

"But none of us know what it was like to lose our memory," Sharon said quickly.

"Just saying that this has been stressful for everyone."

"But put yourself in Bailey's shoes." Now it was Chase who spoke quickly, and Bailey heard an edge to his voice. "How would you handle this?"

"I don't know, but this isn't just her issue. This is a family thing. And I want to make sure Heather and Davis are taken care of and protected."

"Why would this hurt Heather? Bailey is the one that had the accident," Chase said, anger starting to show through his voice.

"Then why did Bailey come here?" Tom continued.

"Because her mother asked her to."

"That is enough!" Sharon said, loud enough that both men stopped talking. "Tom, you know that Heather's part of the will is secure. That has been settled. And I continued to look for Bailey because that was what Nathaniel would have wanted me to do."

"You sure she isn't here only for the money?"

"Tom!" This time, it was Heather that spoke. "We talked about this before we left the house. This is not the time or place."

"When is?"

Bailey felt like she was in a whirlpool, being pulled from side to side, with no way to get out. What was this about a will? Money? People being hurt because of her? Was her mom only looking for her because of her dad, or did she really want to be reunited with her daughter?

"I need to go," Bailey said.

"Bailey, we can talk in the morning. I'm so sorry dinner didn't turn out like I had planned," Sharon said, looking at her daughter.

"No, I have to leave. I can't stay here. It seems I've caused more problems."

"No, you haven't. Please, let us talk more. I've got so much to tell you. And you and Heather need to talk, too."

"According to Tom, maybe Heather doesn't want to talk to her sister." At Chase's statement, Bailey looked at her sister that only hours ago, had seemed like she could be a best friend.

"I do want to talk to Hai-" Heather stopped herself. "Bailey. And my husband needs to apologize."

"I'm sorry, but I just find this all a bit odd. And the timing too perfect,' Tom said angrily.

"My timing?"

"For dividing up your father's estate."

31

"I have no idea what you are talking about." Bailey looked to her mother. "What estate?"

"Your father left both of you girls a sizeable amount of money that you would have access to two years after he was gone. He wanted you to think about what you would do with the money and not just get it and squander it away, though I told him I didn't think either of you would. But he also left you something else, Bailey," Sharon said. "His portion of the house you two owned in Marathon."

"That is worth at least a million dollars, if not more," Tom remarked quickly.

"A house in Marathon?" Chase said, puzzled, looking at Bailey.

"Like I told Bailey this afternoon, she and her dad went to the Keys regularly, and right before her move to San Diego, they purchased a house together in the Keys."

"He purchased it. Bailey, Hailey, whoever couldn't have put any money in it."

"Tom, please!" Heather said, pleading for her husband to be quiet.

Sharon suddenly had her hand on her head.

"Mom, are you OK?" Heather said, looking worried. Bailey looked and saw that her mother looked pained.

"I'm fine, but I will not have any more talk like this, Tom, at my table. If you want to discuss this with Heather at your house, that is fine. You've read everything and know what is to be done with the house. It belonged to Nathaniel and Bailey. I'm sorry you are upset, but that is how it will be."

"Well, it's not fair. Heather deserves more. Just because Nate liked the Keys and Hailey does, too, doesn't mean she deserves more."

"Heather has her money. I'm sorry you are unhappy, but this is the way it was set up. Nathaniel and Bailey purchased the house *together* and legally, it is hers," Sharon said, still looking as though her head was hurting.

"I just think we need to relook at everything."

"I won't say this again. What is done is done. Things will stay the way they are. If you don't like it, then it's something you will have to deal with. But from this point on, we will not talk about it in this house. Have I made myself clear? To everyone?" Sharon's voice was strong, but Bailey could tell this dinner was taking a toll on her.

As Bailey looked around the table, everyone sat quietly. No one was dining on the food before them as it seemed the agitation in the room had taken away everyone's appetite.

What had started out as a nice family meal was now a room full of tension. Bailey only wanted to eat and go to her room. But one thing was for sure. Tomorrow, her mom had to give her the whole story, so she would know what she was dealing with.

Having a toddler at the table did break the silence though. Soon, they were having a cordial conversation, but the unease was still there. As soon as dinner was through, Sharon excused herself, telling Bailey that they would talk in the morning, then made her way to her room.

"Bailey," Heather said before she walked out the door, "I want to apologize. I promise this isn't me. Tom just, well...."

"It's alright. Maybe we can talk later, OK?" This time, it was Bailey giving her newly-found sister some reassurance. Heather shook her head, then walked out to the car that was already started and ready to head to her home.

As soon as Bailey was in her room, she heard a small knock. It was Chase.

"How are you doing?"

"Confused. Tom got so angry! Heather trying to smooth things over and my mom, so upset. I don't know what is going on, so I'm determined to find out tomorrow."

"But you have a house?"

"My mother told me about it when we were walking before dinner. I didn't realize it was a million-dollar home. I thought she was talking about some little cottage type home that we see all the time. I know she said my dad and I loved the Keys and that is why I have the house, but he must have left something for Heather, too."

As Bailey laid back on the bed, Chase came to lay beside her, holding her in his arms. "Why don't you get dressed for bed? And then you can get some rest."

"Will you stay with me tonight?" Bailey asked, wanting him to just hold her.

"What do you think your mom will say?"

"Does it matter? We aren't doing anything wrong, and I've been on my own for so long. Just having you next to me is something I sorely need right now." Bailey practically buried her face into his neck, finding refuge in his strong touch.

"Like I said, change your clothes and relax. I'll be back in a bit."

As Chase shut the door to her room, Bailey looked at her phone to see that it was already nine o'clock, which was really midnight for her and Chase. It had been such a long day, and the tension was already heavy surrounding her newfound family. For some reason, she expected this loving atmosphere, all peaches and roses. Or at least that was what she was hoping for.

But did you really expect that? she thought to herself. *After everything you've been through, you should know by now that's not real life.*

What if she didn't accept anything from her parents? She could walk away from this, knowing who her family was, and maybe just see them occasionally. Right now, she longed to be back in her little apartment in Islamorada, planning weddings and watching happy couples say, "I do." To spend the days and evenings with Chase, getting to know each other better every day. That life seemed so much simpler than what she was facing now.

But like Chase had told Bailey earlier: *find out your past, then you can move on.* And that was what she had to do now that she was here.

When Chase arrived back to Bailey's bedroom, he slipped in to see her lying in bed, underneath the covers. And very much asleep. As he looked at the girl lying there, he wished so much that he could take all the pain and struggle away for her.

He had dealt with a dysfunctional family all his life and knew how to handle it. Bailey had no memories from which to draw strength from. Or to be able to have some defense because when it came to this family, for Bailey, they didn't exist in her mind, except for the few memories that had appeared and the small amount of time she had been here so far.

As tempting as it was to pull the covers up and slide into the bed next to her, only to hold her as she slept, he quietly walked back to his room. She needed rest after this long day, and if he was being truthful, he would welcome some sleep, too. He had to make sure he was rested, for who knew what the next few days would bring.

■ ■ ■

The smell of coffee wafted into her room and acted as a wake-up call for Bailey. Looking around the space, she remembered where she was. The memories of last night flooded back to her, and she sighed. She was also by herself, even though she thought that Chase was going to stay with her last night. But it was time to get up to see what was in store for today.

With a simple glance in her suitcase, Bailey chose her favorite pair of jeans with a colorful shirt and her flat, casual sandals. These clothes made her feel good, and she needed all the confidence she could muster. Today was the time to ask the hard questions. Bailey needed to know more, and she wanted to know it all.

As she stepped out of her room, it felt like the same scene from last night. She could hear voices coming from the family room or kitchen, except the voices were all adult. It was her mother and Chase, but she couldn't make out what they were saying. But this brought a little hope to Bailey that it would only be the three of them this morning and that she would be able to ask the questions and get the answers she so desperately needed.

"Good morning," Chase said as Bailey came around the corner into the spacious kitchen. He greeted her with a sexy smile and gentle kiss. "Your mom and I were just talking about the Keys. I was telling her about my family in Miami, and she thinks that maybe one of our realtors was the one that sold you and your father the house in the Keys."

"I can't be sure, but it does sound familiar. But then, my memory isn't what it used to be," Sharon said lightly. "But we'll go over that in a bit."

"Well, everything smells wonderful. I'm really hungry this morning."

"I wasn't sure what you would like, so Rosita fixed eggs, biscuits, hash browns, and bacon. We have orange juice, milk, tea, or coffee to drink. I know it's not the healthiest breakfast, but it just sounded good this morning." Sharon smiled as she poured herself some hot water over a small tea bag in the cup before her. Bailey could see that her mother's hands were shaking and wondered if it was because of the stress her visit was causing or if it was something else altogether after Heather's account of Sharon's possible health issue.

"To me, it all sounds good," Bailey said, giving her mother an encouraging smile.

"When you were a little girl, your favorite breakfast was biscuits and gravy. Anytime we went anywhere for breakfast, that was all you wanted. Even when we travelled overseas," Sharon laughed. "Plus, if hot chocolate was part of the meal, you thought that was the best. It didn't matter what time of year. It could be very hot outside, but that didn't matter to you. Hot chocolate was a year-round drink for you. If it wasn't available, you would settle for chocolate milk."

"I have to say my love for chocolate hasn't changed," Bailey laughed. "I do try to sneak some each day, and I keep a jar of hot cocoa mix in my cabinet."

Bailey loved the ease in the atmosphere this morning compared to the night before, but she knew it was time to ask more questions. Her hesitation to talk to her mother was bringing on more anxiety, but she decided to be brave and dive in.

"Shar… Mom…"

"For right now, just call me Sharon, OK?" Bailey's mom looked at her across the counter and gave Bailey the reassuring glance that she needed to continue.

"Sharon, can we really talk today? I need to know everything you can share with me. About me, you and my father, this thing with Heather and Tom. I know it's a lot, but I need to know. It's like I've waited so long, wondering, and now here the answers are at my fingertips."

"Let's get a plate of food and go sit out on the back porch and talk. You can ask me anything, and I'll tell you what I can."

"I'll let you two have some privacy then," Chase said quickly.

"No," Bailey said. "I want you there. You are a part of my life now, so there is nothing to hide."

"Is it OK with you, Sharon?" Chase asked to be sure.

"It's whatever Bailey wants."

32

The three of them took seats around the beautiful glass table that was in the back sunroom. With the sunrise, the room seemed so much brighter and colorful than it had the night before. And it felt more welcoming. Bailey was glad that this morning's breakfast was just her mother, herself, and Chase.

"Sharon, tell me about my life. Growing up. Living here. Heather told me that the room I'm staying in was mine when I lived here."

"It was. After you moved out, I redecorated it," Sharon chuckled. "I remember your first visit back, and you couldn't believe that I had already boxed up your things and changed the room around."

"Why would I be upset?"

"You had just graduated from college and were in your first apartment. You were barely scraping by. I wanted to help, but your father was adamant that you do everything on your own. I went ahead and had the room redecorated, then one day, you came home in tears. You wanted to move back here till you could get more stable, and your dad kept telling you that you would be fine. You went off to your room, and when you opened the door, all I heard was, 'Where is my stuff?'" Sharon was laughing at the memory, but Bailey was trying to understand. "You were so frustrated, but it gave you the fuel you needed to get back out there and make your life work."

"What wasn't working?"

Sharon sat back in her chair and sighed. "Everything was working. You were just used to having us to help with everything. But your dad knew you had it in you to make it on your own. And you did. But Bailey..." Sharon paused.

"There is so much I could tell you. All the little details, but I have a feeling that it's going to take more than a couple of days here in California to answer them. It will take time to give you all the details of your life. I wish there was some way I could share everything with you all at once, but there are some important things I think we should discuss first. Hopefully, we'll be able to spend more time together in the future, and you can ask me any question you want when something comes up that you don't understand. But know this: I want to be a part of your life again. I feel like I've been given a second chance. To find out that you were alive – well, like I said in the letter, it was a precious gift."

Bailey sat there, using her fork to slide the food on her plate from one side to the next. Now that she had her mother's attention, she didn't know what to ask next. Then, suddenly, she knew.

"Why didn't anyone notice that I had disappeared? Did we not talk after I moved to San Diego? I remember being in the hospital and the police telling me that it was odd that someone didn't file a missing person report. Were we fighting or something? I don't understand why someone wouldn't have missed me. Did I have a boyfriend? Was I married? Was I working? Was I some horrible person that no one wanted?"

There it was. *Why was I abandoned?* Bailey thought. It was the huge question that had plagued her since she woke from her coma over four years ago.

"First of all, you weren't some terrible person. In fact, you had loads of friends here. As for being married, you certainly weren't, but you were talking about it."

"I was? With who?"

"His name was Daniel. Very sweet boy."

"What happened?"

"You were doing great here. A wonderful job at a local technology company. You had a degree in computer science, and this was a little start-up company that grew extremely fast. Your dad was so excited for you. It was like you were following in his footsteps. But you also had another passion."

"What?"

Sharon smiled at her. "You loved to plan. You wrote everything down and kept notebooks and calendars everywhere. When someone needed help planning a birthday, wedding, bachelorette party – just about any event around here – you offered to help. And the thing was, you were good. Plus, you loved it. I mean, you could be in the biggest mess, but to watch you at a party, it was like you were in your element."

"I went from a technology firm to party planning?" Bailey asked, not quite sure what to think of her past choices.

"A local event planner hired you after a bachelorette party had gone wrong. You were with your friend, Piper, at her party, and I forgot what happened, but you had everything fixed in no time, and the planner asked if she could hire you. You started working with her on the side. Before long, you quit the tech company and were working with her full-time within a few months."

"I guess my father didn't like that too much."

"He wasn't angry, but he always thought you could do better. You weren't making as much money with event planning, but you loved it. I mean, it was all you talked about."

"But what about this guy, Daniel?" Bailey had to know what had happened.

"Well, you met Daniel at one of the weddings you helped coordinate. He was one of the groomsmen. The two of you were together almost all the time from the moment you met. I think within a few months of dating, you were already talking about getting married. That's when you got the call from San Diego."

"What call?" Bailey asked.

"We still don't know who, but someone locally saw how you handled a party they were attending. They worked for one of the largest event planning services in California. They approached you about working as an assistant to the head person in their San Diego office. The pay was more than you had been making at the tech company. You were so excited. Of course, we didn't want you to go, especially your dad. And Daniel. He was adamant about you staying here. To the point that if you left, he wanted to end the relationship. You came to me, and we talked and talked." Sharon spoke the words now so softly, like she was deeply immersed in the past.

"You decided that you were going to go. It was a great opportunity, and you weren't that far away. Your father was upset because he couldn't see a future with this business, and I think for the first time, you two weren't talking. As for Daniel, he made good on his promise. He broke it off as soon as you told him you were leaving. You even asked him to come with you. You were willing to come home on the weekends and try whatever it took to make it work, but he would have nothing to do with it."

"So, my father and Daniel weren't speaking to me, but what about you or Heather? What about any of my friends?" Bailey wanted to know, so she could put the puzzle pieces of her life together.

"I was worried about you. And Heather was working in Los Angeles at the time. We barely heard from her. I think that was another reason your father didn't want you to go because we were going to be all alone. We wondered what our life would be like as empty nesters, and we both knew we wouldn't like it. We loved having you girls here. Your friends. It was always our house everyone came to, and we liked it that way.

"Once you moved to San Diego, I waited a week before I tried to call you. You already had an apartment before you left, and you weren't scheduled to start working for another week. You went early because of Daniel, mostly. You told me that you had to get away and you might as well go ahead with the move now instead of later. That it would give you more time to learn where everything was. You were going to buy furniture and most of the things you needed, so it would give you time to get settled. I offered to come and help, but you insisted that you wanted to do it on your own." Sharon now sat back in her chair and shook her head. Bailey could feel this was the part of the story that would be most painful – for her mother and for herself.

"I wanted to call you. I even wanted to ride down to check on you, but I didn't. Neither did your dad. We both figured that you would call us when you were ready. You were angry. No, that's not the right word. You were very frustrated when you left. You felt like no one supported your decision, even though we did in a way. We were happy to see you excited, but we just didn't show it well. I kept expecting you to reach out to us any day, but we never heard from you. I waited a month before I tried to call because I couldn't wait any longer.

"But you never answered your cell phone. It always went to voice mail. Soon, it said that your voicemail box was full. Then I decided to call your new employer, and that was when we found out that you never showed up for work."

"That I was missing?"

"Yes. Your father and I," Sharon paused, closing her eyes, as though relieving what had happened was too awful to continue. "Your father and I were beyond upset. At ourselves. At your new boss. At the police. We went to San Diego and talked to them. We found out that they had a young woman who had been in an accident and that she had amnesia, but it was six weeks ago. They wouldn't give us much information, except that the woman had amnesia and that she signed herself out of the hospital. They wouldn't even give us a name, but they did describe the woman. When they said, 'dark brown hair', we knew it wasn't you. But we left there and went to the hospital anyway to make sure. But no one there would give us any information and told us to check with the police. We had nowhere else to begin to look. Nowhere to start to try to find you."

"What about my work? Or my new apartment? Why didn't you look there for clues?" Bailey asked.

"Since you never showed up at your new employer, they didn't have your address. As for your apartment, you never told us where it was. That period of time when you were leaving to go was tense at the house, with everyone not speaking to each other.

"I remember one day, about six or seven months after you went missing, your father walked up to me. He was so depressed, looking haggard and tired. We both were. We had searched and even hired someone to investigate everything for us. But it was as though you had just vanished. Nathaniel just said to me, 'She's gone, Sharon.' At that moment is when I lost it. I knew I had to accept that you were never coming home, but I...." There was no way to hold back the tears now. Sharon gently wiped away the water in her eyes.

This time, it was Bailey that sat back slowly in her chair and sighed, as she remembered now what she had done.

"I did have brown hair."

"What?" The words were said in unison from both her mother and Chase.

"I remember. When I was recovering from the accident, I had brown hair. But as it grew, the roots were red. I remember Dena asking me if I could remember why I colored my hair, and I couldn't. Maybe I was mad? Or needed a change?" These were the things Bailey wished she could remember; they were like little holes that needed to be filled.

"You'd never colored your hair, so I have no clue as to why you would've done it, except how frustrated you were with everyone. You were headstrong, like your father, but I sometimes wonder if you didn't get that from your biological parents. Your mother was a pistol. Quick with words. So sure of herself and very determined."

Now that she knew that her family had tried to find her, the mention of her birth parents took Bailey to another huge question. She wanted to know about her biological mother.

33

"What can you tell me about her?" Bailey asked, wanting to know everything about her, too, but at the same time, not wanting to cause her mother any more stress.

Sharon once again delved into the past. "Your father and I decided that we wanted another child soon after Heather was born. We tried for a few years, and I couldn't get pregnant. I brought up adoption a few times, but your father was so against it. He said he didn't know if he could love someone else's child as his own.

"One day, I was at the park with Heather. She was playing with some blocks on a blanket I'd placed on the grass beside the bench I was sitting on. A girl much younger than me sat on the other end. She looked like she was at least six or seven months pregnant. I asked her how she was doing, and she didn't answer, but began to cry. We started talking, and she told me how she had come to California to stay with some friends while she was pregnant. That her family was upset that she had gotten herself into this mess. That her boyfriend wanted to marry her, and she wouldn't. That she had almost had an abortion, but couldn't go through with it. I asked her what she was going to do, and she said she was in the process of selecting parents for her baby and how hard it was.

"We talked for over an hour, and before I knew it, I invited Lynn – that was her name – back to our place. Nathaniel and I helped her go through the papers she was filling out, and she even told us about some of the parents she was considering. After that, we kept meeting at the park, and within a month, we were seeing each other every day. I kept up with her progress and even took her to a few doctor appointments.

"When she was eight months pregnant, she was having dinner with us and just out of the blue asked if we would adopt her child. Your father looked at me, wondering if I'd put her up to this, but I was as shocked as he was. At first, he said that we couldn't, but I quickly said that we would discuss it. Your mom, just like you, wasn't going to take 'no' for an answer. Lynn told us that she had even told the adoption lawyer that she had already picked out parents and gave her our names!" Sharon laughed.

"Within a few days, with Lynn practically begging Nathaniel and me talking to him afterwards, he relented. He really liked your mother and thought she was being responsible by choosing adoption instead of trying to do it all on her own because we both knew she wasn't ready to raise a child."

"I remember the day when Lynn called to tell me she was in labor, and we met her at the hospital. Your father and I both were in the room when you were born. You had these soft red curls and Lynn said that those came from your father. She held you for about ten minutes, and then she placed you into my arms. We were able to take you home with us the next day, but the hardest thing was leaving Lynn at the hospital, by herself."

"Why did you leave her? Weren't you such good friends?" Bailey asked, so keyed up listening to the story.

"We were, but we agreed that it would be best for you that she move on with her life and not see you again. It would be too hard to see you. She told us before we walked out of the door that she knew without any doubt that we were going to give you so much more than she could have dreamed of. "

"Do you know if she is still in California?" Bailey asked, still wanting to know more, but could see Sharon was getting tired.

"I don't know. Lynn never even told me where she was originally from. It seemed like she always evaded the question. I knew she was running away from something, and I assumed it had to be her family. My only prayer was that she would find happiness in life, like we had in you."

"Why didn't you tell me I was adopted?" Bailey asked tentatively.

Bailey saw the shock register on her mother's face. "How did you know?"

"I asked Heather last night."

"I wanted to so many times once you were a teenager, but Nathaniel kept telling me 'no'. You were our child, the one he didn't think he could love. From the moment we brought you home, you were his little ray of sunshine."

"What about Heather? How did that make her feel?"

"Oh, he loved her, too. Both of you girls were priceless to both of us. But there was just this bond between the two of you. It was like magic."

"That didn't bother you?" For the first time during this entire story, it was Chase who asked the question, joining the conversation.

"No, actually, it didn't. We were such a close family. Heather and Hailey were so different. Heather and I liked the indoors, and we shared arts, crafts, reading and more. Hailey, I mean Bailey, was more the outdoor girl, very much like her father. But we always came together as a family, sharing what we did, what we liked. I think that is why our travels were so much fun. My mother used to accuse Nathaniel and I of playing favorites, but we didn't. Did we have squabbles and disagreements? Sure! What family doesn't? We certainly weren't perfect, but we loved each other."

"If everything was so nice, why did Tom go off like he did last night? And what was he talking about?"

"Bailey, I promise I'll answer everything, but if it's OK with you, I'm going to go inside for just a bit. Maybe an hour or so," Sharon said.

"I'm so sorry. I didn't realize we have been sitting here for so long." Bailey was surprised when she looked down at her phone to see the time. With all they had talked about, it felt as though they had only been at the little table a very short time.

"There is no problem. I just seem to tire out a little quicker than normal these days, but I'm fine. Just keep telling everyone it is old age. Why don't you and Chase go into town? Look around. You might see something that jogs your memory. You never know. You are welcome to use my car, and I'll leave the keys on the counter."

"Thanks," Bailey said, clearly some disappointment showing in her voice.

"I promise to answer more questions," Sharon responded. "We've got plenty of time."

They stood up. Her mother came around to Bailey, kissed her on the cheek, then walked into the house.

"I wish we could've gone on. We aren't going to be here long, and I need to know more." Bailey felt like she could cry now. Though she now knew so much more than before, she felt like there was still much to learn.

"We still have the rest of today and tomorrow morning before we head back to San Diego. Your friend isn't expecting you till tomorrow at lunch, right?"

"I know. Now that I'm here, I almost wish I could stay longer. Learn as much as I can. But I also need to see Dena and Stan. Hopefully, she will forgive me for not keeping in touch. But after that, I have to admit, a part of me is ready to get back to the Keys. A place that feels somewhat normal and safe."

34

Using the GPS on his phone, Chase steered the car toward downtown Carlsbad. Bailey was looking from side to side, and Chase wondered if anything would jog her memory.

"Can we go to the beach again?" Bailey asked quietly.

"We can go wherever you'd like. You might enjoy the Village. It's a pretty cool place to shop. Might take your mind off things for a bit."

"You've been here before?"

"Came here for a small conference with my dad and brother when I was younger. That's how I remember the Village. Harris and I thought it was the coolest thing that we got to go by ourselves. It was nice, but of course, we were more interested in the beach – or should I say the girls in bikinis," Chase said, flashing his mischievous grin.

"It seems you have been everywhere," Bailey remarked, relaxing just a bit.

"From what your mom said, it seems you have been all over the world."

"I guess you're right. I wish I could remember it all. I forgot to tell you that she said that I used to love to zipline. That everywhere we went, I always seemed to find a place to zipline. Isn't that strange? I never even thought about ziplining before."

"Did she tell you some of the places you've visited?"

"Europe, Asia, Australia, South America. My father loved to travel, but she said that he and I would always make a trip to the Keys every year, sometimes twice. Sorta like it was our special place."

"That's the reason for the house in Marathon."

"That house. Not that it wouldn't be nice to have my own place, but it seems that is a very sore subject," Bailey recalled, remembering the heated conversation last night.

"No, it sounds like someone needs to grow up. Tom seems to be all about the money. Do you think it might be because he is so much older than Heather?" Chase asked.

"I wonder how old he is."

"I don't know, but he certainly doesn't look the same age as your sister."

"I hope she and I can still talk after what happened last night."

"I'm sure you will," Chase said as he parked the car close to the beach.

As soon as Chase was by her side, he gathered her in his arms before she could take another step. He kissed her so sweetly, his lips caressing hers. "Man, I've been wanting to do that all morning."

He kissed her again, and this time, it was more sensual and deep. He just wanted her all to himself after all this family drama. Watching her go through this wasn't pleasant, but he hoped that when they got back to Islamorada, Bailey would be able to lay down more roots and feel more grounded.

They walked down the pathway to the beach. It was an incredible, sunny day, with mild temperatures. A perfect California day. They walked down the beach, hand in hand, not saying much, but just absorbing the area around them.

"I wonder how much time you spent on the beach?" Chase wondered aloud, giving her hand a squeeze.

"My mom said that she used to have to chase after me to wear sunscreen since I liked to practically live outside."

"I could see that. You running wild, red hair flying in the wind, and her chasing after you, lotion in hand. That's probably where those adorable freckles came from."

Bailey smiled. It was nice to walk in the sand with this wonderful man by her side. Everything she was going through now, she couldn't even comprehend doing this all by herself.

Bailey stopped slowly and looked at Chase. "I know I've already said this I don't know how many times, but thank you so much for disrupting your life to come here with me. Asking these questions, hearing about a life I lived and have no clue about – sometimes, it just overwhelms me. I feel like you're the one keeping me stable, even sane. I can look at you and things just seem to calm down. Thanks so much, Chase."

"No thanks necessary. I already told you there is no place I would rather be. You are a part of my life now, and I want to be here for you. I know that if the roles were reversed, you would do the same for me. I love you, Bailey," Chase said. He cupped her face with his hands before his lips descended onto hers yet again. The kiss was so tender and loving that it almost took Bailey's breath away. She couldn't get enough of this man, and she certainly didn't want him to stop.

"I say we go to the Village now," Chase uttered when they came up for air.

"Sounds good." Bailey wasn't sure how long they had kissed, standing in the sand, but she didn't care. At that moment, her world felt right for a change, and she needed every second of the strength that he had just given her.

The instant they arrived at the Village, Bailey adored the place. The shops and restaurants that lined the streets were so inviting, and even though she didn't remember anything specific, she could feel that she had been here before. It was just a knowing inside of her, similar to the feeling when Bailey knew she was to go to the Florida Keys.

"Are you hungry?" Chase asked, sliding his arm around her waist.

"Absolutely! I feel like I haven't eaten a thing all day. I know this morning, I was just too anxious to hear the stories. I don't know if I ate a bite."

"I watched you, and I think you just pushed the eggs around on your plate. You were too intent on listening to your mom. Even so, I did eat, and I'm already starving, so what sounds good?"

"I'm going to let you pick," Bailey said with a smile.

They found a small Bistro, where they shared a plate of nachos and then a turkey club sandwich. Chase laughed as Bailey picked out the food, neither entrée complementing the other, but he didn't care. They were hungry, and both plates sounded wonderful.

As they ate the gooey, cheese-covered chips, then the huge turkey sandwich, Bailey scrutinized everything around her, even glancing out the window they sat by, hoping for clues to her memory. She was hoping for something – a sign, a store, a street - that would possibly spark a memory or two. But as they sat there, nothing happened.

After finally meeting her family, Bailey was beginning to accept when something didn't magically show up in her mind. But she thought that once she was in the small town, her memory would burst forth in her head, and she would finally be whole. She would know who she truly was. But it didn't quite work like she had hoped.

"Whatcha thinking?" Chase asked as he took the last bite of the sandwich.

"Just looking around and wondering. I've probably been here before."

"Since you grew up in this town, I would say that's a pretty safe bet. Maybe not this restaurant, but then, maybe so. Are you OK if you don't get every little detail?" Chase posed the question, wanting to help her.

"I wasn't sure at first, but I think I can say 'yes' now. I dreaded coming back here. I had even promised that I would never go back to San Diego again. I just wanted to start over, which I did, but I'm glad you convinced me to find out. You were right."

"About what?"

"Even if some unpleasant things surface, at least I know about them and I can put it behind me. I might not understand why things happened the way they did, or why I and the people around me made the choices that led to this point, but at least I know the truth. That's better than nothing."

"I'd venture to say that the thing that still bugs you the most is that you feel no one cares that you went missing. Even though your mom told you this morning that they searched for you." Chase chose his words carefully because he knew before Bailey even answered that this was the case. He knew that if he were in her shoes, it would be the most pressing question for him.

"You're right. I just don't understand why. I'd never stop looking."

"Bailey, you don't know how everyone was feeling back then though your mom explained it pretty well."

"But if you had a missing child, wouldn't you move heaven and earth to find her? It just feels like they quit. Like I wasn't important to them. Maybe because I wasn't their flesh and blood."

"Do you hear yourself?" Chase said incredulously. "Your mom just got through telling you how you and your dad were so close. You even bought a house with him in the Keys! You went on trips all over the world. Bailey, I don't think this couple could have loved you more. It didn't matter that you were adopted. They were and *are* your parents no matter what.

There are people out there that would've loved to have with their birth parents what you got from this couple."

"I know you're right, but it just still doesn't feel right to me. I can't explain what I'm trying to say."

"Just give it some time. But I do want to ask you something."

"What?"

"Has the thought crossed your mind to look for your birth mother now that you know the whole story? At least you have her name and that she lived here while she was pregnant. We could always hire Travis again to help."

"I think I just need to concentrate on one hurdle at a time. But I can't say that the thought didn't cross my mind as soon as I heard the story. Maybe later, after things have settled down, I might look for her. Right now, though, we probably should be heading back to the house."

"Want to go look in a few shops first? Some retail therapy?"

"Not sure about buying anything, but to walk the streets for a bit would be nice."

Bailey took Chase's hand as they walked down the sidewalk, peering into the little shops and boutiques along the way. The colorful window displays and watching the happy people walking by made Bailey smile. She was starting to get used to this rollercoaster of feelings that she seemed to have no control over.

"Oh, I want to go in here," Bailey said, walking into a little shop with beach clothing. Though they had their share of boutiques like this in the Keys, Bailey was drawn to the clothing and the colors that shone through the shop's windows. They reminded her of home.

"Do you see something you like?" A young woman stepped from behind the counter and came to greet her.

"I'm just looking, but I love the 'beachy' feeling you get in here," Bailey said, smiling at the woman. A spark of recognition played in Bailey's mind, but she couldn't grasp it.

"Hailey Palmer?" the woman asked, a look of shock on her face.

"Who are you?" Bailey was suddenly backing away before running into Chase's body.

"Is it really you? I heard that you went missing. Everyone thought you were dead. You are Hailey, right?" The young woman stood in front of Bailey, so close, like she wanted to touch her to make sure Bailey was real.

"Who are you?" Bailey asked the question again because she didn't know what to say. She had not expected anyone to recognize her. But then if she had grown up here, there would be people who knew her and about her disappearance. Why hadn't she thought of that?

"I'm Hailey Palmer, but I don't remember that name. I go by Bailey Parker."

"What happened to you?"

"You still haven't told me who you are," Bailey asked once more, not wanting to give out any more information till she knew who this person was.

"I'm so sorry! I was just so shocked to see you. I'm Piper's little sister, Megan. I can't believe you are here! Does Piper know you're back? What about Daniel? Does he know? We couldn't believe when we heard the story that you had disappeared without a trace. Piper's going to be so happy."

"Megan, I'm sorry, but I don't remember you. Or Piper."

"What are you talking about?"

"I'm sorry, but I have to go," Bailey answered, then turned and fled the store, with Chase hot on her heels.

"Bailey, hold on," Chase said, trying to catch up with her as she practically ran through the crowds along the street.

"Chase, just take me home. To Florida. I don't want to do this anymore. I belong back in the Keys. I don't know these people. I don't know how to talk to them. I can't do it anymore."

Bailey suddenly stopped, practically collapsing against the wall of a vacant building. She could no longer hold back tears. Instantly, it was as though her eyes developed a constant stream of water that she couldn't turn off.

Chase held Bailey as she sobbed. He tried to calm her down by stroking her hair, holding her tight, and telling her everything would be OK. He didn't care about the odd stares they received from passersby. He only wanted to console this woman that had come to mean so much to him.

"It'll be OK. Come on. Let's go back to the house."

"I really want to go home. I feel like I'm going crazy. One minute, I'm laughing, having a good time, enjoying being here with you. Then the next minute, I'm in a panic, feeling like I'm about to have a nervous breakdown. I really can't handle it anymore. I want to be Bailey Parker, the woman I've come to know. Not Hailey Palmer – I have no idea who she is."

When they were finally back at the car, Chase carefully eased Bailey into the passenger seat. Her tears had stopped, but one look at her sweet face let anyone know that she was in distress. Her eyes were swollen and bright red. Bailey had finally cried the tears that she had been holding back so long, releasing the pent-up stress of everything. It was a physical release, but in her mind, she felt that she just wasn't up to going through this barrage of emotions.

"Bailey, do you remember what you told me just a little while earlier?" Chase asked as they began the drive back to her mother's house.

"We've talked about so many things."

"You thanked me. For pushing you to find out who you are."

"But I didn't expect to run into someone who knows me and then stand there like a fool, not knowing what to say. 'Oh, yes, I'm Hailey Palmer, but I have no clue who the hell she is. And I certainly don't know who you are. Because I have amnesia. Don't you feel sorry for me?'" Bailey's words and tone were now sarcastic, but she couldn't help it. She was at such a loss for how to act, what to say, how to feel.

"Dammit, Bailey," Chase said, "can't you see that people want to help you? That they are so happy to see you? Instead of feeling sorry for yourself, start appreciating that you have people who love you and are beyond relieved that you are here — alive!"

The words came out harsh before Chase could censure himself.

Bailey sat, stunned, by the manner of his words. It was like a slap in the face. He had never said anything like this, but his words give her pause to think.

"Hey, Bailey, I'm sorry. I should have never said anything like that. I don't know how you are feeling. I certainly don't know what I would do if I was in your shoes. Forgive me?" Chase reached for her hand and brought it to his lips.

"No, Chase, you are right. I've been making this all about me, and it's not. Like Tom said last night, this has affected the entire family, everyone that was a part of my life. I don't know what I'd do if you went missing and then years later, showed up on my doorstep."

"Bailey, you have a right to your feelings. I didn't mean anything like that, but you have to realize that everyone else is just doing their best, too. This is really hard on everyone, though you are definitely the one who has the worst of it."

Bailey looked at him, then reached over and gave him a kiss on the cheek. "It's really OK. I think I needed that little wake-up call."

35

"There you are," her mother said as Bailey and Chase walked into the house. "I thought you'd be back before now."

"We rode around, went to the beach, then had some lunch at the village. It's really nice."

"You and your friends used to spend quite the time there. Did anything look familiar?" her mother asked.

"Nothing, except someone recognized me. Piper's little sister?" Bailey said with trepidation.

"Oh, goodness! I haven't seen Piper since you went missing. She was devastated. You two were so close, best friends all through school. She is still married and has two children now."

Bailey listened as her mother talked about someone she had no clue about. She could hear the names, listen to the stories, but that really didn't help her, except for Bailey to know that she once had a life here in Carlsbad.

"Sharon, are there any pictures I can look at?" Bailey asked with a bit of hope.

"Pictures! Of course! I have several albums in here."

Bailey and Chase followed her into the family room, and she proceeded to take out one album after another, filled with photos and papers. Bailey finally got to see a picture of her dad, and a spark of recognition shone in her mind.

"This is the man I saw when I had that flash of a memory at the beach. You know, the one about surfing. That was my dad at the beach with me." Bailey looked at the picture, not wanting to let it go. "Can I have this?" she asked.

"Of course," Sharon said.

They sat on the couch for the next hour, going through pictures, Sharon telling Bailey and Chase who was in each one. Bailey found out some family history about aunts, uncles, grandmothers, and grandfathers. At times, Bailey felt like it was too much information to process, but then, like they had talked before, this was probably something her mother needed to do as much as Bailey needed to know about her family, so she let her mother share the stories.

The pictures of the family adventures around the globe sparked her interest the most. Bailey was fascinated over some of the places they had traveled to and suddenly wished she could remember each one. She had been to places that she had told herself that she would go to one day, like Egypt, New Zealand, and Peru. To know that she had already been there was both odd and exciting.

"And here is your personal collection of ziplining pictures. Actually, this was your book of pictures and brochures that you collected. After you went missing, I took it from your room and would look at it from time to time. You loved this so much that just to look at the pictures would bring me a little bit of peace about you being gone."

Bailey took the book from her mother's hands and saw a little redhead girl, in harnesses, ready to take a leap off a platform over trees. Other pictures showed canyons and rivers. The smile on the girl's face was one of pure joy and excitement. Through the photos, Bailey could see the progression of the little girl becoming a teenager, then a young woman. *This is me,* she thought to herself and smiled. For some reason, these images made her happy.

"Can I have this, too?" Bailey asked.

Sharon laughed. "Sweetheart, these are yours. I've just kept them safe for you till you could have them again."

For the first time since entering the house, Bailey suddenly felt something for the woman sitting beside her. It was strange sensation that swept over her. It was like Bailey knew in her soul that this woman loved her like a daughter.

"Thanks, Mom," Bailey said softly.

Sharon looked at Bailey with surprise as tears began to form in her eyes yet again. And before Bailey knew it, she was hugging her mother. It was an instant realization that this person was, in fact, her mother, though Bailey still couldn't remember details. But the love was certainly there.

"Thank you," Sharon said, her voice choked up.

"For what?" Bailey asked.

"For calling me 'mom'. You don't know how long I've waited to hear those words. I longed for them every day I didn't know what happened to you, and even more so after your father died."

"I wish I could have met him. Again," Bailey said tenderly, wondering if she would ever understand the bond that they had.

"I do, too. Just know that he loved you so much. Oh, and wait right here," Sharon said and quickly went to a small desk in the corner of the room. She opened a small drawer, taking something out of a box and bringing it back to the couch, where they were sitting among the pictures.

"I want you to have this." Her mother placed two seashells in her hand, one small and one larger. "Your father looked at these almost daily after you were gone."

"Why?" Bailey asked, staring at the shells in her hand.

"These were your shells. On one trip to the Keys, when you were about eight or so, you found these. You told him that the big one was him and the little one was you. You went on to say that when you found them on the beach that the big one had covered over the small one, protecting it, like he did you."

As Sharon placed the shells in Bailey's hand, Bailey couldn't help the flow of tears. The story was so beautiful, and the man she saw in the many pictures was suddenly coming alive in her mind.

"Are you still leaving tomorrow afternoon?" Sharon asked.

"Yes. We are heading back to San Diego. I need to see Dena and Stan. If it hadn't been for them, I have no clue what would have happened to me. And I need to see the place where the accident happened. I'm hoping that it will help bring me a little bit of closure. I know that sounds silly, but..."

"No, it doesn't. I only wished you didn't have to leave so soon. I have so much more to tell you. We need to talk about the house in Marathon."

"I still can't believe there has been a house there with my name on the deed. Why does it upset Tom so much if I helped purchase it?"

Sharon sat back on the couch and closed her eyes. "Your father's will stated that both of you girls would receive money. He left Heather a larger sum than you because he left you the house in the Keys. Tom feels that the house is worth more money than Heather received and doesn't think it's fair. He tried to get Heather to contest the will, and she refuses. You can imagine that didn't sit well with Tom and has caused a few problems in their marriage."

"Mom, is Tom older than Heather?"

"So, you could tell?" Sharon smiled. "He is eleven years older. He was one of your professors in college, but he and Heather didn't meet till after your disappearance, and they were married within seven months. It was only two months after that she was pregnant with Davis. I sometimes wonder if she got married just because of the strife we all felt with you being gone. Then Davis was born about a month before your dad passed away. It's been difficult for her, but Tom has been good to her. Now Davis keeps her busy. I guess I could say all of us have had our own way of dealing with what happened."

Hearing her mother's words brought back the conversation she and Chase had earlier. Or should she say, when Chase told her to stop the pity party. The statement her mother just made only proved that he was right.

"Have you talked to Heather today?" Bailey asked.

"She is supposed to be here in just a little bit. I know she wants to talk to you, but she was really embarrassed by how Tom acted last night."

"I was hoping we could talk before I go."

"I'm sure she will come by."

No sooner had the conversation ended than the front door opened and shut. Bailey looked up to see her big sister standing in front of her.

■ ■ ■

"I'm sorry that Tom was such a jerk last night. I've tried going over everything with him yet again, but I think right now, all he sees are dollar signs. Bailey, he really isn't the man you saw last night."

The two sisters were walking down the street, through the neighborhood that Bailey was sure she had once been familiar with, but she could remember nothing.

"What about you? How do you feel about how dad left things?"

"I honestly don't have a problem with it. That is where Tom thinks I've lost it. You loved the Keys. I still remember you and Dad down there. You two thought it was the best place in the world. I didn't care as long as we were on a trip. I just loved to travel.

"If we had that house, I would have sold it as soon as I could because the Keys just don't hold my interest. But now that you are living there, I might have to come and visit. You know, a girls' weekend – or maybe make that a week." Heather laughed, making Bailey smile.

"We were really close, weren't we?" Bailey asked.

"You could say that. When you went missing, I was a wreck, but I couldn't let Mom or Dad know. They were feeling so guilty about how things had been when you left. I felt guilty because I was in Los Angeles and was so involved with my career that I didn't even take the time to check up on you. I know that you'd have given me your address if I had just taken your calls. But I was working for an assistant producer for a TV show and thought that I was just too busy for everyone."

"What happened when you found out I was missing?"

"I came home to try to help, and in the process, I lost my job. But now I can see where that was a blessing because Mom and Dad were lost. They needed me here. Then I met Tom, and before I knew it, we were married, and I was pregnant."

"Mom told me that Tom was one of my professors at school?"

"That he was. Now he's working at the tech company that you worked for before you started planning events," Heather laughed.

"What's so funny?" Bailey asked.

"Just how life works. You leave a job that you were basically trained for by my husband. You leave to do what you really love, and then he gets the job you left behind. Well, kinda. He's with the company, but not the same position you had."

"After all this, will your husband ever like me? You know, with the house and all?"

"Just have to give him some time. I know he is already embarrassed about what happened. He let his temper get the best of him after he promised that he would keep his opinions to himself."

"I hope he really doesn't think I planned this. Because believe me, I didn't. I think the timing was just that. Some would call it a coincidence, but then again, I don't believe in that anymore. I think things happen like they are supposed to, so you learn and become a better person."

"Wow, listen to you. You sound like a philosopher instead of a wedding planner," Heather remarked and linked her arm into Bailey's.

"Maybe that smack on the head did me some good?" Bailey smirked.

"Little sister, you were already a sweet person, just very stubborn and headstrong. But I think that has served you well these last years. If I was in your place, I probably would've crumbled and crawled into a hole somewhere."

"After what I've seen – you taking care of your child, taking care of Mom, and married? You seem pretty tough yourself," Bailey said and suddenly remembered a question she wanted to ask. "Last night, you indicated that something was wrong with Mom. You said dementia, but she seemed perfectly fine today."

"It just seems to come and go. There is no rhyme or reason. I'm hoping, now that you are here again, things might get better for her. It might just be stress, at least that's what I'm hoping."

"I think you both should come to the Keys, along with Tom and Davis," Bailey said with a laugh.

"Do you have to leave tomorrow? It's so soon."

"I need to spend tomorrow in San Diego and see Dena. If it wasn't for her, I truly wouldn't be here. I'm going back to that street corner where it all happened. I need closure. But then I need to get back to Florida. My boss was truly wonderful by letting me come out here. She's really a friend now and understood the circumstances, but she is still recuperating from that broken leg, and I have to get back and help her. Can you imagine taking care of a wedding, hobbling around on crutches? I haven't heard from her, so I'm hoping things are going well."

"You like your job?"

"I really do. And I'm good at it. Now I know why," Bailey laughed as she now knew why the business had come so naturally to her. "Weddings in the Keys are pretty popular, and she is probably the most in demand planner in the upper Keys. Chase and I were doing all the weddings after she got hurt. So, I need to get back and help her with some weddings. We have five in a row coming up."

"People get married during the week?" Heather asked as they began their walk back toward the house.

"It's a big destination spot for weddings. I think since I've worked with Mandy, I've done a wedding every day. On beaches, in hotels, on boats, even arranged one that was held underwater, if you can believe that."

"Seriously?" Heather asked.

"Yep."

"No wonder you like this wedding planning stuff. Seems to be exciting."

"Sometimes, it's hectic, but even so, I really enjoy what I do."

"And you love it there, don't you? The Keys?"

"It feels like home," Bailey said.

"So, tell me about Chase. Is this pretty serious between you two? You know I wouldn't be doing my sisterly duties if I didn't ask about it."

Bailey leaned against her, and that same sense of familiarity flooded through her again.

"Yeah, it's getting there. I can't imagine my life without him."

"Then I would call that serious," Heather quipped.

"You're probably right."

"Hai... I mean, Bailey, I hope that we can be close again. I know that things will never be the same, but I want my sister back again. Even if we are three thousand miles apart."

Bailey looked at her sister and was so happy. This was part of what she was seeking when she came to California. That family she so hoped would be there for her.

"I want that, too. You know there is always FaceTime or Skype. That would be a great way to catch up and also allow me to see Davis grow up," Bailey said as they started walking back toward their mother's house. When they reached the home, Tom's car was in the driveway.

"I promise tonight will not be a repeat," Heather said. "I will make sure of that."

"Watch my big sister go," Bailey said, allowing herself to feel something and not be so scared. She was finally letting go of the past and moving forward into her future.

36

"I think I have everything packed up and ready to go," Bailey said as Chase entered her room.

"Did you take any pictures last night of this place?" he said, gesturing around to the place where they stood.

"No, not really. This might have been my room at one time, but it isn't anymore. To me, it is the pictures from the past and that old, beat-up teddy bear that mean so much. Those are the things I want to take back home with me."

"Well, I think I took enough pictures for all of you last night. I'm sure that you don't have any room on your phone till you can download them onto your computer."

"Ha-ha," Bailey said, rolling her eyes at him.

"How do you feel about leaving this morning?"

"I'm OK. I can't say that I still don't have a bunch of questions, but they'll just have to be answered over time. I don't know why I thought that I could learn everything I wanted to know in just a day or two. I guess that was wishful thinking."

"I personally think you have done excellent so far."

"The next big test is San Diego and seeing Dena. She was a lifeline for me, and I never really got back in touch with her. I hope I can make it right."

Chase put his arms around her, hoping that it would give her some comfort and peace as she went on the next leg of this journey. "I know it will work out."

"Especially if I have you around to kick my butt into gear, like you did yesterday," Bailey declared.

"There are other things I would rather do with you than kick your butt. Maybe-" but Chase was cut off by the knock on the door.

"Bailey, is it OK for me to come in?" It was her mom.

"Sure."

"Oh, hi, Chase. Glad you are here, too. I wanted to talk to you both before we went out in the kitchen. Heather, Tom, and Davis are here, but there is one more thing I need to discuss with you before you leave. Come sit," and Sharon sat on the edge of the bed.

"Here is the necessary paperwork you need for the house in Marathon. I have all the papers, deed, the rental agency name – everything you need is in the envelope. I've already talked to my lawyer, and the house is being transferred back into your name. Plus, the money your father left you will be deposited into your bank account when you get back and can give me your bank information. Then make sure you secure a lawyer, too. Let them handle these transactions to make sure you are protected."

"I trust you, mom."

"Bailey, in your mind, you haven't really known me that long. We've only spent a few days together. It's just safer to make sure this is done through a lawyer, OK, sweetheart? Chase, will you make sure she finds someone? Also, with you working in real estate, you can help her with the house?"

"My brother and sister will definitely be able to help out there, but Bailey has a good business sense about her."

"Well, maybe the house will suit you, and you can live in it instead of your apartment. I have a feeling you are going to love it. I know your father did. But every time he went there, he could never get any peace about it because you were gone. So, make that house happy. Fill it up with people and new memories."

"Then that means you are going to come and visit me, right?"

"Not sure about that. This woman is getting old."

"Nonsense," Bailey said. "Let me get things situated, and then you and Heather are coming to see me. Promise?"

Sharon looked at Bailey and smiled broadly. "OK, it's a promise."

They made their way into the family room, where they were promptly greeted by everyone. Heather had a present for her that she made Bailey open right away. It was a picture frame with two photos in it: one of the two of them when they were teenagers on a trip in Australia, and then a picture that

Chase had taken on Heather's phone only the night before. Bailey gave her sister a tight hug and put the treasured frame in her tote bag.

Tom unexpectedly hugged his newly-found sister-in-law and once again apologized for his behavior. Bailey told him that everything was fine and that he had better take very good care of her sister, nephew, and her mother.

"You ready to head to San Diego?" George asked, looking at Bailey with that bright smile of his.

"I think we are."

As they all walked to the car, Bailey could feel the love coming from the house now. She knew that she belonged here. The feeling was seeping into her soul and as far as she was concerned, it was that part of her brain waking up from its deep sleep.

"Thank you for being so welcoming. For answering so many questions. Just be prepared for me to ask many more. I really want to know everything about my life and remember anything if I can. But if the memories don't all come back, it's OK now because I'm making new ones with you." Bailey hugged her sister one more time, then spent a little extra time embracing her mom. "Thank so much. Just remember your promise to me."

"I will. Be safe," Sharon said, and Bailey could see she was doing her best not to cry.

As Bailey and Chase headed toward the waiting vehicle, another car quickly pulled into the driveway, coming to a sudden stop. A man nearly jumped out of the driver's seat and practically ran to where they stood.

Bailey immediately recognized him and the panicky feelings that she thought had finally been erased were suddenly flooding her mind. It was the man from the park at the Seven Mile Bridge in the Keys. What was he doing here?

"Daniel?" Sharon said coming to stand beside Bailey.

Bailey felt shocked as she stood looking at the man, hearing her mother say the name of her ex-boyfriend. She remembered how she felt that day in the park. She was angry and couldn't figure out why. And now as she peered into this man's face, she could put some of the pieces together for why she felt the way she did.

"Hi Hailey," Daniel said looking only at her.

"Daniel, why are you here?" Sharon asked.

"I ran into Morgan and she told me Hailey was back." Daniel continued to stare at Bailey like maybe he was afraid she might disappear.

"Hailey, can we go somewhere and talk?" Daniel asked.

"We're just getting ready to leave," Chase said protectively, putting his arm around Bailey's waist.

"I promise it won't take long but I've got to talk to you. To tell you how sorry I am."

Bailey looked from Chase to her mother and back to the man named Daniel, wondering what to do.

"Why don't we all go back inside for just a minute," Sharon suggested.

"I need to talk to Hailey alone." Daniel tone was emphatic.

"I don't think so." This time Chase spoke up again.

"Daniel, my name is Bailey. I'm sorry but I don't remember you but I did see you in the Keys."

"Can I please come in? We need to talk."

Bailey shook her head "yes" and everyone went back inside, each taking a seat in the family room. To make things a bit quieter, Tom took Davis out back to play so everyone else could talk.

"Can we be alone please?" Daniel asked again.

"Whatever you have to say to me, my family can hear it to." Bailey was not about to be alone with a man that was causing her this much distress inside because she was feeling that same anger like she did when she saw him in Florida.

Daniel hung his head down and sighed. "That's fine."

"So what is going on?" Chase asked.

"I had to come and tell you how sorry I am," Daniel said, his eyes not leaving Bailey. "I didn't think I'd ever get this chance. Everyone told me you were missing, probably dead. When I heard you were here, I couldn't believe it."

"Sorry for what? And why were you in the Florida Keys?" Bailey asked.

"I was searching for you."

"How would you know about Florida?"

"Hell, every time we talked about going on a trip, that was the one place you always brought up," Daniel said, smiling for the first time since arriving.

"But why try to find me? Mom said that you broke up with me when I decided to move to San Diego." Bailey was feeling more aggravated the more he talked.

"Because I was an idiot. I should've never let you go. You were the best thing that ever happened to me." Daniel looked around at the other faces in the room, clearly embarrassed, but not enough to stop saying what he came here for.

"Every time you called, I kept saying that it was over but deep down, I just wanted you to stay here. I kept thinking that if I said no, you would relent and not go. But you did and that made me angry."

"Because you didn't get your way?" Bailey asked curtly.

"I guess you could say that. But then I decided that I wanted to see you but you wouldn't answer my calls. So I sent you a text."

Bailey suddenly felt like she had been hit by electricity as the memory flooded her brain. "I was texting you when Dena pulled me out of the street. I remember."

"Bailey, take deep breaths." Bailey could hear the worried voices of Chase and her mother but didn't want to open her eyes.

"Sweetheart, it's fine. You're OK."

Bailey finally looked out, she could see Chase kneeling in front of her with her mom and Heather close behind. But her eyes found Daniel's as he continued to sit across the room.

"What's wrong?" Daniel asked.

"She has amnesia you asshole!" Chase said, wanting to go across the room and punch the man in the face.

Daniel looked dumbstruck. "I didn't know."

"I'm fine. I just remembered what happened right before the accident. I was sending Daniel a text. I remember feeling so mad then being yanked backwards and that's it. Next thing I can recall was waking up in a hospital."

"Hailey..." Daniel started.

"It's Bailey!"

"Bailey, I'm so sorry. I admit – I was a jerk. When I found out that you were missing, I was a mess. All I could think about was our last conversations and that text."

"What did the text say?" Bailey asked.

"That I was coming to San Diego," Daniel said slowly. "I loved you. In a way I think I still do after all these years. That's why I went searching for you. My parents told me I was being ridiculous to even think I could find you because everyone said you were gone. I refused to believe it. If I could find you, I was hoping we could talk, try to work things out. You saw me at the bridge?"

"I did and I felt so angry. At the time I couldn't understand why seeing a stranger made me feel that way. Daniel, I don't even remember you."

The room was silent, everyone trying to digest what just happened.

Daniel was the first to stand up, looking sheepishly at Bailey and then to Chase. "I really didn't know. I heard you were back in town and I had to see you. To at least apologize if nothing else, though I can't lie and say I didn't want more than that when I planned on coming here."

"I'm sorry I can't help you. I wished I could remember more but even if I did, it wouldn't change the way I feel about things in my life now." Bailey took ahold of Chase's hand, hoping that Daniel would get the hint.

"Well, now that I made a fool of myself, I'm going to go." Daniel heading toward the door quickly but Bailey stopped him.

"I'll walk out with you." Bailey glanced back at Chase who looked concerned but she reassured him with a gentle smile that everything was going to be fine.

"Daniel, I want to thank you," Bailey said once they were alone on the front porch.

"What for?" he said surprised.

"For giving me some more pieces of the puzzle I'm trying to put together called my life. The last four years have been rough, not knowing who I was. I heard that we were pretty close, even talked about getting married."

"Yes we did," Daniel said, a slight grin on his face. "But I can see you have someone else in your life now. Just know that if he doesn't take good care of you, he'll have to answer to me."

"You don't have to worry about that. He already does."

Bailey watched as Daniel's car went out the driveway and down the street. Though the morning had been stressful, she had closed another chapter on her previous life. Though she couldn't remember the events surrounding the relationship between her and her former boyfriend, the anger she had felt when she saw him earlier had melted away. Bailey was finally making peace with her past a little at a time.

37

Bailey helped Chase put their luggage into the back of the rental car. When they were settled in, she put the address for Dena's house into her GPS and soon they were navigating the streets, making their way to another place that would help Bailey connect with her past. She remembered this town, but these memories weren't happy ones. They were of fear, anger, and frustration. The one shining spot here was Dena and how kind she and her husband, Stan, had been to her. But now she said a small prayer, hoping that the couple would accept her apology.

As Bailey looked around she recalled how she had ridden down these roads time and again, looking for clues to her identity.

After she was released from the hospital, she and Dena tried to find out who she was, where she had lived, and more. Bailey's anger would flare, and even though she wasn't verbal,

Dena would soothe her, almost like taking care of a small child. Dena and Stan had even given her a car, the one she still had to this day, and money to start her life over again. How someone could be so unselfish and help a person they didn't know like they did still amazed Bailey. But then she had gone to Florida and lost touch with them.

As they pulled up to the couple's home, Bailey remembered it all. It looked completely the same as it had over four years ago. Bailey recalled coming here the day she had left the hospital and how scared she had been. Those feelings of anxiety were back now, but this time it was for a different reason.

"Are you ready?" Chase asked, once again taking her hand, stroking the back of it like he was giving her a shot of courage.

"I hope they forgive me."

"Well, you don't have to wait too long to find out. They must've heard us pull up."

Bailey turned and looked out her window to see a man and woman standing just outside the door to the house.

"Bailey!" Dena rushed to her and had her in a hug before Bailey knew what was happening. The warm embrace calmed Bailey's fast beating heart about this reunion.

"You look terrific. I'm so happy you are here. Come in!" Dena was pulling Bailey along, and she could only look back to Chase with wide eyes as he followed.

"Thanks for letting us come by," Bailey said.

"We would've been mad if you hadn't," Stan said, giving her a hug as soon as Dena released her hand.

"This is my boyfriend, Chase," Bailey said, making introductions between everyone.

"I hope you have been taking good care of her."

"Only when she lets me. She is pretty independent," Chase said, beaming as he looked at Bailey.

"Don't we know that! Come in and take a seat," Dena said, guiding them to the living room.

"The house still looks great," Bailey said. "And you, too. How have things been?"

"Stan still works at the bank, and I'm the secretary – or should I say assistant – at the church office. Still go hiking as much as possible. Same old stuff. The more important question is: how are _you_?"

Bailey shuffled her feet, wondering how to start. "I'm doing fine. I have a great life in Florida." And then she paused. "Dena – Stan – I'm so sorry. I should've called you more often. I should've paid you back by now. Everything you did for me, most of all saving my life. I feel like I just abandoned you as friends."

"Bailey, don't worry about that. From the moment you stepped into our lives, we knew we wanted to help you. We didn't do it for anything, but to help you find your way," Dena said, coming to sit beside her.

"But you kept me from being hit by a truck! You visited me almost daily, and then you bring me, a complete stranger, into your home. You gave me a car and money when I decided I needed to leave. You deserved better from me as a friend."

"We knew that you had to find your own way, Bailey. And when we gave you that car and money, we did it because we wanted to, not because we expected something in return. We both just agreed it was the right thing to do. Did you come here today, thinking we were going to be mad?"

"Yes!" Bailey exclaimed.

"Didn't you stay with us long enough to know that we aren't like that?" Stan said cheerfully.

"Yes, but people aren't like that."

"There are more people that err on the side of kindness than you realize," Dena said. "It's just that we don't hear about it that often. It seems like everyone likes the hate and drama in society. But then again, we don't help people to gain recognition. We do it because we like helping others."

"Bailey is so lucky that you were on that street that day," Chase said softly.

"I have to admit, I was scared myself after all that happened."

"Dena, can you tell me again what happened? I just talked to my mom, and she said that things were a bit strained in the family because I wanted to move here to work with a large event planning company. I left without even giving them my address. I just moved. What do you remember?" Bailey asked hopefully.

"You were just texting as you walked. I was behind you for about a block, and I do remember thinking that I was surprised that you hadn't walked into a telephone pole or something," Dena laughed. "But then we were slowing down to stop at the street corner. You did, too, but you were still texting. You seemed very keyed up, like you were frustrated, but you never uttered a word. Then, suddenly, you stepped out into traffic.

The only thing I can think of was that you thought it was time to walk across the intersection for some reason.

"When I saw that delivery truck coming, I just acted. I've never done anything like that before or since! I grabbed you by your arm and jerked back so hard. Your phone went flying into the street, but you and I felt back on the pavement. There were several people around, and I remember someone calling 911. I looked over at you to see blood on the pavement. I honestly thought you were dead and that I had killed you by trying to help!

"I crawled over to you and realized that you were breathing, just knocked out. The blood was coming from a cut on the back of your head."

"What about you?" Chase asked. "Were you hurt?"

"Only some scrapes and bruises, but they sent me to the hospital, too, once the emergency people and police got there. After I was cleared to go home, I wanted to see you, but they wouldn't let me. All I knew was that you were in serious condition with head trauma. I came to the hospital every day, but it wasn't till you woke that they let me see you. The doctors were hoping that if you saw me, maybe you would remember something. And that is how we became friends."

"I remember those first days," Bailey said quietly. "It felt surreal. It was like I knew some things, and I didn't know others. I remember when I got out of bed for the first time, thinking, 'How do I know how to do this?' It was such a weird sensation. The doctors would show me objects and ask me questions to see what I knew. Things like forks, shoes, pens. I thought they were nuts, but then I couldn't recall my name, my age, parents, friends. That's when the panic set in. They had to give me medicine to calm me down. It was horrible." Bailey shuddered as she remembered that day.

"But then a little while after the doctor left, you came in," Bailey said, looking at Dena. "You were so sweet. I had no idea who you were until the nurse said that you were the reason I was alive. You sat and told me this story. I'm sorry to ask you to repeat it again. I'm just trying to put puzzle pieces together."

"Have any of your memories returned since you've been back to California?"

"I've had a few flashbacks. It started not too long ago in Florida. Then when we got here to California, I remembered a few things like my Dad, what our house looked like. I also found out that I was texting a boyfriend that had broken up with me for moving to San Diego. That's why I wasn't paying attention that day and stepped out in front of the truck," Bailey said.

"Oh, wow!," Dena said as Stan just looked at her a bit amazed. "Was your family able to help with more details?"

"My mom and sister are great. I have a suitcase full of things they gave me to take back to Florida. I don't really remember the people and places in the pictures or the other things they made me pack to bring back to the Keys, but I'm hoping in time I'll remember."

"At least there is a bit of progress. But tell us about Florida. We only talked a few times after you left. I think the last time was just as you got there." Dena's and Stan's faces were so relaxed and kind that Bailey still couldn't get over the fact that they weren't upset about her leaving and losing touch with them after all they did.

"When I got to Florida, I just knew to keep going south for some reason. I ended up in Key West. It was all so new to me. The city was so relaxed, and I felt like it was where I belonged. Once I crossed over into Key Largo, that feeling came over me. And now I know why."

"What happened?" Stan asked curiously.

"My mom informed me that my dad and I had a particular love of those islands. The two of us would travel there almost every year. So much so that right before my disappearance, it seems that the two of us bought a house together on Marathon. My dad, mostly, but my name was put on the deed."

"You have a house in the Keys you didn't even know of?" Dena asked excitedly.

"Seems that way. We'll be checking it out when we get back home. It caused a bit of family turmoil at first when I found out. Apparently, my brother-in-law didn't think it was fair that my father left it to me in his will."

"Your father is gone?" Dena asked softly.

"Yes," Bailey said, not elaborating any further.

"Oh, Bailey, I'm so sorry."

"My mom gave me a bunch of pictures of him and me, even one of the two of us in front of the house we bought. It's beautiful and looks like nothing I could ever afford, but when my father passed away, the insurance paid it off."

"That's such a blessing. Did you have your own house already?"

"Oh, no. I wasn't making enough as a restaurant manager to afford that. I did have a nice little apartment in Key West, though. I liked it there, but one day, someone asked for me, and when I saw him, I had this creepy feeling, so I left Key West. I just left a note for my boss, packed up my stuff, and basically run away from the city."

"But she ended up in Islamorada. That is where we met," Chase said, placing his hand on her knee.

"I knew I couldn't leave the islands. I kept feeling like there was a connection there, but as much as I wanted to, I couldn't figure it out. After a while, I tried to let it go. Most of the time, I was successful, but other times, I felt like I'd go crazy unless I figured out why I had this feeling about the Keys. But then I met Chase." Bailey looked at him, and the love she felt for him was growing stronger every day, especially how he had been there for her these last few days.

Bailey went on to tell them about her life in Islamorada: her work as a wedding planner, her friends, her apartment, and more.

"I'm actually ready to go back now, especially since I know more about my past. I haven't remembered as many things as I had hoped, but maybe over time and with help from my mom and family, those memories will return. If not, I'm already making new ones. But there is something I learned that was a bit of a shock."

"Other than your father?"

"I also learned that I was adopted at birth."

"Really?" Dena said with surprise.

"Yes, I'm the only redhead in our family," Bailey said with a small laugh.

"Are you going to look for your birth mom?" Stan asked.

"I don't think so. It's hard enough to remember my family now. To bring another stranger into my life at the moment would only complicate things further. Plus, my whole goal was to find out as much as I could about my past, then move on. Start new." With those words, Bailey was transported back to one of the last weddings they did, where she and Chase danced while he sang her that song. *Let go of the past and start anew.*

"Bailey, I'm so impressed. You're handling everything so wonderfully. I can't say I'd do the same if I were in your shoes," Dena remarked.

"I do have a favor to ask you. Can we go to the street where the accident happened? I wondered if it might trigger something for me."

"Of course, but why don't we get a bite to eat first? Stan and I want to take you both to lunch. I know you can't stay all day and you're leaving in the morning, but I want to take you to that little diner we ate at after you came to live with us. Do you remember it?"

Bailey smiled. "I loved that little place. It's still there?"

"Joyce will never shut that diner down. I don't care if the buildings around it are crumbling to the ground," Dena laughed.

"I don't blame her because I do remember the food was good."

"Maybe not good for you, but it sure tastes wonderful. Stan and I splurge there every so often."

"Now you can see why I'm glad you decided to stop by." Stan's laugh was one that Bailey couldn't help but love. These two people in front of her had been a lifeline for her, and there was no way she could ever repay them for their kindness.

"Before we leave, I have to ask you one question. What is your real name?" Dena asked softly.

"Hailey Palmer."

"Wow! When you picked your new name, you were so close. You knew even then, though you couldn't think of it completely. I believe your memories are going to return more quickly now that you came back home," Dena said softly.

"I hope you are right, but after learning some things about our family from my mom, they might be painful, too. I guess it's a blessing and a curse."

"From what I've seen you go through this far, there is not a doubt in my mind that you can handle it, Bailey Parker."

38

Bailey stood on the street corner, surveying all that was around her. She glanced at the buildings, the sidewalk, and the very spot where Dena had pulled her to safety. Nothing. No triggers and no memory. None of the shops looked even remotely familiar. The only thing she did remember was walking and texting plus that horrible feeling of anger.

After the accident, Dena had brought her by here, but it was so fresh that Bailey had only stood on the spot for a few minutes till she was ready to leave. And she had never been back till this day.

"Do you recognize anything?" Chase asked as he stood beside her.

"Nothing," Bailey said, disappointment clearly in her voice.

"Why don't you try taking a bunch of pictures? When you get back home, you can look at them again and see if anything happens. At least you'll have them to look at if you ever feel like you need to."

Bailey nodded and proceeded to take pictures of everything she could that surrounded her. She stood there one last time and told herself that if other memories didn't resurface, it would be OK. She had so many loved ones that they were her priority now.

"I think I'm ready to go," Bailey said, taking Chase's hand and walking back to the car, where Dena and Stan had waited for them.

"Any luck?" Dena said as they got in the car.

"No, except for what I told you about earlier, but it's OK. I'm glad I came back here. I remember when I got to Florida, I swore I'd never return to this spot, but I'm glad Chase convinced me to. He said I needed closure, and I think that is what I got today."

"To close the past and move forward. Sounds like great advice," Stan said.

It wasn't long before they were back at the house, and Bailey knew it was time to leave. They had to get the rental car back to the airport because their flight was leaving early in the morning.

"I sure wish you could spend a couple of days with us," Dena said, her arm wrapped in Bailey's as they headed for the front door.

"I think that you and Stan should come to Florida. If this house is nice and I keep it, I want people to visit. My mom told me to fill it up with new memories, friends, and family. That's what my dad would've wanted."

"She is probably right. I'll let you know on that trip. Stan and I have never been to Florida, and it would be nice to get away."

"I think you would love it, especially the Keys. They are like little tropical islands, with such a soothing mood that it's hard not to fall in love with them. I knew from the minute I was there that it was where I was meant to be. Little did I know that I had been there so many times before."

"I'm so happy for you, Bailey. You deserve it. You've worked hard to get this far, and I think the best is yet to come. Especially with such a handsome young man by your side. I think if I were you, I would hang on to him," Dena said, winking at her.

"I plan to."

Bailey smiled and gave her friend one last hug, but before she walked out the door, she paused.

"There is one more thing," Bailey said, turning to face the couple. "You did so much for me those frightening days after the accident. Coming to the hospital. Letting me talk endlessly about my fears and feelings. Then opening your house to a stranger. You gave me food, shelter, and then when I insisted on leaving, you gave me a car, which I still have, and enough money to live on till I could get on my own two feet. That kindness can never be repaid. I have no idea how to, but I want to do the same thing for someone one day. Just hopefully, not with my circumstances, though," Bailey smirked. "But here." Bailey reached into her tote bag and brought out a large envelope.

"What is this?" Dena asked, unsealing the folded paper that was placed in her hands. Inside was the money that equaled the car and the amount that this generous couple had given her that day she left town.

"I had to give you cash because I knew that if I wrote a check, you'd never cash it."

Dena quickly thrust it out for Bailey to take back. "We can't take this, Bailey. That was for you."

"Dena – Stan – please. I need to give this to you for all that you did for me. Use it to help someone else just like you did me. You two are so special that I don't believe you realize what a blessing you are to all those around you. I don't believe that it was a coincidence that day that you were behind me," Bailey said, looking at Dena and grasping her hands. "Someone put you there because I was going to need help, and you were the one that would do it for me." Bailey hugged her friend again, tears streaming out of both women's eyes. She then hugged Stan once more.

"Thank you for giving me my life back. I tell everyone you were my guardian angel, and I believe that with all my heart."

"Thank you, Bailey," Dena said, her words almost a whisper.

As they drove away from the house, Bailey looked back to see the couple waving, with Dena still wiping tears from her eyes. Bailey realized that this couple had been so instrumental in helping her put her life back together, and there were no words to express the gratitude she felt.

"Are you ready to head home?" Chase said.

"I think so. It's been such an emotional trip, I think I need a bit of routine. The peace and quiet of the Keys sounds so good right now, to help me process all that I've – no, *we've* been through. I'm so lucky that I met you that day. I think you are also my good luck charm."

"What do you mean?"

"Well, my life was a little dull till I met you."

"Is that a good thing or bad?" Chase asked, grinning.

"Well there have been a few bumps, especially a dark-haired girl that is determined that you belong to her, but mostly good. No, make that great."

"Now there is the Bailey I fell in love with. I know these past few days have been rough, but you have handled them so wonderfully. Might have to call you my Wonder Woman."

"Your woman?" Bailey asked.

"Oh, yes, you are definitely mine."

■ ■ ■

Waking up in her own bed felt most wonderful. As a matter of fact, the minute the plane touched down in Miami, Bailey's body seemed to just relax, realizing that she was back home. But now things had more meaning.

As she looked out the window at the swaying palm trees, she realized that she had shared some wonderful times here with her family. That made this place even more special than it was before she left. Plus, now she had a house to go see about. But her first priority had to be checking on Mandy.

The whole time she had been in California, with everything that had happened, she hadn't once called to check on Mandy. But nor did her phone ring, showing that Mandy had not needed her. Bailey could only assume that everything had gone off without any problems. At least she hoped that was the case.

After she got dressed, Bailey quickly put her work tote together again. It felt good to be back, and she really looked forward to seeing her friend, hoping everything had fared well. Also, that she and Dennis were still getting along and not arguing or worse, finding out that he had gone back to Key West, leaving Mandy by herself.

Chase was going to meet with her later at the office to go over the schedule for all the upcoming weddings, but he had a few things he had to do after being gone. Plus, he was going to talk to Harris and contact a lawyer to help Bailey with the new house. With a rental company involved, Chase wasn't sure what the protocol was in case Bailey wanted to make this home her own.

Bailey wasn't sure what to do about the house. She could sell it and have a nice little nest egg in the bank, which would solve a lot of issues, but then her father had left her a large sum of money along with the house. Since the two-year "waiting" agreement had passed while Bailey was missing, the money from her father was hers to use as she saw fit, and her mother was depositing the money in the bank today. At this point, Bailey could get a nice house closer to work, still be near Chase, and continue to rent the other house on Marathon. She had a lot of options, and that helped so much.

Bailey walked into the office and was immediately taken aback by the young girl that sat at her desk.

"Hi! Can I help you?" Her cheerful demeanor was nice, and Bailey smiled, thinking that Mandy had finally hired a receptionist.

"Hi. I'm Bailey, Mandy's assistant."

"Bailey!" The voice from behind the partition seemed to scream out. "You're back! I thought you would be gone longer." Mandy came around her desk as quickly as she could on crutches.

"You'd better slow down, or you are going to be back on bed rest," Bailey said, laughing and hugging the woman tightly. "I found out what I needed to know and came back. You need me, remember?"

"Well, I know how important it was to talk to your family but I'm so glad you're here. Things are super busy! But I have to tell you first I'm so grateful for you. I didn't realize till you were gone just how much you did for me. Lacey has been a sweetheart, answering phone calls and helping where she could."

Bailey turned to the girl. "Nice to meet you, Lacey. Before I left, Mandy was saying how we needed to hire someone to man the office phones. Maybe this is permanent?" Bailey turned to Mandy with hopeful eyes.

"Not sure about that. Lacey is going to college online, so this kinda fits with her schedule, but we have some other things to work out. Come back here and give me details. How did things go?"

Bailey helped Mandy to her desk, then took the seat across from her. "It was a lot to take in. There is so much to tell that I think a lunch date might be in order. Then we will come back, and I'll get to work."

"Sounds wonderful. Lacey, we'll be back in a while. Do you have everything covered here?"

"I sure do, Ms. Thompson. I'll call you if something comes up I can't handle."

The two women went to Bailey's car, Mandy maneuvering her crutches very well, even putting a bit of weight on her leg.

"Are you supposed to be walking like that yet?"

"Maybe not like that, but the doctor said I could put some weight on it now. Have to say it still hurts like hell, but its better. Still can't believe I fell down those damn stairs."

Once they were seated at an outdoor table at the Lorelei Restaurant, Mandy immediately wanted to know all the details of the trip. Bailey recounted everything that she could while Mandy stayed absolutely silent, seeming to soak in every single word that Bailey said.

"I can't believe you were adopted," Mandy remarked. "That had to be another whammy when you found out. But you also own a house in Marathon? I bet you're still reeling from information overload."

"You could certainly say that."

"So, when are you going to go see the house?" Mandy asked before taking a bite of her sandwich.

"As soon as I know what the wedding schedule is. Plus, Chase is helping me find a lawyer, and Harris, his brother, is going to help in case I have problems with the rental company."

"Man, I'm happy you two are together. I always wondered if Chase would stay a lonely bachelor after his break-ups, or if he would finally let that guard down and give in."

"I could say the same about you. How are things going with Dennis since I've been gone?" Bailey asked.

"Things have been fine," Mandy said casually, but Bailey could read between the lines. She saw the little twinkle in Mandy's eyes at the mention of her ex-husband's name.

"Do I see a reunion of sorts for you two?" Bailey asked excitedly.

"Don't go getting your hopes up for us two. We are kinda set in our ways. And Dennis still likes to go out and be part of the crowd. That's why Key West suits him fine. But we've also changed, too. Maybe I could use the words 'mellowed out at bit'. We sure have done our share of talking since my tumble down the steps. Even an argument here and there, but that was mostly when he'd do something at a wedding that was just pure crazy. Couldn't imagine what he was thinking some-times," Mandy said, shaking her head.

"Need to give him some slack. He's not an event planner, remember? He's not used to this business. Speaking of Dennis, where is he now?" Bailey asked curiously.

"He went back to Key West yesterday to get a few things and take care of some business. He is due back today. Kept saying he didn't want to leave me by myself, but I think I did OK. He did make sure that everything I needed for yesterday and today was within my reach. Even fixed my meals ahead of time. It's those things he does where I can tell that he has changed a lot. He would've never done that when we were younger."

"I guess we all evolve over time," Bailey said. "Even though I don't remember my sister and parents, from the stories I heard, they have changed over the years. And my disappearance facilitated a lot of that."

"I can't believe all this time, you were an event planner. No wonder you were such a natural at this job. I remember after that first day, when it seemed like you just knew what to do at the wedding, I was super impressed. Everything you did was like you had worked with a planner before, but all you had on your resume was the restaurant. And I was so desperate that day that I didn't even look to see you had no job history before that. I think things just worked out like they were supposed to."

"It seems like that's the sentiment that has been discussed a lot in my world lately. Almost to the point of being overwhelming."

"I can imagine."

As they sat at the restaurant, enjoying the sunny weather and the view of the water before them, Bailey had a quick thought: had she and her dad ever eaten at this restaurant? She knew that probably for the foreseeable future, this thought would always be in the back of her mind. But she decided that she would just assume that they had been everywhere together since, according to her mother, they had loved these Keys as much as their California home.

"Are you OK?" Mandy asked as she was finishing her sandwich.

"Yeah. Just thinking."

"Well, are you ready for some wedding work? While you were gone, we picked up four more weddings. At least they are a few months away, but one is pretty big, and talk about a bridezilla. Whoa! I was just waiting for you to get back, so I can let you handle her. I don't think I have the patience anymore with some of these younger brides. Give me the older ones any day of the week."

Bailey laughed, and it felt so good to be back where she belonged. Looking forward to getting back into her normal routine was something that she relished right now.

Back at the office, they moved desks around and situated Lacey up front to be able to greet anyone who should happen to walk through the door. Now Bailey had a little private area marked off with partitions, and though she missed her window to the outside world, it felt good not to be so out in the open. For Bailey, everything seemed to be moving smoothly for the first time that she could remember. And it felt so good.

39

As they watched the twinkling lights over the few dancers left from the guests at the wedding, Bailey and Chase stood there, arms at each other's waists. This is what she remembered, and watching the happy couple this evening exchange vows was magical for her.

For Bailey, it didn't matter the couple. She loved watching two people exchange vows that bonded them together for life. Or at least she hoped the marriages lasted that long.

For this wedding, like the others, she had watched Chase as he moved around stealthily, capturing the moments that the bride and groom would have forever to look back upon. After her trip to California and the photos she got to bring back with her, Bailey recognized the importance of pictures more than ever before. She didn't know if Chase realized how invaluable his services were for lasting memories, but one day, she would have to describe it to him the best way she could.

"So, tomorrow, we are making the trip to Marathon?" Chase said, pulling her a little closer.

"I guess. I'm a little bit nervous. The pictures of the house are beautiful, and it looks very big. Not sure if I would want to live there by myself. Plus, I would have a little farther to drive to work."

"It's not that far away. Plus, you know how many people would love to live in a place like that? You have your own beach! Even Harris couldn't believe it when I showed it to him."

"I have to say the beach thing does sound pretty awesome." Bailey turned to him and wrapped her arms around his waist. "You know what this means?"

"What?" Chase said eyeing her warily.

"That we could go skinny dipping," Bailey said with arched eyebrows.

"Well, when you put it like that, I hope you decide to live there." and Chase tenderly placed his lips upon hers. Yes, they were at work, but the event was almost over, and at the moment, he didn't care. They were back in their world now, and it was just them. He wanted – no, *needed* – this closeness with her.

"Um, we are finished for the evening and getting ready to leave. Wanted to let you know." The familiar voice broke their hold, and Bailey and Chase quickly parted like two kids that had been caught doing something they shouldn't. And for all people to catch them in the act, it was Maria.

"Thanks. Make sure to tell your dad thanks too. Everything turned out great, and the couple said the food was delicious."

Maria's face showed no emotion, but her eyes weren't on Bailey. They were on Chase.

"I will do. Goodbye, Chase," the girl said, then turned and walked away.

"Wow," Bailey said. "She just doesn't let up. She has got it bad for you."

"It doesn't matter because I have got it bad for you." Chase kissed her once more, but she had to pull away.

"Sorry, but I have to go get this thing wrapped up. You might as well go home, and I'll see you in the morning."

"I could always wait for you and take you home?"

"As wonderful as that sounds, I'm so tired, and my feet really hurt. But be at the house at eight o'clock. I want to spend the whole day in Marathon. I can't wait to see the house," Bailey said.

"Are we taking a picnic with us? Maybe eat out on the beach."

"I hadn't even thought about that. Can you bring some blankets? I'll put some food together. Sandwiches and chips OK?" Bailey asked excitedly.

"I can do that. I'll see you in the morning," Chase said, then gave her one more kiss goodbye.

Bailey watched the last few people gather their shoes, drinks, and anything the bride and groom had left for their guests and begin to leave. With the event company taking down the lights and putting up tables, Bailey felt it was safe to go.

"You know he likes me."

Bailey turned to see Maria standing on the other side of her car.

"I don't doubt it, but only as a friend." Bailey was doing her best to keep her composure. This woman was persistent.

"No, it's more than that. He has feelings for me. I can tell. Did he tell you we dated before?"

"Yes, he mentioned it. But he said you two were only friends now, and that you understood that."

"I really want him back. Why can't you just leave him alone? Then he would be back with me."

"Maria, I have to go."

Bailey got in her car and quickly backed out of the parking lot. But Maria never moved. She looked so sad, and Bailey could tell something wasn't right. She didn't need this in her world right now. No other complications. Hopefully, Maria would get the message that Chase was with her and move on.

■ ■ ■

"She actually confronted you?" Chase asked, finding it hard to believe the story that Bailey was telling.

"She wants me to leave you alone. Maria honestly feels that if I weren't here, the two of you would be together. She looked so depressed." Bailey didn't like the girl, but at this point she was beginning to feel sorry for her.

"I've done all I can to get the point across to her. If she harasses you again, let me know."

The GPS on the phone told them to take the next left, and Chase followed the instructions. Soon, they found themselves sitting in the car, in front of one of the prettiest houses Bailey had ever seen on these islands.

They both couldn't believe their eyes. It was a two-story house with what looked like a complete wrap-around porch on the second level. The house was painted an ocean-blue with white trim. The island shutters were white, too, only accentuating the outside beauty.

"I can't believe this is my house!" Bailey said as she got out of the car and slowly closed the door.

"I knew it looked nice from the pictures, but I had no idea it would be like this," Chase said as he came around to Bailey's side of the vehicle. "Are you ready to go inside and look?"

"Absolutely!" Bailey said. She grasped Chase's hand and they began the ascent of the stairs to the porch.

They found that the porch went around the entire second floor, with doors in the front and the back. Colorful rocking chairs with tiny tables were placed strategically around the house, giving people privacy if they so desired.

As they walked to the back of the house, the little beach and ocean came into view. They hadn't even walked into the house and Bailey could understand why the house had stayed booked up as a rental. More importantly, she could see why her dad loved it so much. Just the thought that they had been here together at one time made her smile.

"What a view! And with all the palm trees, there is privacy. I can see why my dad and I picked this place. Do you have the keys?" Bailey asked with anticipation.

"Right here in my hands."

"Let's go inside!"

"Well, I think since this is your house, you need to be the first one to open the door." Chase placed the metal objects in Bailey's hand, and she nervously put one of the keys into the slot to open the door.

The inside of the house was stunning. It reminded her of some highly-staged model home that someone had fixed up to sell. Everywhere she looked, from the kitchen to the large family room to the dining room, this house felt like it belonged on this little tropical island.

Bailey went from room to room, looking at each and smiling every time. With three bedrooms, a master bedroom suite with master bath, and two other bathrooms, there was plenty of room for a large family. The colors throughout the house were cool Caribbean colors, and bamboo furniture was used through the entire house. It was so inviting and relaxing that Bailey still couldn't believe that it was all real. And that it was hers!

"Whatcha looking at?" Bailey asked as Chase stood, looking out the back doors.

"There has to be at least fifty feet of sandy beach out there. This is so cool! Do you realize what you can do here? There's even a dock close by. You could have your own boat, go fishing, snorkeling, scuba, and more."

Bailey just stood there, looking out at the scene below. She had never imagined this. Harris told her the house was worth over two million dollars, and now she could understand why. *No wonder Tom was so upset,* Bailey thought as she recalled the scene in California that very first night she had arrived. He wanted to probably sell the house for the money. But right now, she was so glad that her mother had stuck to what her father wanted and kept the house. Now Bailey would have to decide what she wanted to do with this beautiful piece of property.

"I think I could stay here all day. Hell, Bailey, this is the perfect place for you. Please tell me you aren't going to sell it."

"I love it, but I can't imagine living here by myself. This place is huge!"

"But think about when you have company, like your mom. You could probably even put a home office in here and work from home," Chase said as he continued to walk around, inspecting the house. "I know I wouldn't mind spending some nights here with you," Chase said as he came up behind Bailey and gathered her into his arms.

"Let's go take a walk down to the beach," Bailey said.

"Are you sure you want to leave just yet?" Chase asked, giving her feathery kisses down the side of her neck. The sense of delight that came to her wanted to tell him not to stop, but the beach was calling out to her.

"I really want to go see the beach and check out the ground floor, too."

"OK, you win," Chase said as he pulled away from her reluctantly.

They went down the back steps and immediately, their feet hit the sand. The walk on the beach to the water was perfect. They waded out into the crystal-clear water, and though there was some sea grass here and there, the water was mesmerizing. As she gazed out toward the horizon, the colors of the water came into view, showing pretty shades of aqua and blue. The breathtaking waters of the incredible Florida Keys.

"I have to say this again – please don't sell it!" Chase said as he walked along the shoreline, Bailey beside him, splashing water as she walked.

"When we were on our way here, I was seriously considering selling it or just keeping it as a rental. But now that I see this place, it's almost magical. It's like I can feel my dad here. Maybe we looked at a lot of houses and that's why this one just feels right to me. Feels like I belong here. I don't think I could ever sell it, and I don't want to. Like I said, it's big for just me, but maybe it could be my home. I can do just like my mom wanted me to do: fill it with new memories, even a family one day."

"That sounds perfect to me," Chase said as the water lapped around their legs. As he turned around to look at the scenery once more, the house on the left looked a little bit familiar to him. As he continued to walk toward it, instantly, he remembered the home and who its owner was.

"I think I know your new neighbors," Chase said with a smile on his face.

"How can you know my neighbors? You've never been here before, have you?" Bailey asked incredulously.

"I've been at a barbecue at your neighbor's house," Chase said, grinning widely. "They are friends of Garrett and Skylar. Their names are Michael and Josie Garner. Josie used to be Garrett's neighbor when he lived in Key West. Now, that couple has a tale for you. They went through hell and back to be together. It's really very interesting, but I would rather you hear from them. If they're home, let's go over and say 'hi'."

"I can't just drop in on someone like that," Bailey said quickly. "That would be rude, especially since I don't know them."

"But I know them, so it won't be a problem. Come on. Let's go," Chase said. He grabbed her hand, and they quickly walked down the beach.

Chase looked around to see if he saw any movement around the Garners' house. Everything seemed so quiet, but then they heard music coming from an open window. Chase and Bailey both heard a Jimmy Buffett song playing, with a man singing along.

"I promise, they aren't going to mind. They are great, and Garrett and Skylar come see them frequently. And remember when I had to go to Key West for a wedding and I stayed with Abbey and Zach? Abbey is the reason these two found each other again."

"What do you mean again?" Bailey whispered as they walked up the back steps.

"It's long story. Promise to tell you if Josie doesn't." And before Bailey could stop him, Chase was knocking on the door.

"Hi, there, Chase. Come on in," Michael said. He was an older gentleman, but nice-looking. Dressed in his shorts and a colorful t-shirt, he looked like a local, as though he had lived here his whole life. Bailey liked his easygoing demeanor and his cheerful face. "Whatcha doing here, and who did you bring with you?" Michael said.

"This is my girlfriend, Bailey Parker, your new neighbor."

"New neighbor?" This time, a woman chimed into the conversation. Bailey turned to see her coming toward them, smiling, with a newly-potted plant in her hands.

"Wow, we didn't know any of the houses were for sale. My name is Josie." She thrust out her hand toward Bailey. "Oops, I guess I better go wash my hands. Be right back." Josie disappeared around the corner. She looked to be in her early sixties, shorter than her husband, but dressed almost identical with shorts and a tropical shirt. Both looked more like a couple on vacation instead of owning the house. It seemed like only a second later, Josie had rejoined them.

"Now I can give you a proper greeting," and Josie shook Bailey's hand. "What was your name again?"

"Bailey. It's nice to meet you."

"Same here. And Chase, you haven't been around for a while. I did see Abbey and Zach not too long ago, and they said you had stayed with them again. How is Skylar and Garrett, and that little bundle of dark hair that keeps them on their toes?"

"They're doing fine. As for Taylor, she is a handful, but I think she has all us men wrapped around her finger. Especially her grandfather."

"Little girls have a way of doing that," Michael said.

"Won't be much longer before Abbey has that baby of theirs. A little boy, which I know Zach is happy about," Josie said.

"I know. I have to go there in two weeks to photograph their friend's wedding, Everly. She's marrying Abbey's brother, Drew."

"Yes, we'll probably see you there. Everly and Drew almost had their wedding here on the beach, but her parents really wanted her to stay in Key West. I don't think her father is up to traveling right now."

Bailey loved listening to them talk, but almost felt like an outsider. Hopefully, soon, she would get to meet all these people that were a part of Chase's world.

"So, Bailey, which house did you buy?"

"Well, my dad really purchased it. It's a long story," Bailey said quickly.

"Well, let me get some tea, and you can share the details if you'd like. Great way to get to know each other if you are going to be living nearby," Josie said and left the room to get the drinks.

They sat on the back porch of Josie and Michael's house for almost two hours, Bailey telling them of her story. Josie was amazed at what happened.

"Bailey, I'm so sorry. It seems like we've all been through a few rough spots," Michael said. "Take me and Josie. I was the dumbass that left her at the altar over thirty years ago, but she agreed to give this old man another chance."

"It's a long story, but since you are going to be living next door, we'll have to get together, and I'll tell you all the details," Josie said before taking another sip of her drink.

"Well, I'm still deciding on whether to live here or to continue to rent it out," Bailey said.

"I'm asking that you decide to live there. Please. I mean, the renters have been nice for the most part, but it would be great to have someone there permanently and not always see-ing someone new each week."

"I can say after seeing it, the house is pretty amazing. I'm currently staying in a little room on the first floor of Skylar and Garrett's house."

"Girl, you have got to move in," Josie said. "I'll even come and help you get situated."

"I really appreciate it. And I am leaning more toward liv-ing there, but I have a job in Islamorada, and it would be more travel time."

"The real reason is that she doesn't want to leave me back there," Chase said with a laugh.

"Then she just needs to bring you along. There are plenty of rooms in that house, if I remember correctly. We looked at it before buying this one. I guess you and your father were looking at it at the same time, because our realtor said there was someone else interested in the property. And before we could decide between the two, a bid had been placed on it, so we decided that this was the house that we were meant to have," Josie said.

"Wow, that is so hard to believe. I wish so much that I could remember those little details."

"I didn't mean to say anything to make you upset, and if I did, I apologize. But you and your daddy picked a beautiful spot and lovely house."

"Thanks."

"Well, we are going to go. Still have some things to check out in the house and then head back home later," Chase said as he stood up. "It was nice to see you. I'm still trying to process that you guys live next door. At times, it's such a small world. Can't wait to tell Skylar and Garrett. Abbey and Zach, too, will be surprised. But I'm glad that you are going to be Bailey's neighbors. Funny how life works sometimes."

"That's for sure." Josie and Michael stood at the back door, watching as Bailey and Chase walked down the steps. "Let us know if you need anything, Bailey. Anytime." With that, they shut the door.

"I can't believe that Michael and Josie are your neighbors," Chase laughed. "And you saw how nice Josie was? Believe me, she wasn't always like that. She will even tell you so herself. Abbey can give you all the details on that story."

"You keep saying all these stories. You keep running into people you know everywhere we go, almost."

"Bailey, I've lived in south Florida all my life. Spent summers on the waters around here. My sister owns a business here, and so do I. I promise that it's going to be like that for you one day, too."

As soon as they were back at the house, Bailey gazed upon it once again. It still seemed too good to be true. All it took was that one thought, and she knew what she had to do.

"I'm going to do it!"

"What?"

"I'm going to live here, Chase. It isn't that much farther from where I live now, or from you. I mean, I am only one street over right now, but it's not like I would be moving across the country. And to have my own beach, a roomy house where I can have family and friends over, plus no rent? I think I would be crazy not to live here."

"Yes! I couldn't agree more. How many times do you get an opportunity like this? Anyway, it's not a long drive, and I can see us spending lots of time here."

"You can come anytime you like. But right now, I'm a bit hungry."

"Then let's celebrate your new house with dinner. You get the food from the fridge, and I'll get the blankets. We can have a picnic on the porch or down on the beach."

"Let's eat on the porch. We can take the cushions from the chairs and put the blankets over them," Bailey said excitedly.

"Sounds great to me." But before Chase took another step, he stole another kiss from Bailey, and she didn't mind one bit.

40

The little patio picnic was perfect. They had a gorgeous view of the ocean, and a slight breeze kept the porch nice and cool.

"Those sandwiches were wonderful," Chase said as he laid across one of the blanketed pillows.

"It was just because you were hungry," Bailey said, sitting beside him.

"This is going to make a nice home, Bailey. And anything you need help with, you just let me know. This place puts my little house to shame."

"I love your little house. It so cute."

"You don't call a man's house 'cute'," Chase kidded with her.

"Well, I think you're cute, and you don't mind me saying that," Bailey shot back quickly.

"Well, I think you are beautiful. The most loving, incredible woman I've ever been with." His voice was husky and low, and he pulled Bailey down to him slowly.

He found her lips and slowly teased them with a kiss. By now, he had wrapped his arms around her, and she lay next to him on the cushions.

"I love you, Bailey."

"I love you, too, Chase."

This time, Bailey pulled Chase to her, exploring his lips, then making small kisses down his neck. Her hands began to run through his hair, and she was getting lost in the sensations of laying body to body.

Chase couldn't help but moan as Bailey's lips caressed his skin. And then he found her mouth once more, kissing her so deeply and sensuously that it felt like neither of them were breathing.

Chase let his hands wander over her neck, her arms, and down to the small of her back. She was stunning always, and right now, he couldn't think of anything but the woman pressing her body against his.

"Bailey, I…"

"Shh, just be with me, Chase."

"Are you sure?"

"More than you know."

■ ■ ■

Bailey laid with her bare back against Chase's chest. He was sound asleep, and she loved hearing his rhythmic breathing. All around them was dark, and they both lay underneath one of the blankets Chase had brought on their trip.

Bailey smiled. She had never known what it was like to be with a man, and Chase had been so gentle. She felt so content and happy that this man wanted her. When she let her imagination roam, as it was doing now, she could see her and Chase making this grand house into a home. Maybe one day, Chase would feel the same way.

"Hey, there, sweetheart." Bailey turned to see Chase now propped up on one elbow, looking at her from above.

"Hi, yourself."

Chase kissed her yet again, and Bailey felt like she could never get enough of this feeling.

"I'm sorry."

"For what?" Bailey asked quickly.

"I didn't mean for that to happen. I mean, I've been wanting to for a long time now, but I wanted to make sure the time was just right."

"Chase, it was perfect. I never knew something like that could be so magical."

"It's only that way because there is love there. When I told you that you were my everything, I meant it. I love you, Bailey, with all my heart."

"I feel so much the same. Chase, you are my love."

■ ■ ■

The drive home was much later than they had planned, but then again, they hadn't planned on spending the evening together the way they did.

"I did want to ask you something," Chase said as they continued down the highway toward Islamorada. "I have to shoot pics for Everly's wedding in Key West this weekend. Will you come with me? We can stay in one of the little hotels in Key West or come home afterwards. The wedding is in the late afternoon, so I don't think we would be there real late. I would get to introduce you to Abbey and Zach, too. I know that you will love them. Everly and Drew, too."

"As long as there are no weddings on the books that day, I'm all yours."

The ride home was relaxing as they rolled down the windows and let the air flow through the car. Bailey was the happiest she thought she could be. A beautiful new home, her boyfriend by her side, and a shared intimacy that she had never experienced had her smiling like never before. These were some of the new memories she was creating, leaving her past behind.

"This has been a wonderful day. Chase, thanks so much for going with me."

Chase intertwined his hand in hers. "You are wonderful. I wish we could have spent the night in that house."

"Maybe soon."

"And what are the chances that Michael and Josie would be your neighbors? Abbey is going to love that when I talk to her."

"I can't wait to meet all your friends."

"I can't wait to introduce you. They are going to love you, Bailey, but not as much as I do." They were standing at her door, the little porch light giving them just enough light to see each other's face. Even in the dark night, those blue eyes of his never seemed to escape Bailey, and she never wanted them to.

"How about a little TV time before I go home? Just to unwind?" Chase said.

"It's getting really late, and I have to work tomorrow. What about dinner tomorrow night? I'll cook here."

"Well, that sounds good," Chase said.

Bailey reached up and brought his face to hers. She couldn't let him leave without one more mind-blowing kiss.

"You're positive about no TV?" Chase asked once more.

Bailey shook her head. "Like I said, it's getting late, plus I need to call my mom and fill her in on all the details of the house. Then I have to be at work early in the morning, and so do you. Remember the Meyers' wedding at eleven o'clock."

"Damn, I forgot about that."

"See, aren't you glad you have me?"

"Oh, most definitely." His lips found hers once more, but his hands began to explore.

"Chase, I think we had better stop."

"You are a very hard one to leave tonight, but I will let you go — very reluctantly, I might add."

"I love you," Bailey said softly in his ear.

"I love you, too." Chase backed away from her, keeping eye contact until he had to turn around to get in the car. And as he drove away, Bailey went inside her apartment feeling as though she was walking on air.

After spending time at the large house today, it was hard to imagine the little space she was standing in, but she loved her little apartment, and Skylar and Garrett had been more than gracious. But now ideas swirled in her head about making the house on the beach her home. From decorating to having friends over, the anticipation was almost hard to contain.

As soon as she took a shower and was in her shorts and t-shirt, she shared a FaceTime call with her mom. Just giving Sharon all the details about the house was exciting, as Bailey could see the look of wonder on her mom's face. At times, there were tears, too, and she knew that her mom was remembering her father.

"I have a room that is going to be just for you," Bailey said as she described the inside of the house. "And the beach is fantastic. Perfect for skinny dipping."

"Bailey!"

"Just saying, Mom. With all the palm trees around, it would be fun."

Bailey ended the call and laid back on the bed, her hand spreading over to the side that was empty. Now that she was by herself, she wanted Chase with her. She wished that he had spent the night with her. The idea came to her suddenly: she would go and surprise him. She quickly packed up her tote and got in her car.

As she came up to the house, she noticed two people standing outside on the porch of Chase's house. Bailey pulled the car to the side and turned off the headlights. To her surprise and shock, it was Maria and Chase standing on his porch, talking. But suddenly, in a blink of an eye, Chase was kissing the beautiful brunette girl, and Bailey felt shockwaves pulse throughout her body. She looked away, feeling a wave of nausea and didn't know what to do. Without turning on her headlights, she backed up and quickly turned around, heading back to her little place.

By the time she got back to her apartment, she felt like she was hyperventilating. She couldn't believe her own eyes. Had Chase been playing her for a fool this whole time? What about what they had just shared this evening at the house?

Bailey went inside, locked the doors, and turned off the lights, crawling into bed. And then she couldn't hold it back anymore. The tears began to flow fast and furiously, and she didn't hold them back.

■ ■ ■

"What in the hell was that?" Chase said, furious as he pushed Maria away from him.

When he arrived at his house, Maria was sitting on the porch, waiting for him. Before he even got out of the car, he rolled his eyes, took a deep breath, and prepared himself. He wished she would get the hint that he was not interested in her.

Maria had told him once he reached the porch that she just wanted to talk. About her and him. Chase tried to stop her, but she just kept talking. Maria gave every reason why she thought they should be together. Why they were a better couple than he and Bailey would ever be. That they could work together and even maybe spend their lives together.

Chase could hear a hint of desperation in her voice, and it didn't scare him, but it made him realize just how fixated she was on him. He had to let her down gently, and everything he had done so far wasn't working.

Once Maria gave him a chance to talk, Chase explained that they could only be friends. He also told Maria that he was genuinely in love with Bailey and had been for some time. He told her nicely that it wasn't that she was unattractive or anything like that, but they just weren't meant to be together in the way she wanted. They could only be friends, and he hoped that she would finally accept that.

Chase thought that he was giving her encouragement by telling her that there was someone out there for her; she just had to be open to the possibility. But it wasn't going to be him. And before he knew it, Maria practically threw herself at him, wrapping her arms tightly around his neck, kissing him.

Chase grabbed her waist, trying to remove the girl from around him, but he struggled for just a second, her hold was so tight.

"I can't believe you just did that!" Chase yelled, having never been so angry with a woman.

"I just thought-" but Maria didn't have a chance to finish the sentence.

"Maria, I thought you understood everything I just said. I didn't want to hurt your feelings, but I only wanted to be friends. You've ruined that now. Get off my property. I've tried to be nice. I've even told you I'm in love with someone else, and you do something stupid like that? Dammit, Maria! Please leave! Now!"

Chase's voice could probably be heard by his neighbors on both sides of his house. He was so frustrated and angry, but he stayed put until Maria walked to the road and down to her house. Once he could see her no more, he went inside and shut the door, locking it for good measure.

41

"Hey, there," Chase said, coming up to Bailey from behind. They were both at the wedding venue, and Bailey was making sure the flowers were placed properly on the tables. "I tried calling you like nine times this morning. Everything OK?"

Bailey couldn't decide how to handle the situation. She had gone through so many scenarios in her head last night, from breaking up with him to letting him try to explain what she saw. But it seemed just as her life was getting back to normal, the person she trusted most was gone to her. And no matter what she tried to say, she didn't want to lose him but she couldn't erase what she saw last night. The emotional pain she was feeling was almost unbearable.

"Everything is fine. Just had to get here early to make sure everything was ready." Bailey kept her voice steady and calm.

"OK, that's fine, but I can tell something is wrong. What's going on?"

"Nothing. I just have a lot going on. You know with the house, the weddings." Bailey felt like she was going to burst, and she couldn't tell if she wanted to cry or scream.

Chase gave her a quick kiss on the lips, which she couldn't help but respond to, then watched as he went about taking the pictures that all the wedding parties loved. As she watched him from a distance during the entire time, it was hard to keep her own tears at bay. There had to be some explanation for what she saw last night.

Maybe she just hallucinated? No, that was not the answer because she was in front of his house. Even the porch light illuminated both Maria and Chase. As for the kiss, she saw that plain and simple. And just the thought of it brought her anger back to the surface. But then one look at Chase and she wanted to cry.

"Hey, girl, what's going on with you?" Mandy said as she came to stand beside her. She was still walking with crutches, but using them more to make sure she was steady on her feet.

"What are you doing here?" Bailey asked a little too curtly.

"I thought you might need a hand. You weren't talking much this morning at the office, and I thought you would be bouncing off the wall after going to see the house yesterday. You didn't even give me a description, except it was nice with a beach. Don't find many of those around here."

"Hey, Bailey." It was Dennis. This did give Bailey something to smile about. Mandy and Dennis had been together every day since she got back, and she had even caught the two kissing a few times. The love fire was being rekindled by those two, while Maria and Chase had just doused what hope she had for a future romantic relationship with the man she wanted.

"The house was great. As a matter of fact, I'll probably be moving there in a week or so. I already promised Chase I'd go to a wedding with him in Key West this weekend, or I'd start moving sooner. We don't have any weddings on Saturday or Sunday, so I hope that's OK."

"It's fine," Mandy responded, still watching Bailey's face.

"What?" Bailey asked, trying to be her normal self, which she was finding very hard to do.

"You might not want to tell me right now, but when you're ready to talk, just know I'm here."

"Seriously, I'm fine. I really just have a lot on my plate, but it's all OK."

"Well, if you need any help moving, let us know," Mandy said.

"I don't think you'd be any help. No offense. Besides, I wouldn't let you help. I know your leg is healed, but I don't think you should take any chances. Besides, I really don't have that much to move, remember? I do know that my mom is going to ship some things out once I get settled. I talked to her last night. As a matter of fact, she will probably be here in a month or so to stay for a week once I move into the house. I really wanted her to be here since this was my dad's place, too."

"I think that'll be great for you and her. And enjoy the weekend with Chase. Might be nice to get away doing something fun for once."

"I'm looking forward to it." The lie slipped from her tongue like butter. She didn't want anyone to know what was going on between her and Chase till she could figure out what to do. She couldn't remember having her heart broken, and if she had, those were memories she preferred never returned. This hurt too much.

After the wedding was finished and everyone was on their way, Chase wanted to come over again, but Bailey begged off. She told him she wasn't feeling good, which was not a lie because she felt so raw and hurt inside.

Chase immediately thought it was a physical ailment, wanting to come in and take care of her, but she insisted she would be fine. How could he be so nice, like the man she fell in love with, while seeing another woman? As she shut the door to her apartment, the tears she had held back all day began to flow.

No matter what Bailey did, she couldn't get the imagine of Chase and Maria in that embrace out of her mind. How was she going to go to some wedding and pretend that everything was fine between them? She wanted to stay home, but she had already made the promise to be by his side. After everything Chase had done for her, how could she not go?

But Bailey had made up her mind. After this weekend was over, she had to break it off with Chase. The trust was gone. But one thought made her sick to her stomach: how was she going to live without Chase in her life?

■ ■ ■

As they were making their way to Key West, the car was unusually quiet. They left early to make sure Chase had plenty of time to talk to the bride and groom, like he always did before every wedding. Though, this time it was different because these were his close friends. These were the friends that Bailey, only days ago, couldn't wait to meet. Now just being near him in the car had her feeling angry and depressed.

Bailey was doing her best to act as if nothing was wrong, but it was so hard. Every time he reached for her hand, kissed her lips, put his arm around her waist, the same feelings of electricity shot through her body. She still wanted him, body and soul, but those physical touches also made her want to recoil from him. Had he been like this with Maria, too? The kisses? The caresses? She couldn't trust him. She had to remind herself of that every time she felt her resolve start to fail.

"I know I've been asking you this like a hundred times over the past few days, but are you sure you're OK? You just haven't been yourself. You aren't getting the flu or something, are you? I know things have been like a whirlwind lately," Chase asked, a look of concern showing on his face.

"No, really, I'm fine. Like I told Mandy, there is just a lot happening right now. Moving to the house. Getting it fixed up because mom is coming to visit. More weddings on the books."

"Are you sure there isn't something more? I mean, I've seen you handle this much stress without batting an eye before."

"I promise I'm fine," Bailey said, desperate to change the subject. "Are you looking forward to seeing your friends?"

"Yes, but I'm really excited for them to meet you. They've always teased me about being the forever bachelor, even though I'm only thirty. They always said I was too picky, and

I just said I was looking for the right girl. Now I've found her, and I want to show you off," Chase said, giving her a wink.

Bailey thought she might get sick. This was the Chase she knew, but every time he said something sweet, all Bailey could see was a dark-haired girl in his arms.

Chase did most of the talking on their trip, telling her of some plans he had made for more wildlife photography shoots and more. Any other day, they would have been like the perfect couple, but all Bailey could feel was heartache.

Just get through this day, then you can break it off, Bailey reminded herself.

Once they parked, they took a boat shuttle from Key West over to Sunset Key, a tiny, private island where the ceremony and reception would take place on the beach. There had been clouds early this morning, but now the day was turning out to be almost perfect for the wedding couple.

Chase helped Bailey onto the boat that would ferry them across. Even though she was stressed and anxious, she kept up appearances by helping Chase with his camera equipment and holding his hand whenever he reached for her. She smiled dutifully and was determined to see this day through.

But as each minute passed, the charade was getting harder to pull off. She wished she could tell Chase right now what was going on, but she couldn't ruin this for him. Even though he might have broken her heart, he had helped her through a most difficult time. And she wasn't going to go back on a promise.

"Hey, Everly," Chase said, giving the bride a big hug. Everly was beautiful. With her hair pinned up in curls, some loosely falling around her head, she looked almost like a princess in her wedding dress. "This is my girlfriend, Bailey."

"You were telling the truth! Chase kept telling Abbey and me that he had found someone special, but we thought he was just saying that to keep us from trying to set him up again," she laughed.

"It's nice to meet you," Bailey said, reaching to shake Everly's hand, but she received a hug instead.

"I hear you are a wedding planner," Everly said quickly. "If I'd known that, I'd have hired you for our wedding. Don't get me wrong, our planner has been great, but I think I've done more work than her. But now the day is here, so I don't care. I'm just ready to finally marry Drew."

"Are you talking about that brother of mine?" A young woman who looked like she could give birth at any time walked toward them.

"And you must be Bailey," Abbey said, giving her a hug, even though her large belly came between them.

"And you are Abbey. Chase has told me all about both of you. It's nice to finally meet you."

"You're for real!" Abbey said with a laugh, turning to Chase. "I guess you proved us wrong. Now you just better treat her right."

"Oh, I plan to," Chase said, gently pulling Bailey to his side.

Just hearing those words and feeling Chase's hand on her back sent a cold shill down her spine. Again, Bailey had to use her willpower not to explode with the words she wanted to say to him. Instead, she took a deep breath and smiled at Chase.

"So, tell me, what kind of pictures do you want today? Anything in particular?" Chase asked as he turned to Everly.

As Chase and Everly discussed pictures, it almost felt like a workday for Bailey. She had gone through these same scenarios so many times over the last months since she had begun working with Mandy. She felt like the wedding planner instead of a guest. But instead of looking forward to seeing the bride and groom say, "I do," she cringed. It was her favorite moment of her workday, but now it just made her depressed.

"I'm going to go talk to Drew and then start taking pictures," Chase said to Bailey and gave her a quick kiss. "Please take care of my girl, Abbey."

"Will do," Abbey said. "Come on, Bailey. We'll go ahead and get our seats. I should be able to plow our way through the crowd with this tummy of mine. This boy is going to be a big baby."

"I think you look great," Bailey said, thinking that Abbey's mid-section may be full and rounded, but she was so pretty.

"There you are." Bailey watched as a tall, blond-haired man with a slight limp came to Abbey, kissing her sweetly on the cheek. "Was getting worried about you," the man said.

"I'm waddling my way around. Wanted to help Everly get ready, but I think I was more in the way." Then Abbey turned to Bailey. "Bailey, this is Zach, my husband and soon-to-be peewee football coach. Zach, this is Bailey, Chase's girlfriend."

"You exist!" Zach said, and Bailey almost laughed that these friends didn't think that Chase could find a woman to be with. *As a matter of fact*, she wanted to tell them, *he found two*. But she swallowed the words.

"Yes, I do. It's nice to meet you."

"I told you we would see you here." The voices had them all turn around, and here was someone that Bailey knew. They were her new next-door neighbors, Josie and Michael, and she was so glad to see them. Now she didn't feel so much the outsider.

"You came!" Abbey exclaimed, and Josie was at her side quickly, putting her hand on Abbey's extended tummy.

"Wait a minute. You know each other?" Abbey asked, looking from Josie to Bailey.

"This is my new next-door neighbor in Marathon," Josie said as she came to stand beside Bailey.

"Seriously? Which house?"

"The rental house. The one we picked out originally, but now we know Bailey and her father purchased it right before we wanted to make an offer."

"Wow! That house is beautiful," Abbey said.

"My dad and I bought it together before he passed away, but I just found out about it."

"What?" A look of puzzlement shadowed Abbey's face, but she didn't have much time to think about it. Two women came toward her, one with a little girl on her hip.

"Hope! Maddy!"

Bailey stepped back as the three women exchanged hugs, the little girl wanting her grandmother.

"I'm so glad you are here. There is just something about a Florida Keys wedding."

"Well, everyone here except Hope got married somewhere on these islands. Well, Josie and Michael did go to Miami, but that still counts in my book. Oh, Bailey, I'm sorry. Let me introduce you." Abbey took Bailey's arm and lead her back to the group.

"This is Bailey. Her boyfriend, Chase, is the photographer today, but he is also Skylar's brother. Bailey, this is my best friend, Hope, and her mother, Maddy. Maddy is the reason I'm in Key West to begin with."

"How?" Bailey asked turning to Maddy, intrigued, trying to get her mind off of Chase.

"I came down here to get away for a while. I needed a break, and my doctors wanted me to get some sunshine and fresh air. My best friend lives in Islamorada, so I rented a house there for a month. Ended up marrying the guy across the street," Maddy said, laughing.

"Sounds like there is a little more to it than that," Bailey said, enjoying the conversation with these women.

"There is. I certainly didn't come here to look for someone new in my life, but I did. Jason just swept me off my feet. We live on Folly Beach, near Charleston, South Carolina now, but we also own a house in Islamorada. We got married at Anne's Beach."

"And that's how I came to love these islands," Abbey said. "I came down here for Maddy's wedding and went back home, packed my stuff, and moved to Key West. Everyone thought I'd lost my mind, but I loved it here. I met Zach at work. We had a few kinks to work out, but we ended up getting married, and now I'm going to be a mom. Everly, the bride, also worked with us. I'm surprised that she chose a beach wedding. I thought for sure she'd go for some hotel or something."

"Why?" Bailey asked, surprised with all the beautiful outdoor scenery. But also, she wanted to know as a wedding planner.

"Everly literally ran away from Key West. She was born and raised here. When she had enough money, that girl split to New York. My brother, her soon-to-be husband, Drew, was living in New York, and he helped her out. But they didn't realize they were in love till Everly decided New York wasn't for her and moved back to the Keys. He followed her here, and now we are getting ready to watch them exchange their vows on the beach. Everly just always said that she'd never do this, but I think Drew had a big part in that. You see, we grew up in the mountains of North Carolina, and once he embraced island life down here, he was all in." Abbey laughed. "But I think it's time for us to take our seats. Bailey, you come and sit with us."

The outdoor wedding was beautiful, and for Bailey, it was bittersweet. The bride looked gorgeous in her strapless lace gown as she walked down the aisle, and the groom couldn't conceal the tears he had in his eyes as he watched her. Throughout the wedding and the reception, their love shone in every way. Though Bailey was happy for the couple, it only reminded her of what she had hoped she could have possibly had with Chase, and now that dream had disintegrated.

Bailey caught sight of Chase every now and then, and he gave her a wink or blew her a kiss. She tried to show interest, but every gesture was hard, and the more time that passed, the more she watched the activities around her, the more Bailey thought that she would not be able to contain herself anymore.

At this point, Bailey just wanted the wedding festivities to be over and to go home. She didn't want to spend the night and was so glad that she had told Chase that when he first asked her about coming. She didn't care what time it was when the wedding was over. She just wanted to leave.

As the party began to wind down and the newly-married couple left the island, everyone started taking the boat back to Key West. It felt weird for Bailey not to make sure that everything was put up and done for the evening, something she was so used to doing. But Chase found her, and they boarded the next boat that took them to the pier and walked to the car.

"I know you probably aren't hungry, but I'm starved. I only got a few bites to eat in between shots. OK if I get a quick bite to eat before we leave town?" Chase asked as they were finally settled in the car.

"Doesn't matter to me," Bailey said.

"OK, I've tried to play along all day, but enough is enough. I've been around you long enough to know that something isn't right. Even though you keep telling me everything is OK, you're not telling me the truth. You've been acting strange for a few days now, and today, you weren't yourself at all. Even coming down here, I felt like I was pulling teeth to get you to talk. What the hell is going on, Bailey?"

42

"I saw you kiss her!" Bailey's voice was so loud that it vibrated through the car.

"What in the world are you talking about?" Chase said, a look of complete disbelief on his face.

"Maria! I saw you kiss Maria!" Bailey was close to tears now. To finally say what she had been holding in for days seemed like a huge relief, but so miserable at the same time.

"Maria? When? I've never kissed her!" Chase said, his voice matching hers.

"The other evening. The day we went to look at the house. When you dropped me off at home. Remember, you wanted to come in, and I said I needed to rest up for work? No wonder it didn't bother you to go on home."

"Bailey, you are making no sense!"

"I got home that night, and after I talked to my mom, I decided that I did want to see you. I thought I would surprise you at your house. So, I drove to your house just in time to see you kiss Maria on your porch. Have you been seeing her this whole time we have been together? Was this all just a joke to you, Chase?" Bailey's words tumbled out so fast, all the hurt and anger coming forth with them.

Chase sat there, stunned by Bailey's words, trying to remember what happened – and then it hit him. Bailey had seen Maria try to kiss him, but apparently hadn't seen the whole exchange.

"That's what this has been all about? You think I'm a player?" Chase was angry now that she didn't believe in him enough to ask him what had happened. "Did it ever occur to you to come and talk to me? To ask me what happened? After everything we've been through, Bailey, do you really think I would cheat on you? That I'm that kind of person?"

Bailey had tears running down her cheeks and not enough strength to wipe them away. "I don't know. I've never been in love before, so I don't know what to expect. I always heard that men could break your heart, but I thought you were one of the good ones. Mandy even told me you were. All I know is I can't go through this pain I'm feeling right now. It just hurts too bad. We can't be together. Maybe you'd be better off with Maria."

"First of all, I'm not a cheater. Maybe that's why I didn't date like all my other friends. I want someone special in my life, one person to be my only someone, and I thought I had found that in you. For your information, when I came home, Maria was sitting on my porch. She was begging me to give her chance, saying all kinds of weird stuff, like we were meant to be together and stupid shit like that! I told her I was in love with you and nothing would change that. What you saw was me telling her that I didn't want to see her, hear from her, nothing, because I have you. You are my someone. Before I knew what was happening, she threw her arms around me, trying to kiss me!" Chase had to pause for a moment to put his thoughts together because his frustration was getting the best of him.

"I told her to please leave both of us alone. That nothing she did was going to take me from you. Yes, Bailey, those were my words to her. I hated to sound mean because that's not who I am, but she just wasn't getting it. If you think I was kissing her, you are sadly mistaken. I actually pushed her away and had to control myself to keep from pushing her too hard." Chase took another deep breath, trying to regain his composure. His explanation had come out so swiftly because now it made sense why Bailey had been so distant. But he couldn't believe she didn't trust him enough to talk to him.

Bailey sat in dazed silence, not knowing what to say. As she listened to his explanation, she realized what a mistake she had made. She had just assumed the worst instead of talking to him. And now it looked like it was going to cost her the best man she had ever met. The only man, as far as she was concerned, that she had ever loved.

"I didn't know. All I know is what I saw," Bailey said softly.

"Then why didn't you talk to me? Why didn't you ask me what happened? Why did you just assume the worst?"

Bailey could feel the hurt emanating from Chase, and she also saw it in his eyes. And she couldn't blame him. After everything Maria had done to both of them in the past, how Chase had been her champion every time, how did she let this spiral out of control?

"I'm so sorry, Chase. I…" but Bailey could not continue. She laid her head back on the headrest and looked out the window. It was over. This fairytale place that she had been a part of with this dear man was suddenly gone.

"Bailey," Chase said, his voice now calm. He placed his hand on her cheek, encouraging her to look at him. "I love you. Only you. You have to know that by now. I guess I can see where you are coming from. If I'd been in your shoes, I might've assumed the same thing. But I hope you can see why I'm upset. I've never given you any reason to mistrust me, and I'm never going to. I know that things have been rough for you. Learning to trust people and get to know them is still hard. But I really thought that you and I were past that."

"It's my fault. Just when I saw the two of you together, I didn't know what to think except maybe what we had was just too good to be true. The way things have been for me since the accident is like if something good comes into my life, something bad seems to be around the corner. But you're right. You've been nothing but loving and kind to me. It's just that I get so scared sometimes, and then…" Bailey hesitated and couldn't say another word.

"Bailey, what's wrong?" Chase asked her.

Bailey felt like she was in a haze. She could see a young man telling her that there was no way they were going to make it, that they had to break up, and then he walked away from her. It was so clear in her mind that she knew it was real, that it had happened in her past. It was the memory of Daniel ending their relationship. She could feel the hurt as the memory came to life.

"Bailey, you'd better say something soon, or I'm taking you to the hospital!" Chase said, almost yelling at her.

"I remember."

"What do you remember?"

"Daniel breaking up with me. Telling me it couldn't work long distance. I remember the feelings of hurt. Loss. Like I couldn't breathe." Bailey sat so still, looking forward. "I can feel the pain and it was so bad."

"Maybe that's where this is all coming from. Except if he hadn't let you go, I would've never found you. Bailey, just remember that is in the past. Try to let it go. It has nothing to do with you or me. I'm not going to walk away. Not even now. We can work this through. I know it. You just have to trust me."

"I do trust you. And I'm so sorry," Bailey said as she started sobbing and laid her head on Chase's shoulder.

As much as he could adjust his seat in the car, he turned so he could cradle her. At times, she was like a rock, and at others, she was so fragile, but there wasn't anything Chase wouldn't do for her. Even now, when she had accused him of cheating. He loved this woman whole-heartedly, and he knew without a doubt that she loved him.

"I think it's time for the two of us to make a visit to Maria. We will let her know, both of us there at the same time, that we are together. Also, she can clear up this mess."

"No, Chase, we don't need to do that. I believe you, and I don't need you to back up your story. Trust has to start somewhere, so I'm starting right now. I've always believed in you. Will you forgive me and let me back into your life?" Bailey asked him, wondering what he may say.

"Bailey, you never left my world. Nothing you could do or say could drive me away. I guess I should let you know now: you are stuck with me."

43

"You need help with that?" Bailey asked as Chase stood at the bottom of the steps.

"No, I think I have it. But I have no idea what you have in here," Chase said with a struggle in his voice.

"That must be my box of books."

"Then thank goodness we are almost finished. These steps are beautiful when you don't have to climb them fifty times. I definitely got my workout in today." Chase was finally at the porch and put the heavy box in the one of the rocking chairs.

"Why don't we take a break and go sit out back?" Bailey said, reaching for his hand.

"After I take this box inside, that sounds perfect. At least everything is up here instead of in the car. And it's a good thing Garrett let us borrow the truck. I had no idea that your mother was going to send you so much stuff."

"Neither did I! I guess she really wanted me to have some family memories to put in the house since it meant so much to my dad."

"Do you think you'll get this place fixed up like you want before she comes next week?" Chase asked as Bailey handed him a drink out of the refrigerator.

"Most certainly. Mandy is even going to come and help me because we have about three days this week with no weddings, and the ones for next week are all ready to go. Or at least as much as we can do right now. Oh, but I did forget one thing," Bailey said, coming to stand beside him. She gently encouraged him to sit in the chair, then promptly seated herself on his lap.

"And what is that?" he asked, giving her a quick kiss.

"I didn't confirm our photographer. You will be there for the weddings next weekend, right?"

"Did you even have to ask?" Chase said as he began to nuzzle her neck.

"I'm just being thorough, and now I can honestly tell Mandy that everything has been confirmed."

Chase continued to give her light kisses along her throat and across her collarbone that almost tickled, but felt so deliciously good to her.

"Stop that! I'm all dirty."

"I like dirty women," Chase said with a husky voice.

"You do, huh?" Bailey said, matching the sexiness she heard in him. "Well, that can be arranged, you know."

"OK, we better stop right now before things go any further. We have company coming in two hours, expecting dinner. We need to clean up, go get take-out, and be ready."

"We have plenty of time." This time, Bailey was kissing him, and Chase had a hard time saying "no".

"I certainly promise that I will take you up on that offer very soon. But right now, I'm going to take advantage of your guest shower, so you can take one in your new bathroom."

"Or we could take one together," Bailey teased.

"You are making this so very difficult. I'm trying to be a gentleman here, so give me a chance."

"OK, you win. But we will revisit this later, for sure." Bailey promptly removed herself from his lap, gave him a very sensual kiss, then went to take her first shower in her new house.

As the towel clung to her wet skin, she dug through some boxes and suitcases to find her favorite maxi dress. The form-fitting top showcased her feminine curves while the bottom of the dress hung loosely, almost touching the floor. The colorful material was dotted with tropical flowers making Bailey feel like she was definitely a tropical island girl.

Once she was dressed, she went out to the kitchen to make room for their dinner guests. She could hear the guest shower running, Chase singing a country song so loud that she couldn't help but laugh. So, she grabbed her phone, selected some music, and sent it to her Bluetooth speaker. A slow song popped up, and as she cleaned, she danced around the kitchen.

As soon as he turned the shower off, Chase heard music come from somewhere in the large house. He quickly put on the clothes he had brought with him today. He was happy he had planned ahead because he knew that more than likely, he wouldn't have had time to go home to get ready before coming back to Bailey's new house. He followed the music, knowing that he would probably find his girlfriend wherever the sound was coming from and was amazed at what he saw.

When Chase glanced around the corner, he saw Bailey as she danced all around the kitchen, slowly and sensual, moving her hips to the beat of the music. Chase stood, entranced by the movements from the girl in front of him. His heart swelled with joy, just knowing that this woman wanted to be with him, and his love increased for her each time they were together.

But right now, it wasn't only love he felt for Bailey, but he wanted her, too. The way she moved to the music left no denying what was underneath that dress, and now he wondered if taking that shower together might have been the better idea.

Chase took his time and came around the corner slowly just in time to see her look up. And instead of being startled, Bailey pointed to him and motioned for him to come to her, which Chase dutifully obeyed.

The song that she had originally been dancing to ended, and another one took its place. As Bailey wrapped her arms around his shoulders, Chase placed his arms around her waist, slowly pulling her so close to him. They both swayed to the music, bodies as close as they could be, Chase capturing her lips more than once as they moved.

"Hello, there!" The voice boomed out over the music and brought Chase and Bailey back to reality. They looked up to see Mandy and Dennis standing there, smiling so broadly that it seemed like they were on the verge of laughing.

Bailey rushed over and turned the music down. "I'm so sorry. We've just had a long day and needed a break."

"Well, it looks like we interrupted something that was going to be very, um, entertaining," Mandy said as Dennis snickered behind her.

"Just excited about being in the house," Bailey said, trying to take the focus off her and Chase's embarrassment. "Would you like a tour?"

"Of course!" Mandy exclaimed.

"This house is beautiful," Dennis said as he and Mandy began looking around. And while Bailey proudly showed the couple her new house, Chase went to get their dinner: take-out pizza and some beer.

"Everything is so stunning," Mandy said amazed as they went room to room. But a picture frame caught her eye.

"Who is this?" Mandy asked.

Bailey went over and saw what Mandy had in her hand. "That's me and my sister, Heather. She gave this to me right before I left California."

"You know, I never did see any pictures of your trip."

"I didn't show you, did I? I forgot. There was so much happening when we got back. I promise when I get unpacked, I'll show them all to you. My mom even sent more picture albums when she shipped my stuff here. You know, she will be here next week."

"I knew that was coming up, but I had forgotten. Now that is going to be exciting. When was the last time she was here?"

"I think she and Dad came here right after I disappeared. But then she told me it was too hard on my dad since I was gone. I wish he could see the place and know that I'm taking care of it. I might not have known him like I wanted to, but having the pictures helps me feel like I know him. Like he is here in the Keys."

"So, are you excited about her visit?"

"I am, and a little nervous. I want her to like the house. It was so important to my dad. Plus, I want her to have a place she can come and get away from everything. Between losing my dad and my disappearance, I think things were so tough on her, but she keeps pressing on. My sister thought she had early onset dementia, but since I was able to visit, she said Mom is doing so much better."

"Did you give any more thought to looking for your birth parents?" Mandy said softly.

"I haven't right now. I'm still grappling with my memory loss, plus a new house and spending more time with Chase. This may sound terrible, but I don't know if I'll ever look for them. I have great parents, and wherever my birth parents are, I just hope they are happy. The only thing I wish my birth mother could know is what a wonderful thing she did picking out my parents though I sometimes wonder if she could have taken care of me."

"It sounds like she did the right thing. But I can certainly see your point about having so much going on. Plus, I will be keeping you busy at work. That is one of the reasons we wanted to come to dinner tonight. But let's wait to talk until Chase gets back."

No sooner had Mandy said the words than Chase walked through the door with two large pizzas, some breadsticks, a salad, and beer. Bailey pulled out some paper plates and plastic utensils, then they sat around the large table in the dining room.

"So, what did you want to talk about?" Bailey asked before taking a bite of her pizza.

Mandy looked at her, then to Dennis. "Well, Dennis and I have been talking quite a bit. We're going to give our relationship another shot."

"Oh, my gosh! That's terrific! I was wondering about you two. I could see there was something there when Dennis was taking care of you."

"Wow, congratulations to both of you!" Chase said.

"Well, thanks, but there is more. This is where you come in Bailey," Mandy said. "I want to spend more time in Key West. So, I was hoping that you could run the office up here. I'm thinking about opening an office in Key West. There is some competition down there with other wedding planners, but I think we could do it. But then again, I'm not looking to grow a big business down in the city. Just a couple of weddings here and there. Dennis is going to take care of me for a while. Really let me take the time for my leg heal. The doctor said it could be months before I'm truly well."

"Well, I'm so happy for you two! You guys just seem to fit together. I consider you my Florida Keys mom and dad. I would be honored to take care of things here. But I have an idea," Bailey said.

"What?" Mandy said wrinkling her brow.

"I was wondering what you thought about me having an office here at my house. I could meet clients here. I'm going to make one of the rooms a home office anyway and I think it just feels more relaxed here especially when they're talking about one of the biggest days of their lives. If you think about it, we really don't see many clients in the office anyway. Ninety percent of our work is done via the telephone, email, and text messages. The phone number could be rerouted to my house, and I could keep business hours just like we do now. The biggest thing is you wouldn't need the office space anymore, and that would save a lot of cost on rent and utilities. It would just be more intimate here, and you have to admit, I have the space to do it." Bailey finally took a breath.

"Wow, you already had this planned out before I even told you about taking over," Mandy said, surprised.

"I was going to ask you about it next week, once I was settled. But now, I think it could really work."

Mandy sat for a few minutes, in deep thought, then smiled. "I think I like that idea. And you're right. We don't really need an office front. I had it because my mom did. And the money I would save! But where would we keep our supplies, the things we use at a lot of our weddings?"

"I have a large area down stairs, weather-proofed and everything. I think it would work perfect for everything we need to keep in storage. As I was moving in, I just thought about how, when you were out, and I was running things, I worked either from the house or my car. I was barely in the office. And I met most of our clients at hotels or restaurants."

"The more we talk about it, the better it sounds. And if you are willing to take on the job, then you are my new manager. And it will come with a substantial pay raise."

"But I can't yet."

"Why not?" Mandy asked, the smile suddenly fading from her face.

"My mom is coming next week. I promised her that she could show me everywhere my dad loved to go when we came here on family trips. She also said he would tell her of the things he and I used to do when it was just the two of us. This will be her first time back, and I want to make sure she has a good time and can relax. This will be the most time we've spent together since my accident. So, can I take that position after she leaves to go back home?"

"Sounds like a plan. I'm sure Lacey can help until then. Let's toast to this business deal," Mandy said.

"Can we use our pizza slices instead of a drink?" Bailey laughed.

"Sounds good to me."

44

Bailey paced back and forth in the waiting area. She was nervous and couldn't be still, knowing that her mother's plane had already landed. This was only their second time together, as far as Bailey was concerned, and she hoped her mom would come to love the Keys as much as she did.

"Calm down," Chase said. "She is going to love it. It's going to be fun to hear about this place from her point of view. It's been so long since she has been here."

"I know. It just feels like that first day in California all over again."

"But this time, it's only you and your mother. No sister, no other family. No going back to places, trying to remember things. No ex-boyfriends. This time, you can relax and just let her tell you stories. It will be better, I promise."

Bailey looked up and saw Sharon coming toward her. And this time, there was no shaking of hands. The mother and daughter hugged tightly.

"I'm so glad you are here. How was your flight?" Bailey asked excitedly.

"It reminded me of some of those long flights we used to take when we went to Asia, or worse, to London. Wait, no. Make that Australia. That was probably one of the longest flights, and you two girls were about to go stir-crazy in the plane. Oh, hi, Chase," Sharon said and gave him a big hug, too.

"Are you ready to see the Keys?" Bailey asked her mother expectantly.

"I am, but I have to tell you up front: please ignore me if I start to cry. Sometimes, this lady can't help if a memory brings happiness, even if it may be bittersweet. I get a little emotional, so just warning you ahead of time."

"That's no problem with me. You cry all you want to. Just promise that if those tears are because you aren't feeling good or hurting, you will tell me."

"You have a deal."

Soon, they had left the hectic Miami Airport and were heading south.

"Oh, my," Sharon said softly.

"What is it?" Bailey asked.

"The blue highway divider. I remember how on one of the trips here, you were so excited to see they had painted the divider. It was your favorite color because it reminded you of the blue water here."

"It's still my favorite color. I hope you like it because it's all throughout the house."

"Your house. I can't wait to see what you've done with it."

"I hope you like it. You even have your own little room."

"You didn't have to do that."

"Yes, I did because I hope that you are going to come visit me often."

They continued along Highway One, Sharon having them pause or stop sometimes when she saw something that brought back a memory she wanted to share. Bailey hoped to make it to the house soon, but she didn't want to rush her mom. This had to be a happy day, but also brought back a lot of memories of her dad.

They stopped at the Shrimp Shack in Islamorada for lunch. As Bailey sat there, eating her meal, it reminded her of the first dinner she and Chase had at this same restaurant. She couldn't help but smile as she sat beside him now, with her mother across the table.

"Mom, before we get to the house, I want to take you by my office and introduce you to my manager. Well, she's really a good friend of mine now. She is letting me have the week off to be with you, and then I have a brand-new position. I'm going to be her manager here in the Upper Keys. I'm an official wedding planner."

"Oh, honey, that's terrific. You know that your dad wanted you to stay in the technology field, but you loved event planning so much. I remember attending a party that you helped arrange. You were such a natural, making sure everything went as planned. I guess now you've found your passion. I'm so happy for you. To be able to live in the place you loved so much, doing what you always wanted to, and," Sharon said, looking over at Chase, "to have a handsome man by your side. It sounds like you are living the dream."

"Yes, I certainly am."

They pulled up to Bailey's office shortly after leaving the restaurant. "I just need to pick up a few things while I'm here. Come on in, and let me introduce you."

"As long as your office is air-conditioned. I forgot how hot it can get down here," Sharon said, smiling at her daughter.

They walked in to find both Lacey and Mandy on the phone. Bailey told her mom she could sit in the chair across from her desk while she gathered some papers that she needed to work on the next day. Slowly but surely, she was moving things to her house, as she had already begun to set up her home office.

"Bailey, is that you? I thought you were picking up your mother today," Mandy said as she came around the corner.

"I did. Mandy, I would like you to meet my mother, Sharon Palmer."

Both women stood there, looking at each other and not saying a word.

"What's wrong?" Bailey asked, and she quickly looked to Chase for help.

"Lynn?" Sharon was the first to speak, her eyes not leaving Mandy's face.

"Ellen?" Mandy's face suddenly seemed devoid of color.

"Do you two know each other?" Bailey asked, trying figure out what was going on between her mother and her friend.

Mandy looked at Bailey, then back to Sharon, and tears formed in her eyes. But Sharon was quickly by her side, hugging her like a long-lost friend.

"What's going on?" Bailey asked softly.

By now, both women were crying and smiling at the same time.

"I thought that I would never see you again. Have you always lived in the Keys?" Sharon asked as though Bailey wasn't standing there.

"My husband and I moved here a long time ago. We got a divorce, but we are trying to work things out right now. I went back home, and Dennis and I got married."

"Oh, Lynn, that's wonderful."

Mandy looked back at Bailey. "I can't believe this. Is this..." but Mandy couldn't finish her sentence. She only looked from Bailey, then back to Sharon for confirmation.

"Yes, it is."

Mandy's hand flew to her mouth, and the tears came faster.

"I don't understand. How do you two know each other?" Bailey asked, still trying to figure out what was going on.

"Honey, this is your birth mom. Lynn – or should I say, Mandy – is the woman that gave birth to you."

Bailey stood there, almost unable to comprehend what her mother had just said. The feeling was so surreal that she had to run the words through her mind once more. She looked back at Chase for help, only to see his stunned face.

"I don't understand. How? You said my birth mother was in California. Her name was Lynn."

"Lynn is my middle name," Mandy said through tear-stained eyes, coming to stand in front of Bailey. "When I was in California, I went by that name, so no one would know me except the lawyer that handled the adoption. Then he only used my middle name on the paperwork."

"This can't be real," Bailey said, still trying to figure out if this was a joke.

"Oh, this is as real as it gets," Sharon said. "I can't believe all this time has passed, and you find your daughter – our daughter – here in the Florida Keys. All those times we were here on vacation, and you were right here with us."

"So, Dennis is my father?" Bailey asked.

"Yes, and that is where you get your red hair," Mandy said softly. "His hair was red, but not like yours. You have your grandmother's hair. I remember when I saw those red little ringlets. You had inherited more of your father's traits than mine."

"Bailey, I know that this is a lot to take in, especially after you just met all of us in California, but what a wonderful gift. Like we talked about when you were there – this isn't a coincidence. Someone wanted you to meet your birth mother, and now you have the best of both worlds." Sharon looked at her daughter, taking her hand, hoping to ease some of the shock.

But Bailey looked at Mandy. "Why did you give me up? I heard my mother's side of the story, but I don't understand. You didn't want me?"

"Bailey, I wanted to keep you more than you'll ever know," Mandy said, shedding more tears as she tried to explain. "But I also knew that I wasn't capable. I was still a child myself in some ways, and I had no support. My parents were so upset, they were hardly speaking to me, and Dennis was always partying. Do you remember when I told you our story? How we broke up after our first semester in college? This was the reason why. I was pregnant with you. He wanted to get married, but I knew he wasn't ready. He could hardly get to class on time.

"So, I decided to get an abortion. I got to the clinic and couldn't even walk through the doors. I talked to my parents and asked if I could go stay with relatives in California till you were born. They wanted me to get an abortion, but I just couldn't. Since I was going to put the baby up for adoption, they were willing to help with that. And that is where I met Ellen – or Sharon – on that park bench." Mandy grabbed a tissue from her desk and then gave one to Sharon, as both women seemed to be reliving this time in their lives.

"I'll never forget that day. You were there with your little girl. Oh, my, that's your sister, Heather," Mandy said, taking Bailey's hand. "When I saw that picture in your house, the one where you two were young, there was something familiar about her, but I thought I was just feeling things that didn't exist."

Bailey sat there, still trying to comprehend everything that was happening before her eyes. She had her adopted mother on one side and her birth mom on the other. Her birth mom, whom she had been working for all this time, had gotten close to, and for Bailey, Mandy already felt like a mom to her. She couldn't even begin to grasp what the odds were of something like this happening.

"Bailey, I know this is a lot. Believe me, I'm having a bit of a moment myself. But please don't shut me out. I only did what I thought was best for you. And you've been like a daughter to me before this even came to light." Mandy's eyes were silently pleading to Bailey.

"I would never do that, Mandy. It just might take some time for me to adjust. To understand. I'm stilling trying to deal with all the information I found out in California."

"And it will be OK, Bailey. I promise," Sharon said, taking Bailey's hand in hers, then taking Mandy's hand in her other. "We have been given a wonderful gift of finding each other. Let's not waste one precious minute."

EPILOGUE

The tropical flowers were evenly spaced along the handrails of the steps that led to the porch of the house. Beautiful clusters of flowers, seashells, and starfish hung from the edges of the porch, from the front to the back of the house. Each rocking chair had a tiny flower at its peak, giving the porch a festive look.

Behind the house, down at the beach, chairs had been set in rows, with the shell- and flower-covered archway all facing toward the vast Atlantic Ocean. The aisle for the bride to walk upon was dotted with seashells and starfish along the way.

Everything seemed in place for the beachside wedding that was about to occur. Even the tent had been set up outside, tables, chairs, and dance floor ready for the guests to enjoy the reception that was to follow the exchange of vows.

"Are you ready for this, baby brother?" Skylar said as she checked Chase's white, button-down shirt once more. Though the event was meant to be casual – something that Bailey had insisted on – Skylar wanted her brother to look his best.

"Leave him alone. He looks just fine." Garrett came up and rescued Chase from his sister. "That's what the best man is for. But there are a few other people that want to see you."

"Definitely!" Abbey said, waking in with the small infant in her arms. "I had to say 'hi' before I go talk to the bride."

"How is Jessie?" Chase asked.

"She is doing fine," Zach said, looking down on his wife and the sleeping child she held in her arms.

"Were you able to return those gifts and get something for your daughter?"

"Most of them. She still has some of those boy clothes, and she wears them around the house. The doctor has apologized I don't know how many times. Says we are only the second time he got the sex wrong," Abbey said, laughing. She reached up and gave Chase a kiss. "You make one handsome groom."

"Thanks, Abbey. See you two later." Chase watched as the couple walked out of the room. "Man, I'm nervous."

"You shouldn't be. Chase, you couldn't have picked anyone better to spend your life with. Bailey is perfect for you."

"Thanks, Garrett. I know Bailey is the one for me. I just hope I can be a good husband."

"You will."

On the other side of the house, the bride's room was buzzing with excitement. Though Bailey's dress was simple, and she wore just a ring of flowers in her hair, all the women in the room remarked how beautiful she looked.

"This reminds me of my wedding on the beach," Maddy said as she looked on. "It was such a magical day."

"I remember it, too. Gave me the itch to move down here as quick as I could," Abbey said.

"Well, our wedding was on a rocking boat. I think a lot of our wedding party got a bit seasick, but for Garrett and me, it was perfect." Skylar laughed as she remembered her special day.

"I'm the one that said I would never marry on the beach, but Drew really wanted it, so I gave in. But I'm glad I did because it was wonderful. And then we went and honeymooned somewhere cold to get away from the heat!" Everly said.

Bailey turned around to both of her mothers. "Are you ready to do this?"

"Most certainly," Sharon and Mandy said in unison.

"We'll see you in a few minutes," Abbey said as she, Maddy, Skylar, and Everly left the room. They had all become such good friends over the last few months, and she was so grateful they were here today for her and Chase.

Bailey walked out onto the porch with both her mothers and Dennis. As she looked at the scene below, she saw her loved ones all seated. Heather, Tom, and Davis were there. Beside them, Dena and Stan had made the trip, too. Chase's mother, father, sisters, and brother were all seated, ready for the wedding to begin.

Then she saw Chase walk toward the minister by the seashell-covered archway, and her breath caught. How lucky was she that this man loved her even with her complicated past? She felt so loved and so lucky.

Bailey was the last one to place her bare feet into the sand. As she started down the aisle toward the man she loved, Bailey had one arm linked with her adopted mother and the other linked with her birth mother. Dennis walked behind them, and tucked into her bouquet was a picture of her adopted dad. She had everyone she loved here at her home as she was starting the next chapter of her life.

At first, she was nervous as she made her way toward Chase. But just looking at him took all those feelings away. He had a magic about him that was only for her. And she couldn't wait for the minister to announce them as husband and wife. This was the man she was going to spend the rest of her life with. Bailey couldn't wait for it to start.

These were part of the new memories her mother, Sharon, had told her to make here at this house. And what better way than with a wedding? *Her* wedding.

Finally, Bailey stood beside Chase, her parents placing her hand into his. Bailey smiled though happy tears were forming in the corners of her eyes.

"I think this is something we will always remember," Chase whispered to her.

"A wonderful way to start anew," Bailey said.

"I love you, Bailey."

"I love you, too."

ACKNOWLEDGEMENTS

For each book I write, when it comes to this section, there are so many amazing and wonderful people that continue to help me along the path of being an author that I'm afraid I won't mention someone. But I'll do my best.

Family is such a huge and important part of my life. I certainly wouldn't be where I am today without their help and support. My wonderful husband Jeff, that makes it possible for me to be able to write. Taking care of the little things that give me the time to create the stories I envision. My terrific parents that have given me encouragement each and every day to pursue my passion of writing. My daughter, Holly, has taught me to keep going despite any setbacks I may encounter. I've seen her overcome great obstacles and her example keeps me on track especially on those days I feel like I just want to stop for a while. Even my little dog, Emma, who sits beside me as I write each day, is a source of inspiration. It's as if she is making sure I stay on task.

And where would any of us be without our friends? To my many friends who have supported my writing endeavors - Thank You! Each and every one of you mean so much to me and I can't express how your friendship has helped me each and every day. Donna Gauntlett - you are truly a gift. Three years ago when we met, I had no idea that we would become such close friends though we live so far apart. I treasure our conversations and the help you have given me as I continue to write.

To all my readers: Love you guys! You are quite simply the best and I feel blessed to have you in my life.

Though this is the last book (for now) in the Florida Keys Novels, the little islands will always be with me. Since I like to visit once or twice a year, you never know if another novel might pop up in the future.

Love and Hugs to all!

Miki

ABOUT THE AUTHOR

 Miki Bennett is the best-selling author of the Florida Keys Novels and the Camping in High Heels series. She has won the Authors Talk about It Award for romance. When she's not writing, Miki enjoys going to the beach, spending time outdoors, and doing crafts. She lives in Charleston, South Carolina, with her husband, Jeff, and little dog, Emma.

Made in the USA
Columbia, SC
04 August 2019